COURTESAN'S WICKED DESIRE

CLAIR BRETT

CB publications

86 Riverside Ave.

Lisbon, NH 03585

Cover design: Harpy Edits

Author photo: BLC Photography

ISBN:

Ebook: 978-0-9983317-8-2

Mobi: 978-1-7352906-4-5

Paperback:978-1-7352906-4-5

www.clairbrett.com

❋ Created with Vellum

DEDICATION

I am dedicating this book to a very special person in my life that hopefully someday will come back to us and let us love her. We all go through things in life and make choices, always remember those people who truly love you only want what is best for you. They will love you no matter what. And also, always remember in life, there is always a do over!

CHAPTER 1

"ou should be out frolicking in the park with all the others. It is a marvelous day outside."

Lady Sarrafinna Lennox glanced up from the rather modest ledger on her desk. The same ledger she continued to pour her attention into since she received a response to her request of an accounting of her funds from her solicitor.

"Lang, I told you I would go with you later to meet up with Reginald, but these numbers must make sense first. Please, if you want to enjoy the day, don't let me stop you."

One of her dearest friends, Mr. Cedric Langley—Lang to his intimates—was a gem. Loyal to a fault, in his eyes Sarrafinna never misstepped a day in her life. However, he was not a man of leisure, instead one of action. He needed to be in constant motion, so lounging while she poured over her accounts was stifling for the flamboyant man.

"Nonsense, I am at your disposal, I simply do not understand what could be so pressing that you must complete it this instant."

"Lang, you sound like a petulant child. Why don't you call for tea?"

"Did someone say tea?"

Finna looked up as Madame Cantrell, her mentor and now a companion of sorts, swept into the parlor. Since her retirement, Madame Cantrell had been in residence going on five years.

"Yes, I'm ringing for it now. Should we have sandwiches or cakes?" Lang asked the group but answered for himself. "Cakes it is." He pulled the bell, went back and flopped with one leg draped over the arm of the settee where he sat all morning.

"What are you doing, dear?" Madame Contrell asked as she peered over the front of the masculine desk.

"I am trying to work out how I am still short," Finna explained, exasperated. She couldn't understand it. Her calculations were not off, but she didn't have the amount she set as her goal.

"Where do you stand, my dear? Often you are over dramatic about your impending crisis," Madame Contrell offered, sinking into the stuffed chair next to Lang to wait for tea.

"I stand at being short to make the last of the tuition payments and not enough to keep the household afloat, even after I sell the townhouse." Again, she looked at the letter, then back at the ledger. This meant she would have to meet with Mr. Gilbert Knottingword, Esq., her solicitor. She was developing a headache. "I very well may need to take on one last client to come up to snuff before getting out." The thought deflated what had promised to be such a lovely day.

Her plan as she dressed for her day, was that after breakfast she would go over the letter and confirm she, in fact, had enough money in her accounts to cover her retirement and still leave her comfortably wealthy, at which point she and Lang were to meet Reginald in the park for a stroll. It all sounded lovely, but now...

"Excuse me, mi lady," Golding, her butler, said and stepped into the room with the post on a platter. "The post arrived. Where would you like it? It looks like some fancy entertainments for sure," he added, his Cheapside accent slipping in as it often did.

"Thank you, Golding, please set it on the tea table."

"Right, right. Here you go, I will be back with the tea in a few." He turned and left them again.

"You really need to work with him on his diction, Finna. It is bad enough that when you have a dinner party, I must put gentleman's purses back in their overcoats, but when he sounds like where he is from, well your guests will wonder," Madame Contrell complained.

Finna bent back to the ledger and proceeded to add up the last four years of expenses, which would mimic what she assessed would be the same as her next four.

"I know. I have been busy. Perhaps you could work with him?" she suggested.

"Oh, I am no teacher. I learned my own manners by observation and determination. And the tutelage I received would not be in an atmosphere that Golding would approve, I am certain."

"Who is Mr. Dylan Birch? Are you keeping secrets, my

dear?" Lang plucked an envelope with a bright blue wax seal from the pile of letters and invitations on the salver and dangled it in front of Madame Contrell.

"That name is familiar, why?"

Sarrafinna moved from the desk, her money issue pushed to the periphery. What did Mr. Birch have for business with her? They were acquaintances from her only season, but not much more. Over the years, he called on her to ask pointed questions about people she held company with. Unsure what his title in the government was, she had the distinct impression it was not what his job actually entailed.

"Mr. Birch is an acquaintance of another life and time. I can't fathom what he might want."

She sat just as Golding entered with the tea. While her friends settled themselves with tea and cook's famous ginger and cardamom cakes, Finna turned the contents of the letter over in her mind. The letter had no official seals to show it anything but a friendly correspondence. The note itself told another story.

"Well, what does Mr. Birch have to say?" Lang asked around a full bite of cake, with no concern that Finna wouldn't share the letter's contents.

"He needs to meet with me. He says he may need my assistance in a matter, and that I would be handsomely rewarded for my trouble."

"There, you see. You worried about nothing. Perhaps you will not have to take on another client. But would it be so intolerable if you had to?" Madame Contrell asked, sipping her tea.

"The newest group of Lords set upon the Ton are exhausting at best, and tiresome at worst," Finna explained. "I am much too mature to desire to tolerate their ill manners and assumptions of freedoms based on their peerage, and their manhood. When a courtesan feels defeated in her efforts before she begins, it is time to get out. I have nothing to offer these young bucks."

"Oh, but a nice older gentleman who is only wishing for companionship would do, wouldn't it? What was the last one's name?"

"You know full well what his name was, and I am quite finished with prattling around on the arm of an elderly gentleman too hard of hearing to talk with."

Lang reached over and patted her on the hand. "You deserve your retirement, love. You groomed some of the Ton's most powerful men into what they are today. For king and country and all that." He waved a hand in the air to punctuate his statement.

Lang's concern and kind words warmed her heart. She did deserve her retirement. It was time for her to settle into the shadows and disappear. It had been a long road. Not one she would have chosen otherwise, but long just the same and her parents were not young anymore. With every day that passed it was a day closer to her brother gaining the dukedom from father. Once that happened, she was certain he would officially disown her, unlike her father who refused to publicly cast her out. She would prefer to be ensconced in the country and out of society when that happened. She knew better than any, public ruination and humiliation were best done behind closed doors and not on a ballroom floor.

CHAPTER 2

*L*ord Kendrick Rutland, Marquess of Harwich, stood outside the imposing building housing the various diplomatic foreign offices of the British government. Today would put an end to a career, that for all the turbulence it caused, he was proud of. But he was looking forward to taking his place in Parliament and bringing honor back to his family title. A troublesome task from the shores of the Mediterranean.

Over twenty years ago, Harwich stood in the office he was about to enter and signed away his family's life more or less. Today, he was taking it back alone. His days of doing what was right for others and ignoring his own desires and aspirations, were over.

Taking the stairs two at a time had him huffing more than he would like to admit. *Years of experience will do that to you,* he decided. Down the hall, three doors on the left, and Kendrick was at his destination.

"Good morning, how may I assist you?" asked a bright-eyed junior clerk at the desk.

"Good morning. Marquess of Harwich to see Mr. Chamberlain-fields."

The young man stared, then blinked, then stared some more, but gathered himself. "Oh, my Lord. I—we—that is, we rarely get men such as yourself here. I apologize for my rudeness. Please, sit. I will let Mr. Chamberlain-Fields know you are here."

"Thank you, son," was all Kendrick said.

It was the title and not his personal aura that struck the clerk dumb. It was something he was struggling with getting used to. Never in his years was he treated more as a deity than a man. As a child he would have more likely been thrown down the stairs and possibly spit on for daring to dirty the threshold of such an important office in the government. For that matter, he had been thrown down the stairs and spit on in lesser establishments as a boy, just trying to find food for himself and his mother.

Kendrick tamped down the anger from the injustice of it before he behaved unbecomingly toward who was soon to be his old superior. Funny how it was so easy to forget and set aside his old anger when it wasn't staring him in the face every day. The streets of Rome held no memories of hardship for him, so he could put it out of his mind. London, however, was a different situation.

"Harwich, I wasn't expecting you. Good to see you."

Kendrick quelled his anger, for it was not this man's fault for his childhood, and looked up with a wide smile.

"I should have sent word or requested an audience, but I am afraid this cannot wait."

"Come in then. We wouldn't want to hold up a Marquess in his daily dealings." Dameon Chamberlain-Fields motioned for him to enter his office and stood aside as he strode past. Kendrick had years of practice commanding a room. The title merely gave him the rank for those below him, to not argue when he did so now.

"Thank you, Dameon. I am aware this is untoward without advanced notice."

"Nonsense. Anything for you. I was going to call for a meeting with you tomorrow at any rate, so this is fortuitous."

"Well, thank you. As you know, Parliament will soon be in session, and I am planning on claiming my seat. In doing so, I am tendering my resignation as a British diplomat. We both knew that was my plan, but I need to make it final."

Dameon sat back in his chair, with his elbows languidly resting on either armrest, his hands clasped in front of him. Kendrick noted a smirk on his face.

"I am afraid I need your singular skill set for one last diplomatic assignment." Before Kendrick could protest, Dameon raised his hand to silence him. "It is conveniently right here in London and shouldn't take long. You will be sitting elbow to elbow in the House of Lords before the gavel falls."

Kendrick ground his teeth. He was a Marquess. He could say no and there would be no consequence. His overly inflated need to be of service would not allow that, however. He knew even as he stood, staring down his supervisor, that he wouldn't refuse. "What is it?"

"I would rather allow Birch to bring you up to snuff. If, after you speak with him, you still want out, then fine. I will find someone else to assist, but I believe once Birch talks with you, you won't refuse."

He never liked the way Chamberlain-Fields carried out his dictates. Kendrick remembered more than one diplomatic package leaving him to scratch his head, wondering what direction the crown wanted him to take on a matter. He had the strong inclination that had he ever made the wrong decision, he would have been standing alone on the sinking ship that was his career and his supervisor would be in the life raft safe.

"Very well, where should I meet Birch?"

The man behind the desk picked up a slip of paper and thrust it in Kendrick's direction. "He will be here after half passed eleven. He is meeting with another party before that, to convince them to assist as well."

"Am I acquainted with that party?" Kendrick never appreciated working with unknowns, whether they be people or circumstances.

"If they agree to assist, I would assume Birch will connect you."

Kendrick glanced at the address. He hadn't expected they would meet at White's, but this area was not only away from the Ton's prying eyes, any Lord who ventured there dressed as such might well find themselves dead. It seemed a change of clothes was in order.

Nodding once, he said, "I will be there and after we speak, I will send word of my decision, but this task will not stop me from joining Parliament this season, so it better be easy and quick."

"Understood, of course," Dameon agreed, standing to show Kendrick out of his office. "I will look forward to hearing what you decide and thank you in advance for your help in the matter. Once you know the players, I assume you won't be able to refuse."

An hour later, Kendrick jostled along the unkept streets of London's dock district. Gone was his white cravat, clean buckskin breeches, and his signet ring. In their place was, even after all this time, an all too familiar smell of dirty, ragged clothes. He even asked a footman for his bottle of cheap gin, which he promised to replace, and poured it down his front. He would like to think it was the awful, unsprung hack ride that caused his stomach to roil and threaten to unload, but he knew it was an all too clear memory of a time when this was his reality. Trips like this brought him too close to home. Yet here he was traveling along the dirty, infested streets of the docks in the name of king and country, when he'd promised himself only two days ago he was done halting his life for others.

The hack jerked to a stop. "Hey, aye, yer arrived," came the driver's gruff, thickly accented voice.

Clearing his throat and willing his polished accent to the recesses of his mind, he returned in an even gruffer, "Oi, am I dumb? I knows that I'm 'ere."

He let himself out and threw the fare, with no added tip to give him away as anything but another dock worker. The driver lurched the poor horse forward, and he was gone.

Kendrick looked at the dilapidated building occupying the space between the Thames and him. The noise from within almost overtook the noise of the street.

After a deep breath, Kendrick entered the tavern like he

belonged. The ceiling slung low, making it a chore for him not to look like he was hunched, and the two windows in the front of the house were so damaged and dingy that the light coming in was almost of no use. Once Kendrick's eyes adjusted, he found Dylan Birch hunkered over a plate of food in the farthest corner away from the more boisterous patrons.

"I was hoping he would talk you into it," Birch said with no attempt at a greeting when Kendrick came to stand in front of the small table. "Sit, sit. Are you hungry?"

"Ah, no, but thank you." Kendrick looked down at the plate and the roil in his stomach returned. How could Birch sit there and eat whatever that was supposed to be?

"Yeah, don't say it. It would amaze you at what we must count as a passable meal in the field. I guess I have just been in the field longer than some." Kendrick's expression must not have been shielded as much as he thought. "So, what do you think? Are you in?"

Kendrick sat back in his chair, hoping it wouldn't splinter under his weight, and broke the news to his long-ago friend. "Dameon did not tell me any of the details. He said you would fill me in. All he told me was that it was a job that required my expertise."

The expression on Birch's face told Kendrick Birch had not wanted this part of the job. "Damn him. I knew I couldn't trust him."

"Well, of that you should have been certain," Kendrick pointed out.

"Apparently," Birch agreed dryly. He signaled to the server for ale and finished his meal as he waited. "I see you still know how to dress for an occasion."

"Yes, well I assumed by your choice of meeting place; you wouldn't want me entering in my usual attire."

"Welcome back, by the way. I was sorry to hear about your wife's death," Birch said in a more somber tone.

"Thank you. She suffered for quite some time, so it was a blessing when she passed. She no longer has to live in this world that was ever so cruel to her."

"And to you," Birch reminded him.

"I cannot complain. I am happy where I have arrived in life. I have an exceptional daughter who has given me a well-connected son-in-law, and soon to be grandchild. My seat in the house of Lords waits, at long last reclaiming my mother's wish to be reinstated into the world her family kicked her out of."

"Yes, I heard your daughter returned. Married Burton, correct? I didn't realize they were wed long enough to produce an heir."

"My daughter is nothing if not efficient," Kendrick said with a smile and all the love a father could hold for his only child.

"So, you are sitting in Parliament this session?"

"Yes, that is what I told Dameon. I went to his office today to resign my position, and he threw this at me. So, whatever 'this' is, we must handle it in a timely manner, or I am out."

Birch shot a skeptical look at Kendrick.

"I am serious, Dylan. I will be in Parliament this turn, whether or not this is finalized. While we are on the subject, what exactly are we talking about?"

"Are you familiar with the uprisings in the two Scilies?"

"The political unrest in that entire plot of land was one of the reasons I got out. I was under the impression the Austrians quelled the attempted takeover."

"You are correct. However, there is interest among some in our esteemed government who would like to see unification of the entire state happen."

"And how does any of this come to London?" Kendrick didn't disagree about unification. Economically it made sense, however getting the Austrians and Hapsburgs to agree would not happen in his opinion.

"Are you at all familiar with the name Michele Amari?"

"Only by reputation. I spent most of my time in Rome working on trade with the northern parcel. He is a historian or scholar if memory serves."

Dylan nodded. "You remember well. However, were you aware he was a Carbonaro?"

Kendrick sat back in his chair, and just like that he was thrust back into his diplomatic duties, tripping through the intricacies of a dangerous landscape. "I am familiar with the Carboneria but was not aware that Amari belonged."

"Why the worried look, what do you know about this group I do not?" Dylan asked, concern clear on his face. Kendrick still wasn't sure what their job was, but this revelation made it markedly more dangerous for all involved.

Kendrick leaned in, putting his elbows on the table to make sure Dylan got every word of what he was about to say in the loud taproom. "The Carboneria is a secret society that cropped up about six years ago, when they began to suppress Freemasonry. The group started out as a secret discussion group to mull over the political situation and comprise possible solutions."

Dylan seemed interested, as if Dameon had not bothered

to share the dossier that Kendrick sent to him about it. It was becoming clear why Kendrick was needed on this job. "They filled the void Freemasonry being suppressed left. However, this group very clearly aligned themselves with Italian nationalism and soon became a threat to all those in power. And believe me, the Hapsburgs are not the family you want to back into a corner. You did not want to be accused publicly of an association in the group, let me just say. They tried many times to disband or ruin the organization, but it is like a many headed snake, they would cut the head off one and three more would grow back in its place. The Carboneria may well be the group that brings down the current rulers and unifies the country. If what you say is true, and Amari is a Carbonari, no amount of exile will hinder the bounty on his head."

Birch sat back in his chair with an exhausted expression. "Well, damn. This complicates things."

Kendrick only nodded. He wasn't sure to what things Dylan was referring, but they would be more complicated with the Hapsburgs on the trail. Their reach was long and deadly.

"So, what are we dealing with?"

"I—we," he gave Kendrick an apologetic look, "have been put in charge of giving Michele Amari safe passage through England on his way to Belgium, where he will have asylum, or at least have a place to hide until it is safe for his return to his country."

Kendrick closed his eyes and let out the breath he had been holding, hoping that was not the job in question. While there were some in England that wanted unification, there were just as many that liked the way things worked just fine, because the Hapsburgs had a long reach and deep pockets. If Amari was a Carbonari, and if he had information about the group and other members, or possible plans, then there was most assuredly a bounty on his head, and plenty of people looking for money and power, who could do the family's bidding even in London.

"Dameon said I would be finished with this before Parliament convened, so there must be a timeline." Oh God, please let there be a timeline.

"Yes." Dylan had recovered from the knowledge that this was no longer a babysitting mission but a saving life mission, and was ready to do the work. "He is to be here only until we can secure passage for him and I north through Scotland, then on to Belgium. They expect him there by month's end."

Kendrick did the math in his head. He might make it in time to declare his seat for this session. He could help Dylan, at the very least to manage him while he was in London. "Do you have a plan for protecting him while he is here?"

"Yes, I have spoken with someone who has the space, and is not limited to the social whirl as it were. They have agreed to be a safe house for Amari once I collect him from the ship he is currently aboard. I would like for us to take turns monitoring him. If I am to secure passage, I cannot be there all the time. I am to bring him to the house tonight. There is a dinner party with a very few close acquaintances of this person, and it won't seem untoward for more of us arriving."

"Do you think that wise, to let his presence in London be known to more than just you, I, and the homeowner? We do not know where alliances are here."

Dylan smirked. "Once you meet them, you will understand. I have been told that Amari is a bit of a handful and will require a certain amount of amusement and entertainment to keep him accommodated, and I believe this particular party of people will suit."

Kendrick was intrigued, but still skeptical. His friend clearly did not understand the reach of the Hapsburgs, but his friend had been in the spy business for many years, so Kendrick deferred to him.

"Very well, shall I meet you there then?"

Birch nodded and handed him a slip of paper with an address scrolled in a very neat feminine script which Kendrick found odd, but put it in his pocket and rose. "Until this evening then." Dylan reached out his hand.

Kendrick clasped it and shook. He had an uneasy feeling that there was a large bit of information he was missing, but decided he had the important bits and would find out the rest this evening. Now, it was time to flag down another hack and change for a dinner party.

CHAPTER 3

"*Y*ou are radiant this evening, darling," Madame Contrell complimented Fina. "I have always loved emerald on you. Suits your skin tone."

Sarrafinna had to admit, she was feeling as radiant as she looked. Her account issues would soon be solved, and it would not require her to take on one last client.

"I say, I agree, you look much more the thing from earlier. I take it your meeting went well," Lang drawled as he lounged on the chaise with his brandy. It bothered her that she had to miss the park earlier.

"Thank you, I am feeling much more like myself. This little endeavor will solve the issues I had earlier in the day. I am sorry I had to miss the park, Reginald. I had every intention of joining the rest when they met you."

"Do not give it another thought, Lang explained when they arrived. I understand implicitly, love," Mr. Reginald Chesterfield, Lang's partner reassured her. "Besides, I brought a piece of my cook's famous lemon cake for you, so I ate yours along with mine." He smiled.

"I do wish I had not missed that. I do so love Mrs. Compfy's pastries."

"So," Lang interrupted and sat up, making room for Reginald to perch on the end of the chaise with him. "When will you fill us in on what this job will entail?"

Finna, who had been standing by the open window looking out onto the street, turned and settled on the couch beside Madame Contrell.

"It is easy really, I was asked to house a gentleman from Sicily who is making his way to Belgium to seek asylum. He and those tasked to protect him will utilize my spare rooms and he will be ours to entertain."

"Sounds untoward," Reginald pointed out. "Why ask a courtesan— a Lady courtesan, in fact—to house such a person?"

"As I understand it, this man is of the upper class himself, and accustomed to a certain level of luxury and amusement. Mr. Birch thought with my upbringing and my background and knowledge of world affairs, not to mention, there currently will be no men of note being entertained it was safe."

Reginald still had a skeptical expression. "Oh, Regi, always the doubting Debbie," Lang said. "I am sure Birch would never bring a dangerous man into Finna's house. All will be well."

Lang reached out and put a reassuring hand over Reginald's. Finna didn't think Lang's laissez faire attitude swayed him in the least, but he returned the affection and shrugged his shoulders. Lang, being the third son of an Earl, had not been exposed to all the underbelly of the world as Reginald had, and in these matters it showed. Finna was glad Lang had Reginald to look after him, because Lang always thought the best of everyone and as Reginald and Finna knew that was not always the safest way to go through life.

The doorbell pealed and the entire party looked toward the entrance to the parlor. Finna was glad her new guests had arrived before dinner was served, she had not eaten all day, and was famished. She rose once again, standing by the window to greet her guests.

Golding, the butler, entered first, almost having to bend his great shoulders to clear the doorway, which was more than tall enough for most. He filled the entrance. "Lady Sarrafinna, might I present Mr. Birch, Mr. Amari, and Marquess of Harwich."

Golding stepped aside so the three men could enter the room, but Finna did not see them. When Golding had introduced the last name, she seemed to go blind, or dumb, or both.

Other than the one incident at the Burton residence when his daughter was trying to find a husband, Finna had deftly avoided any contact with Kendrick since his return. If he was part and parcel of this, she would need to back out. But she couldn't. She needed the money.

"Good evening, gentlemen, it is lovely to have some new faces joining us. As much as I adore Lang and Reginald, it does get tedious to find new topics to discuss." Madame Contrell jumped to Finna's rescue, because along with being struck dumb and blind, she was now mute.

The men stepped forward and bowed to Madame Contrell, giving Finna another moment to choose. She needed this money, and that was that. She would take Kendrick aside and tell him he needed to step away from the situation. That was all. He would leave—he looked as untethered to find her here as she was to see him. She was London's most sought after courtesan, she could take the reins and control this situation.

With a deep breath, squaring her shoulders, Finna slid her expression into place. A bored, noncommittal smile that never reached her eyes.

"Good evening, gentlemen. Please forgive my rudeness, I wasn't expecting Marquess Harwich to be attending tonight. We are abundantly blessed this evening." She strode up to Birch first. He bowed over her hand, but clearly understood she would have words with him later for not disclosing Kendrick's part. He knew better.

"Lady Sarrafinna, please may I introduce Mr. Michele Amari. He will be your houseguest for the foreseeable future."

Finna caught movement from the corner of her eye. Kendrick stiffened. There was more here than was obvious on the surface.

"Lady Sarrafinna, thank you so much for aiding in my safe passage to Belgium." Mr. Amari also bent over her hand, but he took it and kissed the back of it, then held on a fraction longer than necessary.

Finna deftly slid her hand free and bent her head to her guest. "Mr. Amari, I am happy to assist Mr. Birch in his diplomatic mission. I hope you find my hospitality to your liking."

Then it was Kendrick. He made no move to take her

hand. Since she did not offer it, it was a good choice. He bowed, and she dipped into a perfect curtsy.

"Lord Harwich, I was not informed you would be joining us." She again shot a look at Birch, who cleared his throat and turned away.

"Perfectly understandable, as I also was not informed you would be aiding us in this operation. I am sorry if it has put you out."

"Of course not. My home has long been open to any who desired to enter," she said, with a double meaning hanging in the air. She thought she heard Lang clearing his throat to hold back a chuckle. "May I introduce my other guests?" She turned her back to Kendrick, speaking volumes, especially to him. "You have all met my dear companion Madame Contrel. She lives here with me as part of my household. And this is Mr. Cedric Langley, third son to the Earl of Huntington."

"Mr. Langley, glad to meet you." Kendrick was the first to extend his hand in his welcoming way. Birch and Mr. Amari followed his lead.

"And this," she turned to Reginald, who not surprisingly, had stepped back behind Lang by a step. Little did Reginald know he and Harwich had much in common. "This is Mr. Reginald Chesterfield, a close friend of Mr. Langley's."

Reginald nodded, but didn't make an attempt to step forward with a greeting. No one seemed taken aback by his action, and all the men just nodded as well. Finna had almost forgotten how Kendrick could make any one feel at ease. Well, anyone except her. Finna felt hot and cold at the same time. This was ridiculous. Theirs was a story long ago put to the cobwebs of the mind.

"Lady Sarrafinna, dinner is ready." Golding stepped in and broke any unease her lack of small talk may have created.

"Oh fabulous, Golding, thank you. Shall we?" She motioned to the door, but before she could sink to the back of the group, Harwich proffered his arm.

"May I escort you, Lady Sarrafinna?"

She wanted to refuse and insist he move along, but her breeding won out. "Of course, thank you."

She stepped up to his side and linked her arm with his. The two led the entire party out of the parlor and to the dining room. As the two highest ranking in class it was proper, but considering everything, Finna saw it as the farce it was.

"Oh, this looks delightful!" Mr. Amari exclaimed as they all took their seats. He placed himself on Finna's left, and Kendrick sat at her right. Madame Contrell sat next to their new houseguest, and Finna noted that she managed to move her chair slightly in his direction. Raising her wine glass to her lips to hide her smile, she observed her other guests.

"I always say that your cook must give me the recipe for her cream of leek soup, every time it is served. Isn't it excellent, Reginald?"

Reginald nodded, but offered no more and bent to eating the soup. Finna would have to apologize to him later for not knowing a peer would be at dinner. He would learn soon enough that Kendrick was not the normal peer of the realm, but for now she hated seeing him so uncomfortable.

The rest of dinner passed well. Madame Contrell asked Mr. Amari to talk about his homeland, and his adventure on the ship ride over. He made it clear boat travel was not his preferred mode. He was looking more forward to land travel for most of the duration of his trip.

"Have you ever traveled out of Sicily before?" Lang asked, to keep things moving.

Finna was having a bugger of a time keeping the thread of the conversation going in her mind to interject at the correct time. Having Kendrick so close after so many years was disconcerting. The man emanated heat from his core. Even her fingertips on her right side were heated. It would help, she decided over the quail and spinach, if she called him Harwich or my Lord from now on. Referring to him with his Christian name created a level of intimacy between them that did not exist, and would never, so there was no point in her brain having a trail down that particular thought.

When the meal was finished Finna slid back her chair, as did her usual guests, but her three new ones made no room to move.

"I know the accustomed protocol is for the women to excuse themselves and the men then partake in their port and whatever else, but I do not allow that tradition at my table. There will be port and whatever other beverage you might like in the parlor, along with an extensive assortment of snuffs, and even pipes and cigarillos. There is no reason for you to remain here."

With that she stood and waited for her new guests to acclimate and also rise to leave the room. Mr. Amari and Birch seemed puzzled and off balance from the change in the prescribed behavior, Harwich easily came around and walked out with the group with a bemused smile playing on his lips.

Once back in the parlor Golding got everyone their drink and smoke of choice. He was doing so much better, but Madame Contrell did get her attention to the fact Mr. Birch had been relieved of his wallet. She excused herself to chase him down and retrieve it. Luckily, Madame Contrell also had a knack for pick pocketing and easily returned the wallet without Mr. Birch being any wiser.

The company relaxed and all began talking, but Harwich moved from window to window peering into the darkness. When he made it to the farthest window from interested ears, Finna saw her chance and followed him.

"You need to leave," she hissed in his ear, making him jump.

"I am sorry you were not told of my involvement, but it is impossible for me to stand down." He turned back to the window and seemed to be trying to make out something in the darkness.

"What are you looking at?" she asked, peering over his shoulder on her tiptoes.

"Is that—is that a person standing in the middle of the courtyard?" he asked, looking back at her and almost hitting her nose with his, they were so close. She shot back and stood ramrod straight.

"I do not believe there is anyone in my courtyard, no. Perhaps you are looking at the naked statute of Venus I had commissioned when I first purchased the townhouse."

He blinked at her, then turned and looked harder as if that would make the darkness lighten. "It hasn't moved, so you are most likely correct."

"Harwich, I am serious. I cannot have you in my house. You should understand more than anyone."

He turned and looked down at her with all the compassion she imagined he possessed in his eyes. "I do, and if I had any option I would leave row, but I am afraid we will need to make the best of this. Of course, you could always tell Birch that this entire thing was not going to work, and we needed to find another home for him to stay."

"No." She wasn't about to tell Harwich of all people that she was in need of funds, and that this one inconvenience would most likely keep her out of the bed of the next up and coming duke. Besides, she owned no one an explanation of her decisions least of all him. She took one more attempt to implore him with her eyes, and realizing he was as hard in his decisions now as he was over twenty years ago, she huffed and walked back to the group. It would have to be Birch to pull him.

"Mr. Birch, if I might have a word," she bade as she walked past the seated guests and into the hallway. Golding was just coming up the hall with the tea tray. "Oh good, the tea tray has arrived," she announced back into the room. Hopefully everyone would remain occupied for the moment. Birch wandered out of the room after Golding entered. He looked like a schoolboy who had dipped his sister's braids in wax.

"I know, and I am sorry."

She rounded on him. "I find that hard to believe, when you of all people are aware of our past. You left out the fact that Harwich was part of this on purpose. You knew I wouldn't agree if I knew."

"You are correct. I lied, but in my defense, Kendrick—"

"Harwich."

"I beg your pardon?"

Finna took a calming breath. "I would prefer it if you referred to him as Harwich. That is who he is now, and I would just prefer it." She tried to hide the emotion from her eyes, but knew Birch read her easily.

"Of course," he said, then shifted. "Can we stay or are you going to throw us out?"

"You well know I need the coin you are offering. You have created a situation where I have a bad choice or a worse choice. Please know I will not forget that fact, and I have a long memory."

Birch nodded, knowing he would be repaying this debt at a later time and he would not like the payment. Finna turned on her heels and reentered the room. Harwich stood behind the chaise at the farthest point from her, teacup in hand, observing.

"Here you are, dear." Madame Contrell patted the seat beside her and pointed to the prepared tea. "Just as you like it."

"Thank you." Finna was exhausted. After her concerns about money this morning, then her meeting with Birch and now the realization the money she would get from this deal would come at a price, she was yet sure she would be willing pay. She was just tired.

Golding entered and informed her that Mr. Amari's room had been prepared and was ready for him at his leisure.

"Wonderful," he said, putting his cup down. "I am looking forward to sleeping on a bed that doesn't jostle me about. I think, if I am not being rude, that I will retire."

"Oh, no. Please do what you need to. You must be exhausted from your trip," Finna assured him.

Birch rose and laid his half empty cup on the table. "I will walk you to the stairs, then I must make my leave as well. I will see you all in the morning, I am sure." He nodded to everyone and followed his quarry out the parlor door.

"I will be leaving as well. I am not certain yet, when I will see you all again, but perhaps as early as tomorrow. Thank you, Lady Sarrafinna, for a lovely dinner. I will leave you to it then." And before she could respond, Harwich quit the room as well.

Sarrafinna felt the air once again circulate in the room. She could hear the men talking in the hallway but couldn't make out the words. Golding would bring her up to speed later, but for now, she would enjoy what was left of her tea, then find her own bed. Tomorrow wasn't nearly as far away as she would like, and she was certain it would be a very long day.

CHAPTER 4

*L*ondon bustled around her. Finna forgot people ventured out of their homes so early in the city. Being the daughter of a duke, it was always her custom to rise much later in the morning, not to mention the fact that as a courtesan, her mornings were often her own, as her clients were occupied with their own daily lives.

Her carriage stopped in front of the unassuming rooms of Mr. Dylan Birch. Upon retiring last evening, she was certain her decision made. If she could get through this one assignment, she would be set and free to retire from the world of the beau monde, and the life she made for herself all those years ago. That is what she wanted. However, her sleepless night, and the revolving thoughts of Kendrick Rutland told her otherwise. She had to acknowledge the fact that this one man seemed to be bookending her adult life.

At the one end, the catalyst for her choice to leave the immense safety of being a duke's daughter, and seek a life as a courtesan, instead of standing in the light of the scandal and grief of losing him. Now, he was in the way of her quiet exit from that life, to one of quiet solitude. She sighed. She made a brief list of potential men who might benefit from an association with her, and none on her list would be horrible to contend with over a season. Then she could be done.

Decision made, she banged the roof of the carriage and within seconds her coachman opened the door and handed her down. "Thank you, Felix."

"Shall I stay, mi lady, or would you prefer I drive around the square?" He asked knowing the gossip if they saw her carriage in front of a bachelor's rooms.

"You can wait. I will not be long, and honestly I just don't have the energy to care anymore." She hated hearing the defeat in her own voice, but she was tired.

"Of course, mi lady. I'll be waiting right here for you when you finish." His kind, almost fatherly smile made her think of her own father. Not in all the years since her departure had she seen anything but a kind encouraging smile when they encountered one another.

Felix would stand in the spot until she returned, and he would also be up the steps in a moment's notice if ever she needed his assistance. He was a gem of a person, and in making her upcoming decisions, Finna had realized how lucky she had been over the years with the people she surrounded herself with.

She made the steps and pulled the large bell pull to the right of the door. Being so close to the street, there was nowhere to stand other than on the steps leading to the entrance. After a time, she considered pulling the bell again. She assumed there would be at least one servant available to tell her if their master was about. Footfalls heralded someone at last. The door opened a crack, and a rotund, round faced woman stuck her head out, curls bouncing around the edge of her cap.

"Sorry, the master is no interested in whatever you have to offer." Then she went to shut the door in Finna's face.

"I beg your pardon," she said in a sticky sweet voice, however her booted foot jammed in the door's way, told the woman otherwise. "Please tell your master it is Lady Sarrafinna to see him. And that it is most important I have a word with him... now."

She put the emphasis on Lady, and now, hoping to spark the import of their guest. Not that she had paraded around London since she left as a duke's daughter, she often found her upbringing and her title had certain power when pressed into service.

"Just a min," the woman said and didn't even bother to shut the door the rest of the way, but also did not invite Finna to stop cooling her heels on the steep stairs open to prying eyes.

Deciding an unclosed door was as much of an invitation as anyone would need, she allowed herself entrance, and quietly closed the door behind her. The room was long and narrow, holding a set of stairs as steep as the ones on the stoop, leading to the upstairs of the residence on one wall, and a dark hallway along the other. There were two doors to either side of her. She assumed one would be his study, and the other a parlor for accepting guests.

Before Finna could choose which room to settle in, the woman came bustling down the stairs, and stopped when she noted Finna standing in the room, already in the house.

She hmphed, but continued down the stairs, not speaking until she was on the floor.

"The master said he would see you in his study and that I am to bring tea to you." She turned, not bothering to curtsy or otherwise acknowledge Finna's rank.

In her chosen profession, she was used to this type of treatment from other ladies in a drawing room, and even the servant's in a bachelor's household. If she were to be a regular guest, she would put an end to the behavior with a few chosen words, but this would be the only time she visited Birch, so there was no need. It mattered not to Finna how a maid judged her.

"Sit here and don't touch anything. I'll be back with tea."

"Penny," came the sharp retort of Penny's master from the hall. "Is this how you treat all of my guests, or just the ones you assume are not on as moral a high ground as yourself?"

To her credit, Penny turned as bright red as a poppy. "No, sir. I am sorry, sir, I just—"

"It is not your job to concern yourself with my moral high ground either. You are rather new to my employ, so an apology to my guest—who happens to be of the lineage of a duke's daughter, in case you missed the 'Lady' before her name—and a promise to never behave in such a rude manner to another of my guests, will be all that is required."

He stood and waited for her red to turn to a rather unbecoming purple. Finna was uncertain if it was from embarrassment that she had incorrectly assumed the situation, or that she was being forced to still apologize to a woman who dared to visit an unmarried man at his private establishment.

"I am sorry, mi lady. I did not realize your title, but that matters not. If you are here and welcome by my master, that is all I need know." She bobbed and left the room. Finna was unsure if tea would ever be brought to poor Birch this morning.

"I am so sorry for that. She is new. Hired by my mother, so that should explain quite a bit."

"If after all these years I allow a maid to shatter my mood, I am unworthy. She is not the first nor the last, I assume."

Birch said nothing, but he tightened his jaw at her reply. "Let us sit." He motioned to a small collection of well stuffed chairs around a low tea table. The desk loomed large in the room, but he made no move to stand behind it in a play to establish his importance. They were acquainted too long for that.

"What has you knocking on my door at such an early hour? I assumed matters were settled last evening before I left." He did not bother to ply her with pleasantries. He had a full scheduled today, she was certain, and she also had other places to be.

"Yes, I thought so, but after having a night to consider things, I am afraid I must require without compromise that Harwich be taken from this endeavor you and I are on. He will be a distraction to those in my household, and if he is seen coming and going from my residence, it will create a stir that may bring unwanted attention to your guest." There, that sounded educated and not at all waspish.

"Your tea, Mr. Birch. Where should I put it?" The butler entered pushing a rather delicate looking tray for his size.

"Thank you, Bennett, where is Penny?" Birch asked. He must already understand the answer, Finna thought.

"She, well, she felt it better if she didn't disturb you and your guest again. I sensed from her crying that you as well would prefer my services to hers at the moment," the butler explained dryly.

"Ah, of course, just put it here on the table. I am sure we can serve ourselves."

They waited while Bennett did his best to set out the tea service without dropping one of the delicate cups out of his oversized hands.

When he left the room, Finna asked, "Where did you find him? I could have used a man of that size in my service over the years." She served tea to them both.

"Let's just say Bennett was a found object, that I would not have acquired from one of the services here in town."

Finna nodded. Over the years, she and Dylan had crossed paths in some very questionable situations. They knew what the other was, and they liked it that way. She could be the Duke's daughter in a gaming hell, and he the fourth son of an Earl, playing spy games. They lived in two worlds, and as such understood each other.

After they sipped for a time, Dylan set his cup aside and leaned forward with his elbows on his knees. "Finna, I understand. You know I do. And I was wrong to not tell either of you about the other one's participation, but the truth is, I can't do this without you both. To be honest, I am expecting Kendrick to show up here with the same complaint as you, but for another set of obscure and ridiculous reasons."

Her heart sank to the depths of her chest. "Why do you need him?"

"I need him because he lived there. He speaks the language, and he knows the players. He also may be the only one who can get important information from Amari that I cannot."

She knew there was something else, but Birch would only share what he wanted. She couldn't force the issue.

"I understand if it is more than you can do, Finna. I will not hold this against you. We can find a new safe house, and your world will be as it was."

The words, 'as it was' rang in her mind. She would be back to needing the funds before she could plan retiring. She would be back to worrying that she was too old. Yes, she had a list of gentlemen, but at what point would the young men of the Ton decide she was past her prime? The truth was she was getting closer to being the age of their mothers instead of their lovers. If she was tired cooling her heels on the front stoop, this was downright exhausting. She spent her entire adult life being what other people wanted or needed her to be. What difference would it make if she were being a fetching arm piece to an up-and-coming Lord, or having to pretend the presence of the first man she ever loved was not an inconvenience?

"Very well."

"You'll remain?" She nodded. "Excellent, now, there was something that I got wind of from a note last night once I got back here."

"What?" She didn't like his tone.

"You were correct when you said Harwich's presence at your home would be noticed, but not for the reasons you think. Word has already made the circuit that Amari is possibly in London. And it is widely known that Kendrick has spent the last decade or more in Rome, not to mention he has been less than visible. The home office still wants

Kendrick on this assignment but cautions that there needs to be a deflection of why he is attending you at your home."

No, she didn't like his tone at all. "What are you saying, Dylan?"

He sat up and yanked his cravat to make way for a large breath of air, to fortify himself for what she knew was to come. "The Ton must think you are seeing Kendrick socially. That needs to be why everyone thinks he is visiting."

"So, this is the actual reason you chose us?" she asked, knowing the answer without waiting for a reply.

"Not me, Chamberlain-Fields. He knew of your history and decided if we rekindled the old scandal with a new romantic twist it would keep the gossip mongers so whet with anticipation that they wouldn't notice what the real story was." He looked sheepish. "I am sorry. I never would want either of you to relive that time for anything."

"Other than national security, and England's best interest?" she pointed out. Everyone had their price, and Birch was a true patriot.

She was not surprised that Dameon was behind the farce. If he thought it would advance his career and hurt her at the same time, it was a win for him.

He looked at the floor and didn't bother to argue the fact.

"I suppose they will expect us in public, as a couple."

"Yes."

Her exhaustion was turning to pure red anger at the injustice of the world at large. It would never allow her to slip into the shadows, she knew that to her bones.

"Just to clarify so that I get the persona correct, am I to play the love sick, jilted lover reunited, or am I to play the cold hearted courtesan who will take any man to her bed for money?"

"Finna, I—"

She put up a hand to stop him. She didn't need him to be sorry, or to pity her. She chose her life path and liked to think she brought dignity to her profession, as much as one could.

"I need to know which one you believe will work best for your intention, that is all. How do you think I need to play this?"

He looked at her with genuine remorse in his expression. Perhaps he didn't think there was still so much raw emotion on the surface, regardless the damage had been done, and he knew it.

"I would think however you choose will be fine," he answered, looking away and never looking back.

"Very well," was her tight answer. She rose to leave, and stood fixing the seam on her gloves waiting for him to escort her out. "By the way Mr. Birch, my price just doubled."

"As you wish, Lady Sarrafinna. As you wish." He opened the door and she was thrust into the brightness of the morning. London still bustled around her, but it no longer held the promise it had an hour ago. Felix stood where she left him, a solid anchor to swim to in the changing tide.

"Home, Felix. I just want to go home."

"Yes, mi lady."

CHAPTER 5

*K*endrick sat in the tavern's dankness by the docks. Still not willing to give the food a try, he opted for a mug of ale. His stomach grumbled when the serving girl walked by with hot meat pasties. He hadn't thought about the ones his mother made to sell on the street for years. She always made sure, before she left him for the day, that he would get his pick on the lot for his daily meal. Perhaps he would ask cook if she had any knowledge of how to prepare them.

He looked up as the door swung open, letting a small ray of light in from the street. Dylan strode toward him. "I wasn't sure you would come," Kendrick greeted him.

"I would have sent word at the very least. My expert can't be left waiting around, now can you?" He sat, and the server came at once. Kendrick got the impression she was interested in more than just his order. He waited while Dylan ordered more of that stew and another glass and pitcher of ale.

"I didn't consider it wise for me to visit at your home this morning."

"No, you were right to plan an out of the way meeting," Birch assured him. "So, what can I do for you?"

"It is Sarrafinna, you need to find a different place for Amari. Had I known it was a single woman's home, you were suggesting I would refuse. There are too many variables. It is too dangerous."

"Don't you mean, had you known it was Sarrafinna?"

"Pardon?"

"You said if you had known it was a single woman's home, but didn't you actually mean if you had known it was Sarrafinna?"

Kendrick took a calming breath. It wouldn't do for him to strangle one of his only friends here in London. "I am not interested in having a discussion about verbiage with you. This situation is too tenuous for her involvement. We need to be someplace where our only worry is protecting Amari, not a household filled with defenseless women."

Dylan laughed. He not only laughed, he leaned back on the two back legs of his chair and laughed so hard he drew attention to them.

"What in hell do you find so funny about what I just said?" Kendrick was losing his patience. This should be a quick matter. He would point out how dangerous it was, and Sarrafinna would no longer be a target, and he would not need to press his attentions on her. Simple.

"Have you at all kept up with her life since your departure with your new bride so many years ago?"

"No. I was married, and I assumed she would be as well. I saw no reason to drag out an already awkward situation," he said, but then admitted. "Victoria, however, remained in correspondence with her and from time to time would let something slip, but I never asked. Not once."

Dylan put both hands up in surrender. "I am sure you did," he said, then sobered, adding, "It must have been deuced tough, having to marry another while the woman you loved fell out of your grasp."

"You can say that," Kendrick agreed. "It was more difficult for Victoria, she too had a fancy for another, and was certain he was close to making an offer. In one rash decision, Victoria's mother ruined four lives, but we made the best of things and got on quite well after a fashion."

"As did Sarrafinna," Dylan pointed out.

Kendrick held his jaw tight, so it didn't slack open at the obvious incorrect statement. "I should say not. She became a courtesan. A duke's daughter doesn't just run off and become a courtesan," he scoffed.

"And yet, she did. I have talked with her many times about her choices, Kendrick. It was a choice that in her mind set her free. In a way, she believes she fared better than the two of you."

Dylan was being honest. What did Kendrick know of what she wanted really, beyond what they had talked of while taking long walks in the park, or circling a ballroom? Children's dreams really, nothing more. Once he accepted his fate and made the offer to save Victoria from ruin, he no longer had any say in what she did.

"When I heard the news, I figured it was just gossip. There were any number of men willing to step into my shoes. Her father must have had to bar the doors to keep them out."

"I don't doubt that, she is still by far one of the most beautiful women in all of London, with her mother's Spanish coloring and dark hair, then add to that her maternal grandmother's zest for life, but even she knew there were few men who would allow her to be so willful and outspoken. She chose a life that would not take her life from her."

He made noble attempts at not envisioning her at all. Kendrick had never thought another man would not love the parts of Sarrafinna that made her shine the most, but it made sense now, twenty years later. None of the past had any bearing on the current situation.

"Still, this is too dangerous."

"She came to me this morning," Dylan said.

Kendrick felt the first release of nervous energy since he walked into the parlor and realized whose home he was in.

"Good, I guess I didn't need to worry, she saw the foolishness of her participation." Birch, however, was shaking his head and just like that the pressure of a lifetime of responsibility was back.

"Not exactly. She was hoping to strong arm me into firing you. She had no intention of backing away from this. I got the impression the money is an important enticement. In fact, when she left, she doubled her price."

"Why in hell didn't you refuse? Then she would have backed out."

"Listen, putting the two of you together was not my idea, and it reached higher than my paycheck will allow. I am sorry, but this is the way of things. I will understand if you need to walk away."

"You think the idea of being in close proximity to Sarrafinna is a big enough deterrent to ignore her safety? I seem to be the only one with her wellbeing in mind, including the lady herself."

"Very well then." Birch clearly latched onto the crumb and moved forward. "I do have to tell you one other piece that you will not be happy about, and in all honesty, it was what doubled her price."

Kendrick went cold. What could be so bad that it would force her to double her fee? "What?"

"Because you will be seen coming and going from her home, and there is obvious chatter that Amari has landed on London soil, you will need a very convincing reason to be at her home."

Only in the worst nightmare would Dylan be about to tell him, what he knew was coming. "Explain."

"As I explained to Sarrafinna, you two are going to need to be seen in public together, so there is an assumed interest on your part."

Assumed? As much as Kendrick liked to lie, there had not been a day in his life since the night he had to propose to her closest friend, that he hadn't thought about Sarrafinna. "I cannot fathom that you would willingly put us in such a position."

"I wouldn't, if I had a choice," Dylan assured him. The hard plains of his expression showed his anger to it all.

"What did Sarrafinna say?" He would not agree to anything, if it was going to upset her.

"She agreed, but then doubled her price."

Kendrick didn't blame her in the least. If he was forced to

play the pretty to the man who jilted him, he would double his price as well.

"What is this to look like? Reunited lovers, or is it to be believed I have taken her as my mistress?"

Dylan laughed at the question. "The two of you are more alike than ever, years have not changed that. She asked the same question."

His body was numb and the blood in his veins felt like ice. "And what did you tell her?"

"I told her that the two of you could decide which would work better or have the greater effect. Please remember that your job is to deflect from our assignment."

Kendrick only nodded. Anything he might add at this juncture could not be constructive. "I will leave you then. Lady Sarrafinna and I have much to discuss."

"She asked me to inform you that when you arrive home, there will be an invitation to Lady Ferris's rout this evening. She would prefer to be picked up by eight o'clock. She will be ready. Oh, and please keep me informed which invitations the two of you will be accepting and the times. I will need to be at the house in your absence."

"Of course," he managed as he stalked out of the tavern, into the inky sunlight of the dirty street.

Life was to become rather uncomfortable for the foreseeable future. He needed to make this as easy on her as he could, but if there was not one person concerned for her safety, it left him no choice but to continue. The other niggling part was her need for funds. She would never have another worry about stability and surviving as long as he drew breath.

He would hail a hack, make his way back to his residence and prepare for what may well be the most difficult night of his life...and that was saying something.

CHAPTER 6

"*I* am just sick of trying to convince you of the thousands of ways this will not work." Madame Contrell sat, perched in a chair in Finna's bed chamber.

Once home, Finna made the choice to remain there for the day. The only one foolish enough to enter her room was Madame Contrell who, upon discovering the details, refused to leave her side.

"I am certain you are," Finna answered impassively. Emotion would only be a hindrance.

"Do you remember the first man you took to your bed?"

"Of course," she answered, but failed to see what any of this had to do with that.

"That entire day, I swayed between calling for your family to come get you and feeling the need to prepare you for the rest of your life."

"Well, I am glad you chose the latter. It would have been uncomfortable for my family to be there."

"Finna," she said in exasperation, like a mother would to her petulant child. While, in fact, that was hitting very close to the mark for them. Finna thought of Bethany as a mother figure and mentor. "Remember, I was there. In the darkness with you. When you first arrived in Bath. The notion that your mother would send you away alone to deal with such pain."

"We have discussed this before. She had to remain to limit the damage of the scandal. She would have come if she thought she could. I hold no disregard for my mother's actions. She was dealing the best she knew how."

"Fine." Contrell waved her hand as if to wave that argument away. "But I saw the hurt you endured. I do not wish to help you live through that again."

"Whatever do you mean? I am not the fragile, star struck young child I was at ten and eight. I am well beyond such nonsense."

Contrell looked at her with such sadness, reaching out to place a hand on Finna's arm. "But are you, dear?"

Finna couldn't witness the pity in her eyes anymore. Swinging from the woman's grasp, she walked to the bell pull. It was time to dress. A woman had few weapons available, but those Finna had she knew well, and could exploit when needed. Tonight would be one of those nights.

"I understand your concern, and will not lie and say I won't struggle, but I have others to consider beyond my own ego. I have many years of lessons learned since then. It is my job to make Lord Harwich feel as if he is the only man in the room and make the others see him as the most important man at the fete. I will smile and defer to his wants and needs. Nothing more. At the very least, I now know better how to guard my heart. This will be a memory before we blink."

Madame Contrell shot a skeptical glance at her, and changed the subject. "What dress will you wear?"

"The red, and set it off with the diamonds." Finna walked to the wardrobe and searched until finding deep red silk ballgown with the silver threading accents, and a ruffled neckline which dipped closer to her breasts than her neck.

"Well, that will make a statement. You haven't worn that since you spent the week with that prince from... Oh, where was he from?"

"Denmark, and I think it suits the occasion. We are meant to be seen; this will get us seen."

"Yes, it will do that," she agreed. "I am certain Lord Harwich cannot take his eyes off you. It will be very clear what he missed out on all these years."

"Bethany, I am not wearing this to tempt Kendrick." she protested.

"Of course not, my dear, that would be foolish, and you are many things, but foolish is not one of them. And you know not to call my Bethany, so I will assume I have over-stepped."

Finna looked at Contrell from the mirror, then let the conversation die on that remark. Was she hoping to show Kendrick what he missed? It was not his choice to marry her closest friend, any more than it was hers to allow it. He was an honorable man. That was one thing that drew her to him. After all these years, she was certain he was still one of the most honorable men in her acquaintance. She had plenty of experience with the men who were not.

A knock on the door brought her out of her thoughts. "Come in."

"I'm sorry, mi lady, but your guest is here," a young maid said with trepidation.

"Thank you, Milly, but might I ask why you apologized for coming to let me know a guest was here?"

Finna knew the answer but saw it as her mission to make these young girls own their place in the world. They only had one life, no point in going around apologizing for one's existence.

The young girl came further into the room and dipped her head low, to avoid eye contact. "I was aware you didn't want to be bothered earlier."

"In that you were correct, but as I am going out and will be escorted, it was your job to alert me. Never apologize for doing your job."

"Yes, girl, there are more than enough people who don't apologize for not doing their jobs as it is," Madame Contrell added.

Finna walked up to the young woman, who could be barely twenty. She had found her in the alley between her milliner and a soap shop. The poor thing had more dirt on her than she had clothes.

"And always make eye contact with anyone you are dealing with. It shows that you have presence of mind."

"But you are a lady, mi lady. I could never be a good as you."

Finna's heart sank. She knew on the surface what her maid was saying was true. "Just because a person is higher in station than you, does not make them better, it makes them more privileged and that means they have a responsibility to make others around them feel comfortable. Now, that is a rule that few follow, but you cannot help that. You just hold yourself to a better standard. Everyone deserves to be looked in the eye."

"Yes, mi lady. I will work on that."

Finna pulled the girl in for a quick hug, which she understood scared her a bit every time she did, but her recoil had gotten less.

"I am certain you will, Milly." Finna stepped back and let the maid scurry from the room.

"You are either going to make that girl die from a fit of nerves or make her think she could hold a position in the House of Lords," Contrell stated, shaking her head.

"No woman, no matter their station, should be a timid as she is."

"I do not disagree, but outside of these walls, the culture will tell her something different."

"Well then, it is a good thing she will never be expected to find employ somewhere else as long as I can afford her."

Madame Contrell rose and waited for Finna. "Would you like me to inform Lord Harwich you will not be attending?"

"Of course not, after you." She motioned for her friend to head to the parlor while she inwardly steeled herself for what would be a difficult evening, but one of many to come.

The buzz of voices wafted out of the parlor and greeted her at the top of the stairs. One voice she was getting to know. Mr. Amari chatted in his native language, Italian and the other, deeper with a physical component sending chills along her arms and spine. Kendrick's rich voice danced on her nerves as the first notes of a waltz always did, all heady anticipation for good things to come. Finna forced her foot to make the first step and continued down, but she paused just inside the doorway, hoping to listen for a few more moments, and go unnoticed.

"Ah, Lady Finna." Michele Amari looked up first. "You look ravishing tonight. I was just telling Lord Harwich he needed to spend more time in Sicily than Rome."

"Mr. Amari, thank you, but please just call me Finna. I do not hold to such strict rules," Finna responded, sweeping into the room, trying to not see Harwich's reaction to her gown.

She walked over to the drink stand and poured herself a healthy serving of whiskey. She took a long draw and let it heat down to her stomach before turning back to her guests.

"Good evening, Lord Harwich, thank you for sending word that you received my message about our destination this evening."

He bowed over her offered hand, and ever so slightly rubbed his lips across the back of it. Even with her gloves on, the heat of his breath made her lose her own.

"I am ever so grateful that you made the choice of venue. Since I have returned to England as a widower, I am over-whelmed by the sheer number of invitations. I defer to my daughter and attend whatever event they are."

"My pleasure. Will Zoe and Winn be attending this rout?" she asked, grabbing at a neutral topic.

"No, I got the joyous news that she is carrying my first grandchild. They have opted to remain in the country and forgo the season."

The pride in his expression squeezed her heart. She understood the love he had for his daughter. Zoe was an exceptional young woman. Very like her mother but was blessed with her father's expressive eyes. Perhaps the best parts of them both.

"Has she seen her grandmother since her return? When I saw her at the house party last year she had only just returned to the country."

"Not that she has said to me. She is aware of what her grandmother did to her mother and me. I had to give her slim details, because she was asking. Once she understood the duplicity, she agreed that keeping ties severed would be what her mother wanted."

At the mention of Victoria, Finna couldn't help but notice both she and Kendrick took long drinks from their glasses. She would do well to not bring up the past, as much as it is in the forefront of her mind at the moment.

"Well, congratulations on the coming baby. You are hoping for a grandson, no doubt."

"My only wish is that the baby is healthy and that the birth doesn't tax Zoe over much. Winn invited me to be at the estate when she is due, so that is my plan."

"So, where are we off to?" The question, which came from Amari, had them both turning to offer a puzzled look. "What? I am thinking, if I am your guest it would be—"

"You will stay here with me," Birch explained as he entered the parlor with Golding at his heels.

Finna waved Golding off, and he slipped back out of the room.

"I do not see why one little rout would so affect my status," Michele blustered, attempting to look offended and intimidating. Birch did not appear moved, neither did Harwich.

"That is why I am in charge of your safety. There is

already talk that you may be in London, and this will help to deflect interest from here."

"I do not see why Lady Finna and Lord Harwich going out will change anything."

"It is none of your concern, just know that it is."

Finna walked up to Amari and placed her gloved hand on his arm. "I would love for you to attend. I am certain you would have an exceptional time and add to the interest of the night for all attending. Unfortunately, this event is by invitation only, and it is meant to be a rather exclusive evening. For that reason, our host would not accept any last-minute extras."

He looked at her with appreciation for her attempt. "Thank you, my dear, for at the least saying no, that is less like a prison sentence, and more like a fair estimation of the circumstances."

She smiled. Finna quite liked her temporary guest. He was intelligent, witty, and if he drank a bit too much, who was she to judge? At least he wasn't an angry drunk. Madame Contrell was showing signs of becoming quite smitten with him. Finna just hoped her friend remembered this was a passing thing, and to not get too attached.

"I think we should go, are you ready?" came the deep voice behind her. So close, she realized, that she could almost feel his superfine coat rub the back of her arm.

She cleared her throat. "Yes, I'm ready, I just need my shawl."

Finna needed a moment. If the man could suck all the good air out of an entire parlor, she might die from suffocation in his carriage on the way. Golding stood at the hall closet with the light silk shawl.

"I can send the bugger away, mi lady, if you like," he said with a severe expression.

"Um, which bugger are you referring to?"

"The Lordish one, mi Lady Harwich." He crinkled his nose and sounded as if he were talking about something he stepped in when saying Kendrick's title.

She smiled. "That won't be necessary, I have welcomed him into our home."

"But you are upset whenever he is in a room. I'm sure of it."

Finna laid a hand on his arm. "You are a dear, but that has everything to do with me, and nothing that poor Harwich must suffer for. Please do not treat him as anything less because of my countenance."

Golding looked like he might argue, but then the man in question peered around the corner to see what was taking so long. Finna eyed her butler until he nodded in acquiescence and she turned to face Harwich.

"Ready. Please lead the way." Oh Lord, this screamed of scandal and disaster, but hadn't they already walked that road and came out, if not unscathed, at least in one piece?

CHAPTER 7

Kendrick sent up a prayer of thanks when the cool evening air chilled his heated face on the steps of Finna's townhouse. He then sent a curse to the devil for the evening to come.

Upon arriving at the formidable townhouse, in the heart of Mayfair, Kendrick almost left. He sat for much longer than necessary in his coach, waging a war with himself. Two points forced him to step onto the street and ring the bell. This was the last job he needed to do for Dameon. Then he was free of all his ties to the foreign office, and it was clear he was the only one with any interest in Finna's safety. Well, interest was a poor choice of word. He had no interest in her what-so-ever, but as a gentleman his need to find her safely through this mess was paramount.

Proof being a smug aristocrat would bite one in the tail every time, Kendrick eased once in the parlor chatting with Amari, who he was finding to be an excellent companion.

His wealth of knowledge about not only Italian history, but world news and literature were immense. It wasn't until the hair on the back of his neck prickled and he turned to see Finna standing in the doorway with the light from the hall setting her off in a halo that he realized his fault.

The air rushed from his lungs and had it not been for his ribs, his heart would have burst from his chest. He was a fool to think he would leave this drama unaffected.

Taller than the average woman, when she entered a room, she possessed it. As a green buck hoping to impress the world of the Ton, the same world that cast out his mother for marrying below her station, he had not been prepared to encounter Lady Sarrafinna, daughter to the Duke of Rygate. It seemed a lifetime ago, yet here he stood as struck by her as if seeing her for the first time. Thankfully, Amari greeted her, giving him time to recover, but he had yet to take in a full breath, which he blamed the lightheadedness on.

"I hope you don't mind taking my carriage. I felt it would be more convenient."

"Of course not, thank you," she answered as he handed her up, dismissing the coachman.

He allowed her to settle, then climbed in, taking the seat across from her. Her dress fit her to perfection, accenting her every asset. He was sure all her outfits would have the same effect. Considering her chosen life, it would be to her benefit to always be on display for a potential gentleman. Unsure where the thought derived from, it cooled his ardor by a degree, so he would take it. How the hell was he to find solid footing in all of this? He settled, then looked across at Finna. She was straightening the pearl buttons on her glove, unaware of his inner struggle. Had her life brought her to a point where she no longer struggled with their story? Was she so jaded that she didn't notice his strife?

The carriage jiggled to life and turned them into the street. The silence between them filled the carriage to uncomfortable levels.

"Tonight will not be easy, are you certain you are up for the task?" He wanted to make sure this would not cause her undue pain.

The glare she shot him would have withered an oak tree. "Tonight is not unlike every first engagement with a new client. I am forever a hair's breadth away from outright scandal. It is a line I dance on, to the dismay of everyone in the Ton."

He had nothing to offer of reassurance, so he remained silent.

She continued, "I assume you, on the other hand, are not as accustomed to how this will unravel. Let me help you be more prepared.

When we arrive, our hosts will greet us. The lady of the house will great you with a wide, welcoming smile and some useless chit chat, she will then turn and see the lady on your arm is none other than me. This will cause her smile to slip, but not for long enough to be noticed unless you know what you are looking for. She will paste on her best fake smile, square her shoulders, and dip into a barely recognizable curtsey.

You see, while my father feels it a blessing to me that he never publicly disowned me and cast me from the family, I am an anomaly and a threat to their well-ordered way of thinking of people."

Kendrick watched as emotion played across her face,

certain she was unaware she had let her own mask slip in the inky shadows of the carriage.

"While the hostess would rather throw me out of her house— lest I sully the linens with my hedonistic ways—she cannot, and must defer to my rank, which is almost always above her own.

Now, when it comes to the men in the room. I will warn you that we will be elbows to elbows with many of my past clients. They no doubt will make a comment here or there about your choice upon your return. This will not happen within my hearing, so you should have an answer for them prepared. I am, however, very concerned, knowing your political aspirations, that being seen holding court at my skirts may not be to your benefit."

She looked him in the eye, as much as one can in a dark carriage. He understood her warning. On the one hand, he could look like a pathetic milk sop come back to England to have another go at his once love, or he could also look like the worst cad, by ruining her reputation as a debutante, now back to claim her services when the woman he married passed away.

"I have considered it, but I was under the impression men sought you out because you were in a position to help them in their aspirational goals."

He caught the thin smile on her lips as they stopped momentarily under a streetlamp. The townhouse that was their destination was in sight and the line had backed up the traffic.

"That is true for the young ones," she agreed. "However, you and I are a different story entirely. I am not sure at all how this will play out."

"Aren't you worried it may hurt your reputation?"

"Ah, my reputation," she said in a dreamy tone. "I have not considered my reputation in so long, I am uncertain I would know where to begin, but if you refer to my ability to be a true courtesan and not harbor feelings for the gentlemen I spend time with, I do not believe that will be a problem. I am known for my lack of emotional attachment. It is one of my many positive attributes."

With that the carriage door swung open and a bright-faced young footman in white and lavender livery greeted them. "You have arrived, please enjoy your evening."

Finna left the carriage and Kendrick had no choice but to follow. He would have to wait to further their discussion but was not happy with how it was left. What did she mean lack of emotional attachment?

Once out and on the street, the crush in front of him forced his attention. All eyes were on Finna. The men appreciating every fold and thread of the expertly tailored dress. The women had a mix of expressions on their faces. Many, he noted, were looks of envy or excitement at seeing what Finna considered the latest fashion. Others, however, were openly scowling with disgust reading across their faces.

How Kendrick wished to slap those looks from their faces. Not one of them was without sin themselves, but it was accepted and expected to shun anyone who didn't hide their shames from the public eye.

"I see we are already causing a stir," Finna said in a deep sultry tone only he could hear. But when he looked back at the crowd, it was apparent their attention had shifted to who Lady Sarrafinna held on her arm. Fans were up and women hissed their thoughts to those around them, as if the fan didn't make it obvious. "Too late to walk away now, I am afraid."

When she looked up at him, the sorrow and regret that was deep set in her eyes pooled like a river in a swirling current. The urge to pull her to him and kiss it away was physical.

Instead he tucked her arm tight into his, forcing her to step into the protection of his body and smiled down at her, hoping to give her some reassurance that he wasn't sure existed.

Though Finna thought she prepared herself, nothing could be farther from the truth. In the carriage she had admitted more in thirty minutes time to Kendrick than she did in the last twenty years to another. Now, standing in the comforting strength of his shadow, the heat from his body radiating along her side, she felt safe. Tonight would not be pleasant, but for once in her adult life she was not weathering it alone. Kendrick would not allow a cross word to be heard by her. The problem was, he could create more problems for himself if he snapped at the wrong lady for cruel behavior. Their job tonight was to be seen and create a buzz. It was not to ruin Kendrick's long held political aspirations. She would have to remain close and intervene if she thought him in danger.

Kendrick led them to the door and upon entry the host and hostess stood greeting their guests. The Hostess Lady Ferris had been privy to the fact her party was about to be on everyone's lips in the morning.

"Lord Harwich, I am honored you accepted our invitation; I was sorry to hear that your daughter and son-in-law would not be attending."

"Thank you, they have decided to not partake in the whirl that is the season this year. They will remain at his title estate."

"If only I could talk her into taking a break and enjoying our country place. I would more than happily forgo Parliament for the quiet." Lord Ferris said. "Will we be seeing you in your seat this year, Harwich?"

"I am hoping so. Still tying up things to settle in, but that is my plan."

"Good, good. We need men who have seen the world and have experience to back up their opinions. I will be interested to hear your thoughts on our relations abroad."

And now it was time for Finna to be acknowledged. She steeled herself for the inevitable, as she did every time. One would hope that after twenty years the sting would get less, but it never did.

"Lady Sarrafinna, I am glad you joined us. Your dress is simply perfect. I would like very much to know your modiste." She spoke with, if not a warm smile, at least not a forced one.

A little nudge at her side made her jump as she was not prepared for an actual polite reaction. "Thank you. I would be happy to send you the name of my modiste. I think she would enjoy dressing you, Lady Ferris"

The two women curtsied, and Kendrick moved them on. "That wasn't as bad as you claimed in the carriage," he whispered into her ear, sending a fiery streak down her neck to her belly.

"Ah, no, no it wasn't. I am just uncertain why?" Finna must think on this change and ferret it out.

"Come now, don't you think perhaps you were harsh of your assessment?"

Emotional detachment flew out the window faster than a freed bird. Anger deep and rich flared, making her body hot. He of all people knew the bitter taste of being treated less than by the very group of people you were born into. She took a calming breath. It mattered not what he thought after only one interaction. He would see soon enough.

"I am sure you must be correct in your estimation, my lord."

He shot her a glance that said he believed not a word of her last statement, but they had walked into the parlor and Kendrick was being noticed by several men. She accepted a glass of champagne from a passing tray and deftly unlinked her arm from his, allowing him to advance enough to let her slide behind him, making him more important. It was one of many actions she had perfected over the years. It was of import for men to see her on a gentleman's arm, but once done she was not of import and they would go on as if she were not even in the room.

"Harwich, good to see you," one of the lords whom Sarrafinna had long ago not bothered to acknowledge until they forced her, greeted. She didn't even think of them by name or title. Instead, she had them memorized by what their connection was in Parliament.

This man, though she knew well his name and title, was a Whig with the ear of several committee chairs. Unsure if Kendrick leaned toward the Whigs or Tories, she wasn't certain how much help this one would be but making connections across the chamber could never hurt. With his upbringing, Finna would bet he would lean toward Whig's beliefs, but with his need to reclaim his place in the Ton's world and the government, he would be torn. Not to mention his inflated sense of responsibility would lean him toward the Tories. It was a fine balance.

"Turney, good to see you." The men shook hands in a very familiar manner.

"I heard we will see you on the floor this year, have you decided in who's camp you lie?" Lord Turney didn't bother with niceties. Finna could not blame him, as the tides had turned, and the Whigs were grappling for purchase since Prinny turned tail and abandoned the Whig party in favor of the Tories.

Finna sipped her drink and scanned the room. While this was not a Whig only gathering, the attendees told her a great deal about the leanings of their hostess.

"My plan is to attend this session, yes. As yet, I haven't tipped my cap one way or the other."

"How very vague of you," Turney commented. "I wouldn't waiver too long, chap. It will make these parties less tedious if you declare early on. What say you to that, Lady Sarrafinna?"

"What? Oh." Lord Turney didn't acknowledge her in male conversation. Ever. It took her three beats before she regained her equilibrium. "I agree with that assessment, Lord Turney. I have found that as a new member, once you have declared, it helps you get updated on the policies and ideas before the sessions begin."

"Right, right, Lady Sarrafinna, very observant of you." He beamed with pride like he was her professor and she his student. Tonight was not the night to allow her irritation of the male driven world to affect her.

Turney then went back to his usual ignorance of her existence, however, as if it reminded Kendrick of her presence, he snaked his hand over to take hers and squeeze. Damn man. Awareness shot through her, sending heat to all the places she preferred to ignore. Turney noted the action and also didn't miss her cheeks flushing with the energy humming in her body.

Kendrick said his goodbyes, then moved on. Finna followed but slid her hand from his grasp once out of clear sight. Kendrick looked down at the lost contact, then from her periphery she saw him look at her. She did not acknowledge his reaction. At least outwardly.

"I will take a turn about the room. Introduce yourself to that group of men in the corner. If you are not yet sure who you are aligning yourself with, that is a balanced group and most of the men are reasonable in their politics. You will get a clearer indication of your own leaning."

"I should stay with you—" he protested.

"If you are to come out of this with a career intact, you will do as I say. I have been managing a ballroom alone for many years now. Trust me."

It was sound advice, which she had offered to more than one gentleman in her care. He looked like he would argue, then simply shrugged and left her standing alone. To one end, her entire body relaxed when he stepped away from her. She had not realized the strain she was under with his proximity so close. On the other, standing alone sent a shot of exposed fear through her. This was not like her other experiences with clients. This was Kendrick and all the old memories and gossip that came with him. Women were whispering more behind their fans. She even thought one elderly matron gave her a look of pity. Thank the Lord this would be her last job, because what was left of her reputation would be taken from her, or perhaps it was just her dignity.

Taking another glass of champagne from a footman, she found solace next to an open window with a large potted palm placed to give her cover but afford her a perfect view of Harwich's progress. He would have a long-esteemed career in Parliament, she decided, but she already knew his potential. It was apparent twenty years ago. Even her father saw it, that was why he didn't intervene when she first became interested in the would be Marquess. Back then, he hadn't even gained back the title from the abeyance it had fallen into. He was petitioning for the abeyance to be rescinded, but there was no guarantee. But father saw something in him, and now that she watched him work the room, she understood.

She afforded herself a moment to consider what life might have been had they not been torn apart by a selfish woman bent on moving up the ladder of society through her daughter. Would they have had children together? Probably an entire brood of dark haired, brown eyed Kendricks would have laid siege to the Ton, breaking hearts wherever they appeared.

The years had been cruel to them both, but neither looked any worse for it. Kendrick with a few more lines around his eyes, showing many moments of smiles and good humor, and perhaps more specks of gray than a man of his same age. But on Harwich it only accented his rugged good looks and the intelligence swimming in the deep pools of his soft brown eyes.

Shaking herself, when did she spout poetic? In reality she never liked love poems and rarely found any man or woman who pontificated on the appeal of the genre as a person she wanted to converse for long periods.

They hadn't deserved what happened to them, they were both as much as children at the time, but there was no taking back what they had lost. Finna squared her shoulders, poured what was left of the champagne into the plant pot, because clear thinking would be the only thing to get her through the next days, and made her way back into the throng of party goers. She would take these nights under the watchful eyes of the Ton to do what she could to assist Kendrick in his endeavors. It was the least she could do. He was, after all at one time, a dear friend. If she could find a way to not lose what was left of her hardened heart to him in the process, it would be a small blessing.

CHAPTER 8

The morning sun was a cruel mistress as her rays barged into the sanctity of his bedchamber at an ungodly hour. After years of attending such parties in Italy, Kendrick decided the time home had turned him soft. The one sliver of good luck was his choice not to drink over much. He was working, after all, and his primary aim was to protect Finna, so it required a level head.

Throwing his head back into the bank of pillows he thought of Finna. Since he saw her in her parlor dressed in the red confection, she had been at least every third thought running through his mind. That was until he fell asleep, then his mind played her on a loop. With the disarray of his bed coverings, one would think she was in the room with him, not just playing the starring role in his fantasies.

If the feel of her in a dream could slay him so thoroughly, would he survive a night of lovemaking in the flesh? He would like to find out, but she spent enough time last night making it clear she was not at all interested in such.

He rose and splashed water on his face to clear his mind. She was right. Anything beyond a professional relationship would be disastrous. He stood listening to the water lap in the bowl as he filled his hand and let the droplets slide back into it.

Wasn't her professional life, though, all about the sex? She had been one of London's most sought after courtesans for the last twenty years. How many of the men he talked to and connected with last night had been in her bed? Water splashed out of the bowl as he slapped the surface, turning from it and his train of thought.

Rage, hot and strong, shot through him at the thought of any man bedding her. If she had loved them, he would understand. He wouldn't like it anymore, but it was only logical that in twenty years she would have found love, but there was no indication she allowed that particular emotion to dirty the waters for her.

He rang for Fletcher to get his day moving. If he stayed in the room and continued with this way of thinking he would go mad, or go out to murder half of London. Well not half, it couldn't be half. The beast beneath the calm facade of his Lordship persona screamed to life. He had no claim to Finna; he gave that up when he married another and ran to the continent. They left her to stand in the light of scandal alone. Not only did he not have a claim to her, he had no right to even hope for a chance to reconnect.

"Good morning, my lord, I hope you slumbered well," Fletcher chirped as he entered with a tray holding a hot cup of black coffee. Beating the beast back into its cave, he managed to not yell at his unsuspecting servant.

"I did not sleep well, to be honest. I hope this coffee will do its magic."

"Perhaps you should begin taking a tonic at night to help with digestion. My mother used to swear by a tonic for digestion."

Kendrick was a moment away from telling him no tonic would get the vision of a naked Finna splayed across his bed out of his head. "I am certain it has more to do with my current work than my lack of digestion."

He sat back and allowed Fletcher to shave and get him ready for the day. Birch didn't say he needed him early on, so the plan was to spend the day catching up on the paperwork piling up on his desk. One thing he missed from his time in Italy was having a secretary.

When he entered the study, his shoulders slumped at the pile. Would he be considered pompous if he hired a private secretary? It wouldn't help him at the moment, so he pushed the idea aside, steeling himself for the boring day. When had he considered his daily tasks as boring? When he could be in the company of Finna, that was when.

Shaking himself, he strode with more purpose to dive into his business and get out of his thoughts. That would only cause him more frustration.

"Fletcher, what is this?" he asked as he settled into his chair, but on top of his ledger was a salver of letters. There had to be at least thirty of them.

"Your post, my lord. I was uncertain where to put them, so decided to let you sort them," he said with a satisfied smile.

Fletcher had been uninspired by Kendrick's lack of social interaction. The servant seemed to thrive on a busy household, and a widower who never accepted an invitation was clearly not aiding in his work satisfaction.

"Thank you," he answered and went to set the salver aside.

Finna would let him know which events they would attend. He did not need to waste his time, but the top two envelopes caught his eye. One from Birch, which could give him an excuse to leave his desk and delve into something more energizing.

He snatched it from the pile and tore the seal. The note, though short, sent an icy chill down his spine and set off all the warning bells in his protective nature. It simply read, "We have been found out." This was not good. Not good at all.

He set it aside for the moment because the next envelope set his warning signals off as well. The familiar long elegant script brought back memories, though he had not seen it in many years. The ducal seal made no question about where it had originated, if the script had not told him. The Duke of Rygate. Their last meeting had been amicable. The duke understood the problem and commended him for his sense of right and his concern for any lady's reputation. However, since it was his daughter about to be jilted, Kendrick remembered a few choice comments about his lack of discretion and his horrible timing. Even today the words rang the truest of all the comments he dealt with over that time.

Kendrick slit the seal and opened the smooth, rich velum. It too was short just as Birch's; however, he could not decide which note carried the heavier weight at the moment. It simply said, 'Today at 1:00. Do not be late.' It was not signed, but there was no need. He still had the better portion of the morning to contend with. He grabbed a sheet of paper and penned a quick not to Birch asking him to come over and discuss their next move. He called to Fletcher and asked him to see it delivered immediately. At the very least Kendrick knew they would need more security, and he was afraid personal feelings aside, Finna and he might have to up the interest level on their relationship to further divert interested parties.

A quick sort of the envelopes left assured him none required his attention, and he took a restorative sip of his coffee, then bent to keep his mind occupied and his pile of correspondence less before Birch arrived.

Three hours later, Kendrick sat in his carriage in London traffic, not moving. He fought through the lion's share of his business and was reassured when Birch said he would find some additional help with protection. To his chagrin, though, Birch agreed that Finna and Kendrick would need to be more salacious in their antics in public. Though he could have pawned that conversation off onto Birch, he was her contact after all. The idea of Finna talking about salacious anything with another man, didn't sit well. Today was already filled with uncomfortable conversations. What was one more?

"Hold on, mi lord, I'm gonna make a break for it up ahead. Twill be a hard right, it will," the coachman called back to him.

"Thank you for the warning, I shall ready myself." He had no desire to be flung from a carriage into the dirty streets of London. The coachman was correct.

The horses lurched forward, and Kendrick wouldn't be

surprised if the carriage took the corner on two wheels. One was not late when summoned by a duke, so he was happy the coachman took the initiative.

Once away from the main thoroughfare, they made good time and reached the ducal town house, which was many townhouses interconnected. If he remembered, it encompassed almost an entire block of buildings.

He was admitted by a stern looking footman and greeted in the entry hall by the family's long-standing butler, Knivins.

"Knivins, it is good to see you are still on the job."

Knivins motioned to the footman to take their guest's hat before answering. "Yes, my lord. I have never left. I see you did not die in Italy," was his only comment, but it said all Kendrick needed to understand where he stood with the long-time help.

"His Grace is expecting you. He is in the study." And with that he turned and walked down the hall. Kendrick, having no other option, followed in silence. He hoped his reception by the duke would be more palatable.

"Your Grace, the Marquess of Harwich has arrived," Knivins said when he entered the room, leaving their guest to cool his heels. When his head popped back into the hall, it carried a rather disgusted expression. "His grace will see you now."

He opened the door, and allowed Kendrick to enter the room, but closed it, almost hitting him in the back it was so quick after he entered.

"Don't mind Knivins, he has some very clear opinions on a great many things," the duke of Rygate said in welcome when he rose from his desk and extended his hand.

"I have to admit, I was surprised at the invitation this morning," Kendrick said, moving to the crux of the matter.

"Please sit." The duke motioned at the chair in front of the desk. It was clearly meant to remain a business call. Kendrick sat. The sooner he did, the sooner he could be leaving.

"I am certain, if either my wife or my daughter get wind of my meddling, I will pay dearly, but as I am a duke, I have to take on the dangers I see fit."

Good to see he still had his sense of humor, but how long it would last was the question.

"What is it you need of me, your grace? I will be happy to help if it is within my power."

"What are your intentions this time around with my daughter?"

Oh, that was where this was going. If the chair could swallow him, it would be a kindness, but instead Kendrick sat perched on a very solid chair cushion with the piercing eyes of a duke, the same eyes as his daughter staring at him. Assuming the duke would not accept that he had yet to figure that out himself, he needed an answer. Was Rygate aware of their duplicity or just the rumors of them being spotted together?

"What is it you think you know about us at present?"

The look Rygate shot him told Kendrick he did not appreciate being questioned anymore now then he did twenty years ago.

After a moment's scowl Rygate cleared his throat. "I am aware the two of you were seen as a couple at a gathering." He paused for a moment to glare more deeply in Kendrick's direction. "I have also heard stirrings that my daughter may be involved in something more dangerous than her usual fare."

Kendrick nodded. For the Duke of Rygate to not be up to date on such as Michele Amari being in London would have shocked him. This would allow Kendrick a margin of error with the truth of what was happening.

"My supervisor in the foreign office brought me in. When I realized it also involved Finna, my first instinct was to back away. Unfortunately, my circumstances will not allow that, and if I am involved I have more of a chance to protect her if needed."

"At what point, my boy, are you going to stop allowing your circumstances to dictate your actions?"

"Pardon?"

"The last time you sat in that chair, you told me essentially the same thing, but then it was why you were abandoning my daughter to marry another. Has your entire career been based on your current circumstances?"

"I'm sorry, your grace, would you rather I walk away from the situation and leave your daughter in a dangerous situation?"

Kendrick was not the young foundling he was twenty years ago and was more capable of meeting Lord Rygate on his own ground.

"Are you so certain there is danger afoot?"

"Yes, I am afraid there is." He didn't figure there was any harm in the duke being filled in. Kendrick over the years had paid attention to the leanings Rygate had in the political realm. He was, after all, a mentor to the younger version, and Kendrick valued his opinions.

The duke listened in silence and when Kendrick finished,

he sat back in his chair and bowed his head. That was when Kendrick noticed how tired and old the duke looked.

Rygate made eye contact once again, but his eyes were not as sharp and angry as when he arrived. "I have been forced by my birthright and by my daughter's refusal to reach out, to watch over the years as she struggled and fought her way through life. One's child doesn't always make the decisions we would make on their behalf."

There was nothing Kendrick could say to that. He knew how lucky he was with Zoe but didn't think that could add anything to this conversation.

"I hoped she would tire of it and come back home. I never knew what to do. Attempts to reach out only pushed her away. She never allowed me or anyone to put demands on her, so forcing her home would have been disastrous. The only thing I could do was not disown her and hope my title would protect her to the extent she would allow. This situation, however, seems more reckless than her usual rash choices."

Kendrick was speechless. For a father to admit his fear of losing his child, and for a duke to admit any weakness was unfathomable. He understood the trust just handed him.

"I cannot imagine how the last twenty years have been for you, your grace. However, I do not seem to have anything in this situation to lose and will not back down until I am certain there is no danger to Finna." His mind screamed that he could lose her for the second time in his life. Forcing the voice into the recesses of his mind, he forged ahead, seeing an opportunity for an ally. "I am concerned about her reasoning, even after learning of the danger, to continue allowing Amari to stay in her home. Do you know why she needs the money?"

The duke scrutinized him for a long moment, then deciding, he sat back again in his chair. "That is not my tale to tell. I have my suspicions, but we have not spoken for over two years now, and the last time was at a ball where we greeted each other under the watchful eye of the Ton, so it was not a long interlude. I am afraid you will have to ask her."

Kendrick understood his reluctance, but felt it imperative to understand her motivation. "I understand your grace, but if I knew her motivation I could better gauge how to assist."

He shook his head. "There are things that a father just understands. If she has not told you herself, then she may not want you to know. It will not be I who says a word. You need not know her motivations to keep her safe, if that is your goal. I will expect updates as you proceed, however."

"That may be a problem, I shouldn't even be here talking to you now—"

"Please do not for a moment think anyone in the foreign office is beyond my grasp. You are not in Italy anymore, and I have ears bent to me very high up. I may not have been directly involved in my daughter's life and her decisions, but I will not say I didn't influence the direction now and then."

Kendrick knew if he wanted to have any chance of political success in Parliament, he needed to give the duke of Rygate what he wanted. "Very well. I will update you, but only on things that directly relate to Finna."

"Very well." He rose and offered his hand again. Kendrick shook it and turned to leave. "Oh, and Harwich, I expect you to give her an offer of marriage before you lose the chance again. I will be watching."

CHAPTER 9

"Fletcher, who in bloody hell is that?" Kendrick shouted over the banging on his front door, as he descended the stairs still tying his robe.

Fletcher held a candle high to shine a light on the window next to the door.

"Hell, It's Golding. Let him in," he instructed. At two o'clock in the morning, having Finna's butler banging on his door could only be a bad omen.

"You need to come, my lord. Tis a mess over there."

"What happened? Wait, come with me. Talk while I dress," Kendrick turned to rush up the stairs, then stopped. "Is Birch aware there is trouble?"

Golding shook his head. "You were closer, my lord."

"Fletcher wake a footman and send them to Mr. Birch's rooms. Instruct them to send him right away. Tell him there has been an incident." Fletcher strode to the back stairs to carry out his order and Kendrick ran up the stairs with the older, yet nimble Golding following.

"Talk," he instructed.

"Well, my lord, all was well. They had dinner and spent the eve in the parlor playing cards. Then everyone retired, but I—well, I don't sleep well, you see, ever since the war. I had just left the kitchens from finding a snack, and that's when I heard it."

Kendrick strode into his room and didn't bother with a candle. The drapes pulled open, giving plenty of moonlight to see by. "What did you hear?"

"Breaking glass, my lord. It came from the parlor and sure enough, when I got in there, I saw a shadow slinking into the hall. I didn't know there was more than one until I saw them at the top of the stairs heading for the bed chambers. One had a gun, another a knife. I bellowed as loud as I could and that stopped them for a moment. Long enough for Mr. Lang and Mr. Chesterfield to come see about the commotion."

Kendrick's blood ran cold at the thought of Finna having strangers break into her home and put her in danger. This had been a bad idea. It would end tonight.

"Did you apprehend them?" Kendrick asked as he slouched into his coat and grabbed his hat on the way out the door with Golding on his heels.

"One, my lord. The other, not sure if he was the bravest lout, or the dumbest, but he jumped from the balcony and left by the way he came. I was already on the stairs and had no hope of getting a hand on him."

Kendrick heard a loud crunching, and glanced back to see Golding cracking his knuckles like he was pulverizing something. "Is the braggart you collected still alive?"

"Yes, my lord, I thought you ought to question him beforehand."

Again, as he opened the front door, Kendrick glanced back and saw no sign of humor on the butler's face. Kendrick just might save that man's life tonight. It buoyed him a fraction to think there were people in Finna's life willing to kill to protect her, but from here on out that was his job.

"Let us take the back street, so not to arouse any undo curiosity," Kendrick suggested.

"Of course, my lord, but I'm not sure who we would make curious at this hour?"

Golding had a point, but Kendrick knew that there were always eyes where the Ton was concerned. They ducked down an alley and off Mayfair. The moon lit their way. It wasn't ten minutes when they came upon Finna's townhouse ablaze with candlelight. Not sure what he was walking into, he needed to know she was safe.

"Was Lady Sarrafinna injured in any way?"

"No, my lord, I would never allow that to happen, I promise you." He answered with hurt in his voice at the very idea he would allow something to happen to her.

"I know you would do everything in your power to protect her, Golding," Kendrick assured the servant.

When they entered, Kendrick noted there was not a soul in the front parlor, or on the first floor at all. Lookie loos would get no satisfaction. In fact, the house was silent, eerily so.

"Where is everyone?" Kendrick whispered, but wasn't sure why he bothered.

"In the lady's parlor, my lord. Lady Finna said it was to

the back of the house and would not transfer noise if there was any."

"Smart girl," Kendrick said to no one. They continued up the stairs and about halfway down the hall, before the first rumblings of voices met them.

Kendrick would never forget the scene inside Finna's private parlor. It was something out of a comic stage production. In the middle of the feminine space colored in a light lavender with cream accents, a large angry street thug sat in an ornate dressing chair of gold leaf accents and deep pink velvet cushions. They tied him to said chair by a cacophony of scarves and silks of myriad colors and designs. These contrasted the irony of the scene with his dingy black torn breeches and matching jacket. The man looked at Kendrick and Golding when they entered with desperation about him.

Lady Contrell sat on the edge of a matching pink settee with a handkerchief in her hand, dabbing her nose and eyes as she railed about such a braggart interfering with her beauty sleep. While pacing from one end of the room to the other, Lang argued with Mr. Chesterfield, who was perched on a lavender and mint green cushion sat on the floor next to a window.

Chesterfield, from what Kendrick gathered, was trying to calm Lang down and assure him all would be well. Lang on the other hand was having none of it and just as he would have spoken to Finna, who stood unaware of the surrounding chaos with her back turned against the room, watching out the window, Lang looked up and noticed Kendrick.

"Well, it is nice of you to join us. I hope you are all satisfied. While you and your colleagues were at your homes safe and in your slumber, we were all awoken to these men, attempting to violate Finna's private residence!"

"Lang—" Chesterfield tried, but Lang was beyond listening. Kendrick knew he would need to have his say, so he waited.

"How dare you come here after how many years? And as if nothing at all ask her to harbor such a dangerous person. You must have the gull of—"

"That is enough, Lang." Finna's voice was not a yell, but she said it in such a way that it brokered no question about her meaning. "Lord Harwich is neither to blame for this current situation any more than he is responsible for my part in it. As usual, this was my choice. I do nothing against my will, Lang, you know that." She turned then to face Kendrick. The stark expression on her face struck him to his core. "Lang and Reginald stopped the men from advancing down the hall, but one got away."

Without thought of their audience, Kendrick crossed the room and pulled her into the safety of his arms. Her response was not to fold into his embrace and allow the comfort offered there. Instead, she went rigid. To hell with appearances. He knew he had no claim of rights to her, but she was alive. Her heart beat heavy against his chest and her breathing, though not calm and metered, indicated her life. She did not return the embrace, but he noted she didn't pull out of it either. Once his own heart and mind had slowed to a reasonable speed, he let his arms fall to his side and took a step back.

Silence had fallen in the room, he realized, and to his relief when next he looked at Finna the color was back in her cheeks. He turned to Lang and Reginald then, ignoring the grins on their faces.

"Thank you for being here. You are correct. Though Finna would argue otherwise, there should have been more protection here. I will make sure that is a problem remedied before the sun rises."

Both Lang and his partner nodded, lulled for the moment that their concerns were acknowledged.

"I need tea. I think I will go make tea and check on Michele. Would anyone like tea?" Madame Contrell said out of the blue. She would need a new handkerchief, because the one she had been wringing in her hands was all but shredded.

"Tea is a good idea. Golding please help her with a tray for Mr. Amari and for us," Finna directed.

"Golding, I think, perhaps some food as well. Nothing complicated, but it has been my experience it helps to settle the nerves after such an event."

Golding nodded solemnly, glancing at his patroness with concern. Though there was still some color to her dark olive complexion, it was not as vibrant as he would like, certainly due to the shock of being attacked in her own home in the middle of the night.

Now, with Golding out of the room for the moment, Kendrick thought it a good time to focus on the pink and lace clad culprit.

"I will ask some pertinent questions. I suggest if you do not care to have Mr. Golding assist in your memory jogging that you answer before he returns." Kendrick slipped the barely there pink silk stocking from the thug's mouth. Did she empty her entire lingerie drawer on this man?

"Why did you break in here?"

The man looked around the room but stuck his chin high and refused to speak.

"Fine then, who hired you? I am certain you and your companion are not of the level of mind to plan this attack."

"I ave' notin' t' say t' the like o' you," he spat with an all too familiar accent. It used to be Kendrick's. Even today, he could easily slide back into it with no effort.

"Very well, I have another colleague on his way, and then we will also have Golding back in a few moments."

The look on the man's face told the group what he thought of Golding taking another turn. The black swollen eye and dried blood stream emanating from his right ear were from their last encounter.

Before Kendrick could ask again, the door swung open and Birch came through the door looking as harried as Kendrick felt. He also didn't have a cravat or even a jacket. He entered in just his shirt sleeves, not even tucked into his breeches.

"Is everyone safe? Where is Michele?" He scanned the room, then landed his eyes on Kendrick and the assailant.

"Everyone is safe, and Mr. Amari is in his room. We felt it best not to give these men a face to match with a description," Finna answered, her voice more like her usual self-composed person. "This," she waved a hand toward the prisoner, "was one of two men, who broke a window in my front parlor and attempted to gain entry. Mr. Langley and Mr. Chesterfield, with help from my butler Golding, foiled the plans. I will expect you to replace the window with all speed, Mr. Birch."

"Yes, of course. I will have men here at first light," he assured her. Then looked to Kendrick. "What has he told us?"

"Nothing yet. I believe he would rather wait and be persuaded by Golding."

"No, I'll tell ye' I will." He spoke up at last.

Kendrick breathed a sigh of relief because he didn't trust that Golding would take heed not to render him speechless. Before he could re ask the question, the doorbell peeled. All eyes shot to the mantle clock. Fifteen minutes passed the three o'clock hour.

"Stay here," Kendrick ordered and followed Dylan from the room. "Finna, lock this behind me and do not open it to anyone other than myself or Birch."

She nodded once and began crossing the room. He shut the door and remained there until he heard the lock slide into place. The bell rang again.

"Golding, we will take this," Birch called down to the butler on the verge of opening the door. "Stand over in the shadows in case we need your assistance," he continued as the two men made their way down the stairs. Golding slipped back into the shadows like Kendrick felt he had done before.

Kendrick stood with his hand poised on the door latch and Dylan stepped to the side ready to strike. A nod by Dylan and Kendrick wretched open the door. To their surprise, on the step sat a bedraggled street rat, tied at the wrist and ankles. There was an expensive piece of vellum pinned to his shoulder. The man looked up at the two of them with shame and resignation on his gagged face.

"What's it say?" Dylan asked.

Kendrick took the note and opened it. A familiar scroll

curved and curled across the paper. "It says that it appears we were missing something, and it has been caught and returned to us."

Birch leaned out the door and looked down the street in both directions, but Kendrick knew he would see no one. He also knew that did not mean they were not there.

"Who in hell?" Dylan rubbed his neck.

"I'll explain later. It will make sense to you then, help me with him before someone sees." Kendrick and Birch leaned over and hauled their missing culprit to standing and got him inside.

"Golding, is there a free room where we can house our new guest until we have a need for him?" Birch asked, not wanting to get the two men in the same room for now.

"Yes sir, we can put him in one of the unused guest rooms. Shall I get more silks?"

"Perhaps you have some sturdy rope lying about," Kendrick suggested. He could not stand to see another man brought so low as the one tied up in Finna's dressing parlor, no matter how unscrupulous he was.

"Yes, mi lord. I'll get it, meet you there. Third door from Lady Finna's."

After freeing the second assailant's feet, the men made their way to the room in question. They stood at the door for only a moment before Golding came trotting down the hallway from the other direction.

"Something tells me I am glad he is on our side," Birch said dryly.

Kendrick nodded in agreement. He needed to learn Golding's story because it was sure to be a good one. After securing the prisoner, they returned to the group. One glance at Golding had that prisoner sweating. Madame Contrell had arrived with a tea tray and was about to leave to see to Mr. Amari. Lang and Reginald also took their tea and a plate of cold offerings and headed back to their room.

Birch escorted Madame Contrell to check on their primary objective. Then he would be back to question the suspects.

That left Finna and Kendrick alone with the prisoner and Golding. He sat and waited. She had been through enough already, he would not force her to talk about it, and he knew his recalculated plan would not come as a welcome option on a good night. She turned back to the window, putting the entire scene to her back.

Birch entered the room and broke the silence. "All right, let's question this braggart so we can get them out before London wakes up."

Neither suspect had much useful information at the moment. They were hired by another local bloke from the docks who had been asked to find two such individuals. They were paid half before the job and would meet the same bloke for the second half, only if successful at their purpose to kill Amari.

By the time they got the same story from the relocated assailant, another ring came from the doorbell.

"Those will be my men. I sent word when I left my house," Birch explained and led the first man from the room, and Golding came out of the parlor with the other one.

Birch handed them off to two of the men, then stepped back for three more to enter. "These men will keep guard."

"Absolutely not," Finna countered. "My home is not a jail and therefore does not need guards."

Birch ran his hand around his neck, tired and ready to have the sun come up so he could go on with his day. "Finna, this is not a request. You need more protection."

Kendrick leaned against the banister of the stairs, out of the way. This had nothing to do with him. As he stood, he took a better look at the guards Dylan selected. Clearly not far above the station of the men escorted out in bondage. They were dressed better, but with no cravats and a clear layer of street dust covering their coats and breeches. One gave the others a frustrated look, then leaned over and whispered something to one of them who nodded and chuckled.

"I believe, Birch, one of your men has some ideas about this situation. Perhaps a second perspective is worth hearing." Kendrick was certain Birch would not be happy.

"Oh, what ideas do you have?" He turned to the group. The one in question looked to Kendrick, who nodded for him to share.

"I, well, I don't think what I said will assist you, sir."

Birch started turning a bright purple in his frustrated state. "Speak."

"He said he wasn't sure why it was important to protect a prostitute, but the money would all spend the same."

Before Birch could react, Kendrick was off the banister and had the man whose words might be his last, pinned by the neck with his elbow against the door. The other guards slid to the wall out of the way.

"Let me introduce Lady Sarrafinna, daughter to the Duke of Rutland. She is none of your concern, or your business, except for you will give her the deference you would give myself or her father. Do I make myself clear?"

The man blubbered, unable to talk, but made no signal of

acquiescence, so to punctuate his point Kendrick leaned into his elbow. The man turned the same purple that Birch was. "I said, do you understand?"

"Harwich, he can't answer you if you kill him," Dylan pointed out.

Kendrick didn't lighten his pressure, but informed the room, while never breaking eye contact. "Lady Sarrafinna does not need these men. I will reside here until we settle this. You can have them leave."

Kendrick backed away and let the man slide to the floor, grasping at his throat and gasping for air. It was nice to get his own way for a change.

Finna had long ago ceased to care what anyone thought, much less said about her. She knew what she was and who she was. But the speed at which Kendrick flew at that man left her stunned. There had been men who, in a token gesture, asked others to mind their tones, but never had anyone with such murderous intent fought for her honor. She was certain her father had picked up the gauntlet once or twice after seeing a person who spoke badly of her a second time in public. She should be outraged. Never had she needed anyone to stand up for her, but at four o'clock in the morning after dealing with intruders seemed to be the limit to her strength.

Her tears, however, remained banked until Kendrick made the grand announcement he was moving in. "No. No, no, no, no. Absolutely not."

The entry hall, filled to the gills with powerful, strong

men, went silent. The look on Kendrick's face bordered on comedic. Birch's expression showed his utter exasperation with them all, and the three guards all seemed to be looking at something on the floor.

"Finna, I can't leave you here overnight unguarded. You won't always have a house full of guests to assist. I am happy to hire different men, or you can take Harwich's offer, but you need help." Birch, finally done with her dramatics it seemed, rose to his full height, and gave her an ultimatum.

The tears burned, fighting for release. Doing what she always did in the face of a world against her, Finna squared her shoulders and took a deep breath. "We can discuss the details when we have all gotten some rest, however I do not want these, or any other strange men in my home. And I do not appreciate you assuming it appropriate to come into my home, not my husband's, not my father's home, my home. Mine. That means you have no right to dictate anything concerning it." Finna stopped because she could hear the panic rising in her voice. This one instance punctuated her need to finish this assignment to gain the funds.

Kendrick, for his part, kept blessedly quiet. She knew he was scheming and was too tired to worry about it.

"I am sorry. You are correct. I allowed my overly robust need to protect those in my purview and overstepped. Nothing more will occur before we can get this sorted," Birch answered as he gave a look at the now unemployed men, who all nodded and found their way to the door as quickly as possible.

"Very well, then. If you will excuse me, I will return to my room and see if I can gain back any of my lost sleep. Please let yourselves out."

Finna turned to go back upstairs but was stopped when a warm hand settled on her arm. "Wait," was all Kendrick said, but that one word held all the meaning in the world between them. The tears, which had faded, sprang back to life and threatened.

She turned to refuse, but he continued. "I know you must be wrung out, but none of us will get a moment's rest until we settle this. Please just go sit in the parlor and we will be in in a moment. It won't take long, as long as you can be reasonable."

At the last of his words she bristled but nodded. He was correct. When anything threatened her independence, she never handled that with as much aplomb as she would like.

Settling into her favorite chair, she laid her head back and closed her eyes. Tonight had rattled her. She had dealt with trouble in the past, for sure, but she had always been so careful not to bring it into her home. Now it seemed she had not only allowed it, but she invited it in. Now, Harwich wanted to come live in her house.

When he left for Italy, she was of two minds. On the one hand her very heart was ripped out of her chest and handed back to her, but on the other it wasn't until she got word from her mother that their ship had sailed that she could take a full breath of air. And last year when he returned in the middle of the house party planned to help his daughter find a husband, her emotions again swept over her and would have drowned her in their stickiness had she not had the good sense to leave.

Knowing he was in England and in the same city made her feverish and uncomfortable. The knowledge they could meet each other walking in the park at any moment created a storm in her that if unleashed she feared would never be beaten back. Him sleeping just doors down from her might be the only thing that could bring her to knees.

"Now, to get this settled," Birch said briskly. She didn't blame him. Being difficult was not her intent. She observed Kendrick elbowing Dylan and exchange an expression. Birch cleared his throat. "I want to apologize for the caliber of men I allowed into your home. It has reminded me that this is not the usual circumstances I operate in. It will not happen again, but I must insist you have more protection here. I cannot be here all the time, so if you are not willing to have Harwich stay until this is over, then I will need to find others."

Kendrick sat on the settee and had not said a word. She eyed him, and he looked at her with a ferocity that hit her. Not taking into account how this would affect him, it was plain he knew her mind better than anyone. Lang and Reginald would soon leave, and that left her and Madame Contrell with only Golding who could be counted as a protector. It was obvious he didn't want this to drag out and get murky. They were not the children of twenty years ago.

"Fine, Kendrick can move in. He and I can discuss any particulars," she said, unable to look either man in the eye. They both knew the entirety of this farce, and neither of them had ever acted out of pity, which she appreciated.

"I know how deuced difficult this must be, and I want to thank the two of you for helping me," Birch admitted.

"You are helping us both as much as we are helping you," Finna admitted.

"I will need to get my things together and inform Fletcher we will reside here for the foreseeable future."

Dylan looked at the clock with a pained expression. "I can stay until you return."

"Gentlemen, it is now daylight. I do not believe, other than men to fix my window, that anyone else will invade me right now. And the household is waking up so there will be servants about for the rest of the day. We will be safe for the time being." Finna stood, exhaustion pulling on her. "I thank you both for coming to our rescue. I am not accustomed to such gallantry."

Both men stood and bowed. "Do not forget, Harwich, we have the Stinton's musicale this evening."

"How could I forget?" He smiled and winked, flipping her stomach oddly, sending sensations as far down as her toes.

"I shall see you then," she said and swept past them, not even bothering to show them out. A sudden need to be safe in her own room washed over her and for once in her life she indulged in letting her emotions have the reins. She was at her door when she heard the front door click shut and all at once, like before, she could breathe.

CHAPTER 10

*K*endrick entered his townhouse on a jog, having to stop and back up to inform the housekeeper, who jumped, that he and Fletcher would take a trip. She would need to inform the cook and the rest of the staff. Then, he made his way to his study to pen a note to his solicitor instructing him to send any missives to Lady Sarrafinna's residence for the near future.

The panic of hours ago had lifted and in its place a lightness he had not known in a long time. Not being a man to dwell on such unreliable things as emotions, he enjoyed this new wrinkle while it lasted and didn't go beyond that. Finna was not filled with jubilation at their new arrangement, in fact the term he would use was resigned.

As he posted the note, ready to leave the study to get Fletcher packing, he saw an envelope. Identical to the one pinned to the errant assailant this morning. Rygate. He broke the seal, and all there was inside was a time, not even a signature. Glancing at the clock as he quit the room, he had time to pack and gather what he would need to run his life from Finna's before he would need his carriage. He asked a footman to call for the carriage in two hours, then proceeded to his room where Fletcher was already selecting and folding his wardrobe.

"I heard we will reside elsewhere for a time."

"Yes, we will stay with Lady Sarrafinna as a bit of protection while she aids us in this current situation."

To Fletcher's credit the look of shocked indignation only brushed across his face, then it was as placid as a lake once again. "Of course, my lord," was his answer.

This was twice in almost as many hours that the prejudice against Finna had been thrown in his face. Was that what she lived with every time she left her home? She was the daughter of a Duke, after all. He stamped down the urge to pistol whip his manservant, because if he didn't learn to contend with the guttural urge to hurt every person who spoke or thought badly of Finna, he would be in gaol before the season ended. He took a calming breath.

"Fletcher, where I am asking you to go may well put you in situations you are not comfortable with. If you don't think you can remain respectful to Lady Finna and her guests I understand if you would rather remain here. I can find someone else to assist me for the time being."

Fletcher stopped his folding and assessed Kendrick. "Thank you for that option, but I believe if I am to serve you best, I need to broaden my experiences. I may have been too long in the employ of closed-minded people. I am certain I can at the very least learn to understand others who choose an unconventional life. If I find it too taxing on my sensibilities, I would go to you before saying anything to cause harm to another."

Kendrick nodded, appreciating Fletcher's honesty and willingness to try. "Do not go overboard. I am thinking I will need only two weeks' worth of clothes and essentials. I will attend events in that time, so please pack what you think I will need for that. If we forget something it is a small matter to come and collect it."

While his manservant bustled about, Kendrick took a smaller bag and packed a pile of books sitting on his bedside table, then went to collect items from his study he wanted to bring with him. When the carriage was announced, Kendrick felt prepared at least physically, but knew a fine dinner jacket did not guarantee a peaceful way with Finna.

The meeting with Rygate ended soon after it began, and it was less of a conversation and more of a tirade about his lack of understanding on the topic of protection. He managed to find out that Rygate never left Finna unattended. He had a list of revolving men hired to keep watch over his daughter. It was one of them that apprehended the black guard last night. Rygate let Kendrick slink out of his office only after a promise of not letting her out of his sight and a dire warning about his upcoming seat in Parliament if harm of any sort came to his Finna.

Kendrick had the carriage drop him at Finna's town-house, with instructions to collect Fletcher and whatever luggage he had and bring them all here. It would take upwards of an hour before Fletcher descended on the town-house, so perhaps if Finna was still abed, he should grab some needed sleep in the parlor.

His dream of sleep was dashed when he entered the

parlor and found Madame Contrell and Mr. Amari seated, playing a card game.

"Oh, good day, Lord Harwich, I hear you will join our little rag tag family," Madame Contrell greeted him first.

"What? Oh, very good indeed. Welcome, welcome," Amari commented upon hearing the news. "I will feel much safer now my friend. Good of you."

Kendrick sat heavily on the sofa and looked longingly at the perfect spot for his feet to rest were he left alone to stretch out. He knew it was not to be. For all their worldly experience, neither Contrell nor Amari were talented at reading when a person preferred to be alone, or if they did, they didn't bother to indulge a person. Instead, he used this span of time sans Finna to see what he could learn.

"I am happy to be of service," he said as he moved from the sofa and slid a chair closer to their table. "I am afraid I am at a disadvantage, Madame Contrell; I am uncertain when you and Finna became close."

She smiled at what must be a fond memory, took her turn at the cards, then turned to Kendrick. "Why, I met Finna in Bath. She was not but a figment of the woman she would become, but you could still see it."

Kendrick's stomach seized. He didn't have to ask what trip to Bath. It was when the scandal hit, and her mother sent her away. The shame of it all washed over him.

"If I had to choose a word for her it would be fragile, but in true Finna fashion she pulled through the turmoil and made her own way." She didn't seem to show any anger toward him about the whole situation which puzzled him. It must have shown on his face, because she placed a hand over his own and leaned toward him. "Do not despair, she never blamed you. And look how everything turned out. Right as rain."

He did not agree with her last statement, not if Finna continued to go through life having to deal with small-minded people.

Instead of arguing, he forged ahead. "I am puzzled about this new turn of events, however. I am concerned she may lack funds."

She turned from the game and gave him an assessing glance. "I will admit, I was not in favor of this current scheme. I felt she could accomplish her goal without this nonsense, but alas, just because I have her ear does not mean I have any more influence."

"This morning she seemed broken by the stress of it all," Kendrick said aloud, not meaning to voice that particular thought.

"Oh dear, what you saw this morning was not a broken Finna. Tired, yes. Rattled certainly, but I have seen that child as close to being broken as anyone, and even then, to an outsider you would not have been the wiser. That one has a constitution a general would be envious of."

Kendrick chewed on that for a moment. He knew she was strong. Her Spanish grandmother passed that along. He worried, though, that even the strongest people could crumble under pressure. "Do you know why she needs funds so badly?"

"Of course," she answered, not willing to give more information. "Gin! Ha, that is three games in a row, Michele, I am afraid you are not very good at this game."

Kendrick watched as Madame Contrell leaned forward to grasp the shillings they were wagering with to add to her growing pile. He also noticed that her position gave Amari a perfect view of her cleavage. He chuckled to himself, realizing that Amari was winning in his own way.

"I think I just need more practice with this game that I am unfamiliar with." He looked toward Kendrick and winked as Contrell counted her winnings.

"If you continue losing, Mr. Amari, you may well have to take me with you to Belgium as payment for your losses."

Kendrick realized she was done handing her friend over on a platter, and he would get no more information until such time as she decided it was necessary. He bid his farewells and headed to his room, giving the footman direction to send Fletcher and his things there once they arrived.

It seemed he was no closer to discovering why Finna felt the need to endanger herself for monetary gain, except that this was Finna. Her independence was the trait that called to him twenty years ago, and it seemed he was not yet immune to her charms. At her door, he listened. What for, he didn't know. An excuse to enter and just be in her sphere was the likely cause. It was obvious they still attracted each other, but she seemed determined to ignore it. Kendrick would never force her, but he didn't see why indulging and letting life do as it would couldn't hurt.

With that one thought foremost in his mind, he continued down to the next door, which would be his room until they saw Amari safely to Belgium. Perhaps it was time to not force the matter, but to tip the odds more in his favor. He would see if she was willing but scared tonight. Scared was one thing, uninterested, a deal breaker. But if fear led her apprehension, then he could ease her concerns, he was certain. After all, they were two grown adults, with no real ties and responsibilities to anyone anymore. Who would be harmed if they were to take this opportunity and enjoy each other's company?

Later that night, Kendrick sat in the carriage as it jostled through the throng of party goers leaving the musicale. True, he was exhausted, having only managed a brief nap before Fletcher and the luggage overtook his room. Not to mention his sleep had not been of the restful sort. Visions of him and Finna kept him restless and aroused.

In the flashes of light landing on her face he saw, if not happiness, at least not the lines of concern marring her otherwise perfect features. The only stress filled moment to the evening was an unexpected interlude with Finna and her brother Darrin, Viscount Wentworth. While it was cordial, and her brother seemed genuine in his assertion that it was nice to see her, there was an underlying current that could not be ignored. It took a few moments after to bring back her vibrant smile, but he had done it.

"I had a lovely time tonight. I never thought a musicale would be an entertainment worth my time," he said to her, pulling her attention from the open window back to his presence.

She smiled warmly. "No man ever does, I am afraid. They too often concentrate on the poor young girls forced to perform for a crowd, which never ends well. Instead, I try to concentrate on the people and the conversation."

"Thank you for enlightening me." Finna was a bit feral in his estimation, so to not corner her, he slid over on his bench, so they were facing. His leg brushed by her knee, sending shock waves through him. All he needed to do was lean forward and slide his hand under her skirts and—

"Is something wrong?" she questioned when he did not speak.

"No, nothing. In fact, I enjoyed myself more tonight than I have in a long time. I can't help but think the company I am keeping is a large part of that."

Her smile slipped. But in the shadows, he would have missed it, had he not been watching for it? Her brow furrowed slightly. "Kendrick, I do not think it wise for us—"

"To get involved. I agree, it has the potential to be disastrous."

"Then what?" she said, annoyance high in her tone.

He leaned in, but did not reach out to touch her. "What is the danger of enjoying the time it has given us? We had much more time stolen from us in our youth. If we stole some of that back, what is the harm?"

He knew the moment her reserve threatened to throw up a wall, and he needed to stop her from locking herself away.

Before thinking, he leaned in and captured her mouth with his. She could have pulled away. She would be within her right to slap him hard, but instead, she stilled. The air around them ceased to move. Kendrick made no move to pull her into him, even though his muscles screamed for the action.

After what passed for an eternity, she kissed back and leaned into it. The air flowed again, and Kendrick's body vibrated from an energy he thought lost to him with his youth. In a fluid motion, he brought his arms around Finna and pulled her onto his lap, leaning back into his seat. He may have taken the first move, but with her perched on his lap, she now held the reins. They both knew she had the power to pull back and walk away from the implications. Damn, he hoped with all hope she would not.

Warning bells rang like the chimes at St. Peters in her head. There were more ways this would go wrong than she cared to count, but despite her every instinct, her body rebelled. It was a simple kiss, fraught with more emotion and turmoil than a loaded cannon. She was lost.

Of the many kisses she had exchanged with men in carriages over the years, this one outshone them all. She was helpless to fight the attraction, though she must find a way. Now was not that time.

His lips were firm and full, gentle in their attention to her. He was not taking from her but offering. And, oh, what he was offering.

She inhaled the scent of him that had been bewitching her all night. A whiff as he led her into the main parlor, or a scant smell as they passed an open window. It was a mix of tobacco and leather, with the spice of sandalwood. It was the sweetest of poisons. Sweet on her tongue, but deadly to her livelihood.

She leaned in more, absorbed his heat into her bodice. The carriage lurched, and Kendrick encircled her with his arms to not lose the connection.

If this is what succumbing to your greatest weakness was, she would be the first in line. To die in his embrace would be a fitting end. His arms tightened a fraction, allowing her to sense his hands exploring curves new to his remembered touch. Years of lessons and mistakes had happened between those touches. None had the power that this embrace did.

Was he right? Was it time for them to take back what the years had taken? Did they have the right? She knew Kendrick deserved all that was good in the world. No one could begrudge him after his years of service, but did she? Her service differed vastly from his. She chose to not bend to the will of those around her and make her own path, but in so doing she knew the turmoil and pain she caused. How, after all the years and all the men, did she think she deserved a happy ending?

Finna wretched herself from his embrace and the kiss. The warmth had turned to hot angry embers threatening to consume her into the hell she knew she deserved.

"You are wrong, Harwich. We have no right to retake that which was taken from us. We were meant to go down the paths we did. With our own choices made. It would be wrong to come back years later and claim a foul. It would besmirch the memory of Victoria, not to mention all the pain I have brought onto my family. Please—" She cut off the words, because the carriage rolled to a halt at last.

Before she could throw herself back into the safety of his arms, and the fantasy he could weave, she bolted from the carriage and all but ran into the house, ignoring Birch standing in the parlor shaken by the sudden action. There was one place she was safe, one place no one, well, no man had ever been allowed. Her bedchamber. Her private vestige of space that was her own.

With the door shut and locked behind her, the air was no longer thick. Her lungs drank in blessed air as she walked to the window and looked out over her little piece of London.

When she purchased this townhouse, she had been so young. It had been on a whim. She had just received a rather large payment with a bonus, because her connections placed her client at the head of an important committee in the government. That had been a hard year, during which her brother reached his majority and was out in the world and vocal about what he thought of her life choices. He was not wrong on any of his estimations, and they cut her deep. The townhouse purchase had been a means of thumbing her nose at her brother and what he stood for. As it was still rare, and almost impossible for a woman to own anything, she had to do it through several accounts that did not trace back to her. And the one rule she made when she stepped foot in this very bedchamber was to never allow a man to enter here.

She came close to breaking that rule once, and regretted even the consideration, because it made for a hurtful memory to be associated with her sanctuary. She learned a hard lesson. This was the only place she could just be. It was where she held tight to the innocence she lost many times over throughout the years. Where she found calm, when there was no other place for her. But now, she wasn't as calm as she would like.

Heavy footsteps passed by the door, slowing then picking back up as he passed. He was more a fool than she suspected if he thought they could just pick up where they left off. Life did not work that way. It was a series of actions and reactions that once put into motion barreled along like a boulder rolling down a hill. But what if they could, if not start where they left off, at least sample what could have been?

Over the years, Finna had experienced the pleasures men and women could experience. Would she be able to accept just the physical pleasure of an interlude with him or would this decision be the one that broke her forever?

His kiss in the carriage burned hot in her memory. Her entire body buzzed. Did it matter if she had to fight her way back after losing him a second time? She had done it once, and she understood the world more now. It was dangerous to take pleasure for herself, and censure was sure to follow.

Only once, after Kendrick married and moved, did she allow a glimmer of that youthful hope to fracture her carefully created walls. And where did it get her? She was older now, and much wiser. It was possible she could take the pleasure and guard herself against the heartache. When she bedded a man, she remained aloof and separate of the act. She didn't let her heart become engaged. It stood to reason if she could do that then, it was possible to just dismiss her old feelings and concentrate on the pleasure.

Finna turned from the window and began undressing, letting clothes drop where they fell. No need to call for her maid. She sat in just her stays, stockings and high heels, a favorable attire which brought great enthusiasm from many men. Her hair, released from its pins, tumbled down her back and around her shoulders. Her beauty was not lost on her. She was not vain about it but saw it as fact. If she were to go to Kendrick, she would not go as Lady Sarrafinna. He deserved better of her. No, she would go to him as just Finna, with none of her usual protections or provocations.

Standing, she removed her stockings and stays and opted for her simple pale purple dressing gown. It was neither revealing nor fashionable, but it was her favorite.

Taking one last look in the mirror and asking her reflection, "What in bloody hell do you think you are doing? This may well break you," she squared her shoulders and went to barge in on the one man she would always desire above all others.

The hall was empty, thank God, and she padded to the door next to her own. She didn't bother to knock, but turned the knob and walked in. Kendrick stood in only his breeches, looking out the window as she had been doing.

"Thank you, Fletcher, but as I told you, I do not need your services this evening, and don't feel like company."

"I am sorry, but I am not your valet." Her voice was not her own, it sounded like it was miles away, instead of coming from her mouth.

Kendrick stilled and slowly, as if to not scare her away, turned. "Are you all right? Is there something wrong?"

This was her out. She could claim there was a spider in her room, or some such nonsense if she wanted to turn back. Instead, she let her dressing gown fall to the floor, exposing her nakedness to the only man she ever wanted to see it and never had.

Her mouth went dry and she froze, uncertain how to continue. If she advanced, she would never know how he felt, because in her experience, once you offered yourself to man, it allowed only moments for him to turn away. After physiology took over it wasn't until later that he might regret it. She wanted no regrets on either side of the sheets.

Thankfully, it took only a moment before he crossed the room and pulled her into the circle of his arms. The roughness of his chest hair abraded her already swollen nipples. She would have to fight to be present. All her training taught her not to be as present, to keep it unemotional for her. Now was not the time. She wanted to enjoy every second. It felt like they were both cheating death by taking the chance to be together, even if for a night.

Kendrick kissed a line from her jaw down the dip at the base of her neck. Tears sprang to life in her eyes. Could she do this? Was it possible for her to enjoy the experience and not leave broken beyond repair? Finna had experienced physical pleasure many times. She would have to pull back and not allow the rawness of this one situation to rip away the barrier to her heart she created.

Throwing her head back, she sucked in a deep breath and opened the flood gates until she could sit unaffected by it all, or so she hoped.

CHAPTER 11

*L*ord help him. When he saw Finna standing in his room after her quick escape he feared the worst. Then when she let the robe drop to expose her naked glory, he was lost. His heart would pound out of his chest before tonight ended for sure.

Taking her into his arms, the sensation of skin on skin was almost his undoing. Could a man pass out from attraction? The fact she melted into his embrace, seeming to want the same as he only made his passion ratchet up another notch. She wanted to be there. It was her choice. How many nights had he dreamed this very thing only to wake the next morning with unrelenting guilt of being unfaithful—if not in deed, then in mind—to his wife?

That was, until he left her mouth to trail kisses down her neck. The change, like an icy breeze, swept over him. Finna had cut herself off. A subtle shift, perhaps a change in her breathing, or a mere shift in her weight, but it was obvious to him. She was willing to only give him so much.

Without so much as a word, he continued spreading kisses across the top of her chest to the other side of her neck, while he determined his next move. Should he step back and send her back to her room until she came to him prepared to strip herself bare and give him everything? Kendrick had no right to ask that of her. He had not lived her life. He knew nothing of what she had to give up to follow her path, he couldn't expect her to abandon it all on a hint of a promise, if what they were doing was even that. Hell, he didn't know what he wanted.

Perhaps it was just nerves. He made his way up the column of her slender neck. His goal to coax her to dismiss her guard, he made his way back to her full, luscious lips. Just as he was on the precipice of drinking her in, she turned from him and offered her neck again. A chill sliced through his desire and cooled the surrounding air.

Kendrick stepped back even though the act cost him more than he could explain. "Finna," he whispered. "Finna, look at me."

She turned her face up to him, with her defiant chin leading the way. In the moonlight her eyes glowed with unshed tears, making him certain this was the right path.

"When we come together it needs to be an equal desire," he said.

"I would not be here if I did not have a desire for you."

Kendrick leaned forward and rested his forehead on hers. It took all this strength not to shake from his need for her. "Then why won't you let me kiss you?"

"I will let you kiss me."

"You just turned away," he pointed out.

"Did I? It was not my intent. Here, I won't pull away this time." She pulled back and puckered her lips.

Not willing to argue the point, he just waited. After a moment she opened her eyes, confusion clear in her expressive eyes. "What?"

"I want you, Finna. I have wanted you for more years than I should. But I want you. I do not want the shell you offer to your clients."

She pulled away and turned from him as she fumbled around to cover herself with her discarded robe. He waited until she turned back toward him and took her shoulders to still her. He lifted her chin to see her face. Tears had freed themselves from her eyes and streamed down her cheeks. It was enough to slay him. He helped her get the robe around her shoulders, to reclaim what dignity remained, and pulled her into him and just held her. She fought it for a moment, but then calmed. He wouldn't say she gave into the need for comfort, but she didn't turn from it.

After time to let her gain more composure he asked, "What is it you want from me, Finna? I will give you all that I can, but remember you came to me, what end were you expecting?"

She stood still with her head buried in his shoulder and took a long-ragged breath before pulling back to look at him. "I want to lie with you," she said without further explanation.

This unfamiliar territory was not anything either of them expected. If anyone should understand her it was him, but he was prepared to be laid bare and broken after this. If in fact he could sleep with her and allow her to walk away, a piece of him would go with her. What he wasn't sure of was how big of a piece and if it would wreck him for the rest of his life. It was, however, a chance he was ready to take.

She stepped from his arms and walked to the window. After what seemed an eternity she turned back toward him. "I agree that we had our opportunities taken from us and when you pointed out there was nothing to keep us from indulging and gaining back that which we lost, I assumed you meant a physical relationship. I thought about it and find I agree with you."

Her expression showed how much this conversation was taking from her. She had stood alone for the last twenty years. She would see it as an affront if he tried to comfort her now. "So, you want sex?"

"Well, yes, isn't that what you want?"

Damned if he knew anymore. "I believe what I want is to see where this could lead," he continued with caution. "However, that means we both need to be open to the possibilities."

She drew in another breath that wracked her body with shivers. He left her standing alone once, could not stand to do it again.

Taking her hand, Kendrick led her to the reading chair by the fireplace and tugged her down to sit on his lap. She settled in and leaned her head on his chest. He breathed in deep the smell of her midnight black hair and settled his lips on the top of her head.

"It doesn't bother me."

Not pulling away, she replied, "You cannot possibly know that."

"I believe I am aware of my mind, madame," he said in a light tone.

She pulled back then and looked at him with a hard expression. "Maybe here in your bedroom, where you can shut out the reality, but in the light of day, when you will no doubt be mingling with my old clients daily."

"Were all the current members of Parliament your former clients?" he asked, trying to make light of a serious concern. The truth was he could not promise her it would never grate on him.

"I was very good at my job," was all she said.

He leaned up and kissed a rather delectable spot on the tip of her shoulder. "You have done nothing by half my dear. The truth is I cannot promise I won't want to challenge every member of Parliament to a duel to defend your honor, but what I can promise you is that I will not."

"You would get nothing done if you were dueling someone every day. I believe there are few who would speak ill of me, but you should not have to live with wondering if whoever you talk to had been connected with me. You would grow to resent me."

He kissed that spot again, then reached up and turned her head to face him. "We, more than anyone, should know we can make plans all we care to, but if fate has its own plan then we have no control. However, the one thing we can control is to take what we can and make the most of it. That can only happen if we are both willing to lay ourselves bare. We can't hold back."

She looked away and instead concentrated on an invisible speck on her robe. Kendrick took her hand in his and brought it to his mouth, placing a gentle kiss on her knuckles.

"I am not sure I can do what you are asking of me." Her

confession was the most truth she had offered him since he set foot in her home.

"Well, I am not sure I can do this any other way. After trying to engage a mistress when we were early in our life in Italy, it was clear I needed more. Victoria was not the most amorous of wives, and I thought it a suitable compromise. To be honest, I think Victoria was relieved."

"What do you mean you tried?" she asked, still paying attention to their entwined hands.

"I could not separate sex from my feelings. It was awkward and cold. I went once, and never again. So, to answer your question from earlier, no, I do not want just sex."

The silence stretched, but he let her consider what he was saying. After much time she slipped off his lap and stood in front of him. "I understand, of course. I am afraid though that I do not have the emotions you need."

Anger hot and fast surged in Kendrick. Rising from his chair, he pulled her into an embrace and a kiss with all the emotion he could pull from the last twenty years. To his satisfaction, she reacted not by pulling away, but leaning in and becoming an active player.

By the time he ripped his mouth from hers, they were both panting and spent from the impact of it. "I see you can feel as strongly as I," he managed.

She pulled away, the magic of the moment gone. "You have had the luxury for your entire adult life to not hide your feelings in any circumstance. I have not had that privilege."

It was on the tip of his tongue to point out. She had the option before she chose her road, but what good would it have done? After her first encounter as a courtesan, he imagined her options dwindled considerably and there was no turning back. Unlike his experience with a mistress where he just pretended it never happened, and the world allowed him to live as he had always.

"That is very true. I suspect it will not ease your mind if I apologized for myself and the entire world created to further a man in life, but to hinder a woman. But for what it is worth, I do."

She said nothing, but he knew their encounter was over. There would be no love making tonight. He would have to see the win as her coming to his door at all. He made no move to stop her, even though the need to whisk her the ten paces to his bed and fall asleep with her in his arms was palpable.

"I am sorry I cannot be what you are asking," she said, her face flushed in the moonlight. Though her skin held the distinct hue from her Spanish mother, it was not so dark to hide her cheeks when she was high in color.

"Finna, you need not be anything more than who you are when we are together. I don't believe you and I were ever anything but honest with each other, and even after twenty years, I would hope that one piece of our relationship held true."

She nodded but did not offer any reassurance either way and slipped from the room, a gentle click as the door shut behind her.

Kendrick stood in the dark silence for a moment. He looked at the bed, as yet untouched. Running a hand through his hair and rubbing the back of his neck, he instead sat in the reading chair. He didn't need to drift off to know his dreams would be filled with dark lustrous hair and smooth, sun kissed dusky skin. Finna standing in his room with her robe puddled on the floor, emblazoned in his mind. No, sleep would not come tonight. Instead, perhaps he should take the time to get his mind right about what in bloody hell he wanted from himself, Finna, and life in general. It was time.

CHAPTER 12

*M*ornings were more preferable when one slept the night before. This had become Kendrick's truth of the day as he sat in the breakfast room hoping the strong coffee would help to buoy him. He opted for coddled eggs and toast, not wanting any heavy sausage or scones to act against him and make him more tired.

"Good morning, Lord Harwich. It is a lovely day, is it not?" Contrell floated into the room with enough lightheartedness to be the sun itself. Following close behind was Amari, looking as tired, but more energized than him hence the broad smile set on his face.

"Good morning, Ms. Contrell, Mr. Amari. It seems you are both well energized this morning." He took a long sip of his coffee, hoping against hope it would have some effect.

"Oh, there is nothing that a solid night's sleep won't cure," she said brightly and sat down.

Kendrick gave them both time to get their meals and their beverage of choice. In the meantime, he continued to peruse the newssheet for anything untoward or bothersome. Thankfully, it seemed the gossips at least had not gotten word of their guest.

"Is Lady Finna joining us to break the fast?" he asked once they seemed settled.

Contrell looked over her toast points with a very assessing gaze. A bit much for the time of day and the innocent question.

"She had an errand to see to this morning. I would have thought you knew."

Kendrick sat up and placed the newssheet on the table. All this time he thought her tucked away in the sanctity of her bedchamber hiding from him. "No, she said nothing yesterday or last evening about having something to attend to this morning. Where was this errand?"

She sipped her tea and took her time before she decided if she would answer. With a decision made, she set down the bread in her hand and wiped the corner of her mouth with her napkin. "Lady Finna had a business matter to attend to at her solicitor's. She received a letter late yesterday afternoon about a matter that needed her immediate attention."

Kendrick's stomach dropped. She took this opportunity because of the money it afforded her, but he was not privy to the level of her financial distress. "Is there a problem with her accounts? It seems questionable that she is called in such a manner?"

Ms. Contrell snorted her disgust, before offering her assessment of the matter. "If you ask me, that man—her solicitor, is nothing but a crook. She has had nothing but ill outcomes since he took over for his uncle. It has been over a year now, and I swear she loses money daily under his watch."

He had never known Finna to be led by anyone, and her head for finances was more than respectable out of the schoolroom. "How can she sit by and allow that?"

She snorted. "If you ask me, she is trying to catch him in a lie, but to what result I do not understand. Tis not as if the powers that be would take it seriously."

"Well, I think a woman should trust the men who know more of those things," Michele interjected, not paying any attention to his companion sitting next to him. The look Contrell shot him would have withered him had he been aware.

"I beg your pardon, sir, but Lady Finna has directed more than one budding viscount how to invest both his private and entitled fortunes and has never been wrong."

As soon as Amari heard her tone, he sent a pleading glance to Kendrick. To which Kendrick shook his head, letting Amari know he was alone in this battle. It was the job of those put to protect him, to do so from threats outside of the house. Any cannonballs sent at him from within were his to manage.

"I know Finna's head for business and finance, so that is why I am confused."

"Well, to be honest, she won't admit it, but I do not believe there is a brokerage or solicitor other than the one she works with that will take her on." Contrell spoke over Amari trying to profess his apologies for such limited and dated thinking. "Oh be, quite won't you? Do you think you are any different from any other man I have taken to my bed? It just so happens that I must sup and break my fast with you, so I am forced to hear your backward notions. I am terribly glad there is little time for discourse in bed."

Amari turned a bright puce color but was silenced. Kendrick guzzled the rest of his coffee to hide his laughter, then motioned for another cup to a waiting footman.

"Since this braggart took the reins of the business, Finna pours over her accounts and has regular meetings to discuss everything. She often returns in a foul mood."

Kendrick remembered the note from Finna's father suggesting he look into the solicitor. It appeared as usual the Duke knew things he had yet to discover. If that man was cheating her out of a ha-penny it ended today. If her accounts were threatened enough that she had to take on Amari and all that entailed to get her accounts right, this had been happening for far too long. She should have gone to her father or come to him.

"You wouldn't know where the solicitor's offices are?" he asked as he downed the remainder of what was now his third cup of coffee. Not knowing if having a plan kicked him into gear or if the coffee was taking effect.

"Yes, he has an office off of Bond Street, at the corner near the haberdasher with the beautiful peacock feathered bonnet."

Nodding like he knew the exact bonnet she spoke of, he rose and said his goodbyes. It didn't sound too difficult to find with those directions.

Kendrick turned from the breakfast room and went into

the parlor. Finna's writing desk sat open with a stack of vellum note cards ready to use. He would need Birch to come cover the house while he was gone. Golding and Fletcher could keep an eye until he arrived. Kendrick rang for Golding and handed off the note. Golding would see to it the note was delivered and assured Kendrick no one would get in in the light of day.

Heading upstairs to get his coat and fill Fletcher in at the top, Mr. Chesterfield almost bumped into him in his hurry to get down the stairs.

"Oh, my apologies Lord Harwich. I meant no disrespect," he said with genuine fear in his voice.

"Not at all, Chesterfield, it is fine. Where are you off to in such a rush? I hope there is no trouble?" Kendrick quite liked Lang and his companion Chesterfield. He could understand why Finna cared so for them.

"Nothing really, Lang is having a bit of trouble completing a task Finna put him to. I am heading out to assist. It has nothing to do with your current issues, so there is no need for concern."

"Well, thank you for that. Please send word if the two of you are in need of support. I am happy to help."

Chesterfield smiled at that. "You know, my lord, I think you are honest in that. I do not interact with many men of your station honorable as that. I am sure we will have this handled by this evening, though."

The two men shook hands and Kendrick let him on his way. Life was difficult for many people in England who lived outside of what society saw as acceptable. Kendrick got the impression that Reginald Chesterfield had experienced that side of England for most of his life. It was fortuitous that he found someone such as Lang, who could use his family's title and fortune to shield them both.

Kendrick found Fletcher brushing his jacket and filled him in with an assurance that Birch would be there soon, when Fletcher went white at the thought of having to defend the house against anyone.

Next stop, to find Finna, and have yet another conversation she would not care to discuss, and then to force his aid where it wasn't wanted. After a long night with only his thoughts, he was becoming clear on what his life needed to look like. But it appeared it would not be easily won and may be far more difficult to bring into existence, than peace in Italy.

The office, once a cozy jewel box of a room, had turned dingier since the last time. How she missed Mr. Henry. His nephew was nothing like him. He gave no care to his surroundings, and even little to his clients, well, to her. Finna was certain if a peer were to be treated thusly, the man would not only be out of business but on a fast coach to gaol.

"I must insist that you not take up my time every time there is a discrepancy in what you think should be in your account and what the correct amount is. I would also point out that sums this large could well give a woman a headache and cause her to not tally correctly."

Finna took a deep breath. The disrespectful street rat would not be happy in a month's time when she withdrew all her funds from his care. She smiled sweetly, ignoring her desire to stab him with whatever implement she could get her hands on.

"I believe that my account was much larger when Mr. Henry was still here, and I do not get headaches from doing sums, no matter the size. What gives me a headache are men who dismiss the abilities of women, namely clients who keep food on your table." She rose to leave, sending him into a fit of the flutters.

It appeared he remembered who he was speaking to, but still it wasn't enough to give her the answers she sought. As he blustered on about not meaning any disrespect a commotion in the outer room grabbed their attention.

Before either could react, Kendrick strode through the door, like a man wanting to murder. "Ah, there you are Lady Finna," He bowed low over her hand, which he scooped up and kissed.

"Lord Harwich, I was not aware you were in search of me," she said not at all certain how to play this.

"I was hoping to have a word with you, didn't mean to interrupt—"

"I say, you barged into my private office, what did you think you would do other than interrupt a private meeting?" Mr. Knottingword all but yelled.

Finna took a step back to see how the little man fared against a Marquis.

"I do not believe you know me; I am Marquess of Harwich. You may call me my lord," Kendrick said, then turned to Finna, giving him his back.

"You were not at home this morning, and it worried me

since you had not mentioned a meeting at such an early hour."

"Lord Harwich, I did not realize, please let me apologize for my rudeness."

Kendrick winked at her, then turned to give Knottingword his full attention. If she was not at her wit's end, she would step in and not let him speak for her, but it appeared if she didn't step back, she would lose more money.

"Do you mean your rudeness toward me, or toward Lady Finna?"

"I, well, I do not believe Lady Finna has any complaint toward me. I in fact handle all her accounts," he blustered.

"Yes, I am aware, however it has been brought to my attention that you have not been running things as your uncle did."

"He was an old man. I am working to bring his systems up to date."

"Really? Does that include draining the coffers of the accounts belonging to those who may not otherwise be able to defend themselves?"

Knottingword made to speak and Kendrick shot up a hand. "Are you aware of who Lady Finna is?"

The younger man fidgeted and pulled at his cravat. Only making the color flush his face more quickly. "Well, I am aware of what my uncle has passed along."

"And what is that?" Harwich asked, not letting him out from under his harsh glare.

"She is London's foremost courtesan's with good connections, as my uncle tells it. He also mentioned that several clients were acquired because of her endorsement."

He then either found some bravery, or slid completely

into madness. Finna thought it a balanced wager when he hitched his chin up a notch and said with not even a hint of remorse, "I am an upstanding business man, and will not align my business's success to a common whore. I would think, as a Marquess, you would be very careful who you did business with."

By instinct, Finna reached out and placed her hand on Kendrick's forearm. He registered the slight pressure but struggled to know anything beyond the red streak of fury that coursed through every fiber of his body. It was however enough to remind him, he was not there to slay her demons, but to convince them of their best options.

Again, Knottingword yanked on his cravat and took a step back from the apparent murderous expression Kendrick did not hide, his social mask gone.

He moved around the desk at a slow pace. He learned as a youth never to react without first making sure of one's opponent. On the streets you learn that young. Once around the desk, he put his hands behind his back and clasped them. Another lesson learned as a young man hoping to gain back his family's title. It would not have benefited him to strike every upstart that tried to provoke him. By keeping his hands clasped behind him, it gave him time to consider before acting.

"Perhaps, you sir, would benefit from doing some of your own background of your clients. She is in fact London's most sought after companion, but not for the reasons someone like you would assume, although, I am certain the lady is above par in all of life's endeavors. The reason this woman is in demand," he pointed in her direction, to bring him back to the reason they were all there, "is that she is the eldest daughter of the Duke of Rygate."

Finna covered her mouth with her gloved hand to hide the smile and small giggle that bubbled up when Mr. Knottingword blanched. In fact, Finna feared he might in fact faint.

"Ridiculous!" Mr. Knottingword yelled, once he got himself together. "A duke's daughter has no reason to—to—"

"To choose the life of a courtesan?" Kendrick asked. "I will suggest that people regardless of their station make life choices all the time that some would balk at. Like how an upstart who took over his uncle's lucrative business would want to treat one of his best clients like a common light skirt, because he was too ignorant to see the possibilities."

Knottingword's mouth opened, closed, and opened again, with no sound coming out.

"Now you will listen and listen well. I am uncertain where all of Lady Finna's money is going, but she has her ledgers at her home, and I will follow up in a week's time to see that her calculations match with the one's you have. If I am unsatisfied about the outcome of that auditing, I can assure you the next visitor you receive in this office will be the duke himself. If you care at all to keep the clients you currently have, I would suggest any lost funds are found, and all are squared away."

"I, yes, yes sir—I mean, my lord, Lord Harwich."

"See that it is done." Before he could land his fist on the man's jaw he walked back around the desk and straight out of the building. Finna would come when she was finished.

Outside, he sucked in a breath of cool London air that started the tension leaving his body. He had not been so infuriated for a very long time, and it reminded him why he never allowed such emotion. It rarely accomplished what he wanted. In this instance, though, he felt it warranted.

He looked to his left, and there in the haberdasher's window stood an ostentatious confection of a hat sporting peacock feathers. Ms. Contrell was not wrong, it was easily found. A smiled warmed his face and the rest of his anger fell away.

Just then, Finna appeared in the solicitor's doorway's office. He could not read her face, because it was blank. Damn, how did women do that? He let her walk to him before he said anything.

"I'm sorry—"

"Thank you," she said over his apology.

"I'm sorry, what?"

She smiled at his joke, but it hadn't been a joke. He expected her to be livid.

She smiled, and he noted a slight blush to her cheeks giving her a youthful expression. "That horrible little man has been dismissing me for a year now. I am fully aware he has been draining money, but not enough that I had a strong enough argument, so I had just decided that monthly I would demand a meeting to go over the accounts. But he was becoming more dismissive by the meeting. Had you not arrived; he would have sent me away yet again. I will confess I am not used to being treated so badly."

"Why did you not let it slip who your father was?" Kendrick asked.

"I have never been outright disowned by my family, and so I have tried not to force the issue over the years. I know it is silly of me, but on bad days it is reassuring to feel I am not alone."

Kendrick balled his hands into fists to stave off the need to pull her into him. They were on a busy London street, after all. He cleared his throat to take away the emotion building in him.

"I will be one moment, would you join me in the store?" he asked as he turned and offered his arm.

She smiled warmly, and cocked her head to the side, unsure of his intent, but looped her arm in his and followed along. Moments later they emerged with the largest hat box Kendrick had ever seen but was certain it would not be unappreciated. They turned down the street and headed toward their carriages, parked along the wider expanse of the thoroughfare.

"You know bribing my closest companion is unfair play?" She pointed to the hat box.

"As I have yet to be given a rule book, I will play the board as I see the need. Besides, as much as she spoke of the hat in the way of giving me direction, I am certain she will gain more joy out of this hat than I would to keep those funds I just spent in my accounts. If that gains me her confidence, I am not responsible for that."

Finna smiled and appeared less tense than when he barged into the office. He had no more answers than he had this morning about her reasons she for keeping a poor solicitor or doing dangerous duties for the government for extra funds, but he was closer to making sure she was protected and that was important.

At their carriages, parked one in front of the other, he stopped to hand her in.

"Will I see you back at the townhouse then?" she asked before stepping in.

"Yes, Birch should be there and I want to compare notes to see where he is with getting Amari off British soil and out of your home, and I have gifts to deliver." He held up the large hatbox and swung it from its ribbons.

She chuckled settling in her carriage. Once the door shut, he moved to his own, satisfied for the moment.

CHAPTER 13

$\mathcal{I}$n the carriage, Finna let out the breath she was holding. How was it her entire life was a convoluted system of blocks all balanced precariously one on top of the other? If one block toppled, the weight of it would crush her.

In the office today, confronting that awful man about how he was mis-handling her funds, she felt the foundation they were on shift. Had Harwich not entered when he did, she feared the tears may have overtaken her and her world would collapse with it. He intervened out of a misplaced sense of responsibility for her current situation.

London jostled by as she sat and replayed all the decisions in her adult life, no wiser to her distress than they would be if they were in the carriage with her. One of the marvels of the world of the Ton was that nothing was as it seemed. Many could go their entire lives without the realization, but a courtesan to the rich and famous was painfully aware. She spent much of her time as a mistress mending the marriages the men ran from, or patching holes left behind by errant mothers and distant fathers. They could all go to the devil for all she cared. They all thought they understood her, but in retrospect it was her who knew where the demons resided among them.

The carriage slowed in traffic and Finna watched the young ladies in the park gathering to stroll among the fashionable. She remembered her time as a debutante. It was all baubles and balls, champagne and pastries. Then she saw Kendrick—at the time merely Mr. Rutland—at a dinner party, and she was lost. She had to admit however, that with time, and some well-placed lines to show he lived a happy life, all accentuated with a splatter of silver in his midnight black waves he was more dangerous to her now.

Never one to bother with looking back in the past. It did nothing to move you into the future, however she considered how her life would have been different had they wed. Was she the type who would have settled into married life? At the young age of only eighteen years, she would not have known better. They would have been happy; they were in love. Now, she was not so certain. Most would think it was because she was a loose woman and being true to just one man was beyond her capabilities.

The carriage lurched back into motion, making Finna frown at the direction of her thoughts. Other people's opinions mattered not to her. There had been exactly two men in her life who made her consider it, and both times she was ready to take it on. It was not a problem with her monogamy.

"And we are here, mi' lady," the coachman called from his box.

Before she gathered her shawl and reticule the door opened and Kendrick poked his head in, smile wide and playful. "All set, my lady?"

"Well, such treatment. I feel special."

"You should feel special every day of your life, my dear."

The endearment hit her in the chest, addling her brain at the same time. She cleared her expression and followed him to the door.

"We are home," Finna called out when they entered.

"In here, dear heart," Contrell called back.

The parlor was a wash of quiet comfort with Birch and Amari deep into a chess game and Contrell seated at the small writing desk penning a letter to her sister. When they cleared the threshold Contrell looked up concern in her eyes. Once looking at Finna a smile broke out on her face.

"Oh, you look much better than I expected."

Finna sat on the edge of the sofa wanting to escape and take the time to calm the storm brewing inside her. "Yes, well, someone gave Lord Harwich directions to my solicitor's office and he barged in uninvited and intervened."

Contrell dipped her head and looked like the contrite child Finna knew her to be at heart.

"And speaking of those directions. I have to say your description of the hat in the window was spot on." He lifted the huge box onto the chair in front of him. "I saw it and knew it needed a home with you."

Emotion filled Finna's throat as she watched her long-time friend and confidant's face shine as it had never done before.

COURTESAN'S WICKED DESIRE

"Oh, Lord Harwich, it is too much. I could not accept such a gift. After all, I have done nothing that would constitute such an extravagance."

"Contrell, you have my undying gratitude for being so kind. Besides, it is my fortune. What good would a fortune be if I can't spend my money to my pleasure?"

Contrell still didn't move from the chair and looked at Finna for the proper thing to do. "Come, Contrell, to separate a man from his purse for doing nothing but being kind is a win for womankind as a whole. And I cannot wait to see it on you."

Kendrick waited for her to take the box, then made his way to Birch, who had sat back from his play and observed her strange little family. Amari joined Contrell at the hat box and began showering her with compliments.

"Oh, you look marvelous, it brings out the cornflower blue of your eyes. That settles it, I must commission a new dress for you. A hat that spectacular requires a dress to set it off."

"Oh no, Finna, I couldn't—"

"Nonsense, I will buy you a dress if that is your desire, my love," Amari piped up.

With that, Finna moved to the two men with their heads bent.

"Is this a meeting I am not invited to?" she asked.

Kendrick jumped up and offered her his chair and walked to the back of the parlor to procure another.

"What are we talking about?" she asked, leaning in.

"I was just telling Harwich I believe there may be someone in the foreign office working against us. I am having a bugger of a time to find an escape from London."

Kendrick's expression said it for them all. If they couldn't get Amari out safely, they would have to keep him safe in a town where the enemy could be disguised as a friend.

"Birch has connections outside the reach of the home office, and he will reach out. All will be well," he assured her, even though his expression belayed his words.

"I am afraid I need to meet someone for that reason soon, so I will take my leave. I will see you all tomorrow. Hopefully with more promising news. If you need me, I have a man at my apartments who can find me."

"Let us hope we will not need to," Finna said as she rose.

Kendrick and Birch shook hands, and she couldn't help but miss the looks they exchanged without a word.

As Birch quit the room, Kendrick took the chance to make an escape. "I have some correspondence I need to take care of. I will be in my room. I will see you all at dinner."

"Oh, Lord Harwich, thank you again." Contrell shuffled around the settee to meet him at the door. Without warning, she flung her arms around him, and raised up on her tiptoes to plant a kiss on his cheek. "I will never for the rest of my days forget your kindness."

Kendrick whispered something to Contrell, then made his way to the stairs. Finna couldn't help but stand and watch him walk up to the landing. His fawn breeches stretching across his backside, like he was born in them, not sized for them. And the tails of his jacket set just so as his hips swayed his perfect backside would peek out teasing the watcher.

"My dear, I haven't seen you blush like that since your first month with me. Have you forgotten yourself?" Contrell walked up to her and joked.

Finna sighed as she opened her fan to cool her very core.

"No, I haven't forgotten myself, but some things are just meant to be enjoyed."

"You have the right of that, my dear. A smart woman would take what was being offered from that one."

"What is that supposed to mean?" Finna asked, suddenly reminded of their false start last night. She was certain Contrell was not aware of that, however.

"I am just saying a man who moves from his own comfortable establishment to live in a guestroom just to protect a lady, has more interest than her safety."

"Stop with your scheming," Finna warned.

"Mr. Amari, would you assist me in taking my new hat to my room? I think the box may be too unwieldy for me."

"Of course, I cannot think of anything I would rather be doing. I am at your service."

It warmed her heart to see Contrell enjoying their guest. She was concerned that it would throw her into a melancholy when they found safe passage for him and he was out of her life. She would take care of the woman who shielded her from so much in the early years.

With the parlor empty, Finna flopped down onto the sofa in a less than ladylike maneuver. Lord, she was tired. Perhaps with the household occupied, she would sneak to her room and take a nap. Naps always seemed like such a lazy thing to do when there was living to be done, but its benefits may have been under rated. Before she could haul herself up from the sofa to find her bed, a commotion in the entry hall had her freezing.

Lang came bursting into the room. "Oh, blessed day you are alone. Where are our spy men?"

"What? They are not in here, but Harwich is in his room,

so please be quiet. Where is Bryant? I thought we agreed you and Reginald would remain with him."

"We tried, love. Tried like you cannot imagine, but you would think that boy was raised by a stubborn, headstrong woman or something. He was having none of it."

"Lang?"

There was no point in Lang speaking further. "Mother! See Reginald, I told you it would be fine."

"Bryant, dear," Finna greeted her son with arms wide, inviting him in for a hug. As always, the sight of her son coming from school for a visit was beyond her happiest of moments, but this was the worst of times possible. "You are fully aware I dislike you coming into town. Now, as happy as I am to see you, I believe before we go any further you owe Lang and Reginald an apology. They were only doing what I asked of them."

The young man, who had turned from a boy to a young man overnight it seemed, turned to the two harried men standing in the parlor's doorway catching their breath. "I am sorry, chaps. I meant no disrespect. I just hadn't seen mother for so long, I missed her terribly."

Lord help the women of the Ton when he came to his majority. Not one person, including her, had ever stayed angry with him long enough for a good scolding.

"Um, excuse me," Finna said instead of saying what her thoughts really were. "When did I get demoted to mother? Where did mama go?"

"Mother, gentlemen do not refer to their mothers as mama," he said over his shoulder as he shook hands with his overwrought babysitters.

"Well, we shall discuss that later, but for now this

gentleman is going to get back into the carriage and return to the country house with Lang and Reginald as I asked. When I finish here, I will join you. You are on holiday for the next month, we will have more than enough time—"

Her words died in her mouth. On the stairs for who knew how long, stood Kendrick.

From his expression, he had been there long enough. A lesser woman would choose this time when her two worlds, that of her past and her present, collided to orchestrate a well-placed fainting spell. Finna had never mastered that particular skill, to her mother's chagrin.

The fact he had not yet dropped from an apoplectic fit was a sign of his good health, but Kendrick had yet to will his heartbeat to slow to a manageable tattoo. The whooshing in his ears proof.

Never one to shut himself off to anyone who may need him, when he settled in his room, he left the door to the hall open. A habit from his days as a diplomat in Italy. The only time the door was closed was when he could not be disturbed. He sat at his desk and penned a note first to his grace, to tell him he was thankful for the warning of the solicitor and that he had been in contact with him already. Then, the next note was to his own solicitor to make sure his accounts were up to date. As he sanded the last page of that note the front door slammed, and feet could be heard. Kendrick was four doors down from the top of the main staircase, so to hear voices meant they were raised.

Contrell and Amari had passed a while ago. That meant

Finna was alone. He was out of his chair and on the top landing, still with his quill in his hand. It was such an impulse. What he saw stopped him dead.

Lang and Reginald stood at the bottom of the stairs just outside the parlor door. Both looked like a mob had clawed them off and in good shape. But that was not what had his heart doubling in beats. His attention went to the young man standing just inside the parlor talking to Finna of perhaps fifteen years of age, with all the signs of being her son. Was he the only one who didn't know?

Just then, Finna looked up and her expression would have brought him to tears had he not mustered the strength to force the emotion down deep. Was she ashamed of her son? Or did she just not care to have him be privy to that much about her life? Squaring his shoulders, he plastered a welcoming smile on his face and made the rest of the way down the stairs.

"I had my door open and heard a commotion. After the other night I expected we were being taken over." He explained his condition away easily enough as he greeted the gentlemen, who clearly needed a drink and some quiet time to collect themselves.

"Hello, I am Bryant Lennox, and you are?" The young man stepped between his mother as an instinctive barrier to protect her, he was sure.

Kendrick reached out his hand to the lad. "I am honored. I am Marquess Harwich, but my friends all call me Kendrick. I was not aware your mother was expecting you to visit." He shot a telling look over the young man's shoulder to a red faced Finna. Behind them, Reginald and Lang cleared their throats.

"I hate to interrupt, but we need to be going if we are to make the country house before dark," Lang said in a sheepish tone.

All eyes turned to Finna, who squared her shoulders and sucked in a deep breath. "Fine, you may stay the night, but, Bryant," she pointed to her son and waited for him to look at her, "mark my word you are headed to the country house first thing on the morrow."

The young man, who had just informed her that gentlemen used the term mother, threw his arms around her like the child he still was and kissed her cheek. "Thank you! I have so much to tell you about the semester. So much more than I could fit into your letters. Where is Contrell? I want to tell her about the theatrics production?"

"I will fetch her," Lang said, and turned to go upstairs.

Kendrick grabbed his elbow and whispered, "I would knock first if I were you," into Lang's ear. Lang looked puzzled for a moment, then acknowledgment lighted his eyes and he nodded.

"Come, let us have a seat and I will call for tea. Are you hungry?" Finna asked, the epitome of domestic bliss. Her face changed when she was looking at her son, Kendrick noticed. It was softer and a reminder of her younger, less jaded self. "Of course, you are hungry, you are always hungry."

Reginald and Kendrick followed and sat in chairs to hear all about the schooling of Finna's son. As they chatted, Kendrick's mind pushed to decide who he resembled other than Finna. Did he know the man? Was this just a by-blow never to be acknowledged by his proper father? Had Finna loved the man? So many questions whose answers could take him to a dark place he did not wish to visit.

"I am sorry, Reginald, I gave you and Lang such trouble," the boy said with genuine regret.

"I won't be cross with you for long, but I still have a few hours ahead of me yet." Reginald smiled at the boy.

Just then Golding came in carrying a tray laden with food. "I know how the master likes to eat, so as soon as I heard he was home, I set cook to making a plate. The tea will be out shortly."

"Golding, you are the best old chap." Bryant grabbed two sandwiches off the tray before Golding settled it onto the table.

"So, Kendrick—"

"That will be Lord Harwich to a whelp that won't listen to his mother," Finna interjected.

"So, Lord Harwich," without missing a beat, "why are you in residence at my mother's?"

Kendrick was not prepared to explain his very existence in Finna's life to her son, and as luck would have it, Finna was interrupted in her attempt.

"They are gone. Gone. Can this day never end?!" Lang came rushing down the stairs more disheveled than he was when he went up them.

"Did you check Mr. Amari's rooms?" Finna asked, rising and putting her hand to her chest.

"Who's Mr. Amari?" Bryant asked.

"No one of note," both Reginald and Finna answered at the same time.

Kendrick's stomach seized. He knew Michele was getting

more housebound by the day, but being he had no knowledge of London, it had not worried him.

"Contrell." The name slipped from his lips without his warrant, but looking around at the adults in the room, they all knew the truth of it.

"She wanted to show off her hat," Finna nodded, and explained her probable reasoning.

"Where would she take him?" Kendrick asked.

Reginald went straight to the liquor tray and Lang followed, while Finna began pacing with her hand to her head. "I'm uncertain. It has been ages since she has wanted to go about anywhere but the—" She stopped and looked at Kendrick with realization.

"Where," he prodded.

"The park. That has to be where they are. She wanted to parade in the park."

"Help us all from fools and lovers," Kendrick said on a sigh. "It would have been better to hear they headed to an opium den on Cheapside. At least every member of Parliament wouldn't be out escorting their wives and daughters."

"Golding!" Kendrick yelled as he raced out of the room.

"What?" Golding came running around the corner.

"Go to Birch's rooms, tell the man that Amari has left the building and we are mounting a search. We think we have a lead but are unsure."

"Yes, mi' lord. Bloody rich fools," he grumbled, then stopped and turned back to Kendrick. "Meant nothin' of that to you, sir."

Kendrick patted him on the arm but was heading out to the park across the street. He dodged a carriage, and got yelled at by the driver, but made it.

The park, at this hour of the day, was not as full as it soon would be, but there was still enough of a crowd to warrant alarm. Kendrick, for the third time today, willed his heart to not beat out of his chest. Metering his steps in his head to keep from breaking into a dead run, he searched the open areas of the park where a couple might go to be seen. It was no use; they were not at the park. The momentary relief of their primary reason for this farce not being in the park was dashed with the realization of him being out in the thick of London unprotected.

Back at the house, Birch was coming from the direction of his rooms with Golding hot on his heels. They met at the door and neither spoke until they were inside, and the door was shut.

"What the hell, Harwich? All you needed to do was keep him safe. One thing." Birch let the flood gates open and rounded on Kendrick.

"I was charged with assisting you in keeping him and the household safe. I was not put in charge of babysitting an overgrown child who has no care about the danger people are putting themselves in to see him safely off to Belgium." He knew Birch was at his end, but Kendrick was not at fault here.

Birch said no more in argument and marched into the parlor where he stopped. "Bryant, I didn't know you were visiting."

Did the whole of London know of this boy's existence except him?

"Mr. Birch, I am happy to see you, but I'm not sure what's going on." Bryant rose with yet another sandwich in his hand to greet the new guest.

"You must discuss that with your mother, I am afraid." He walked past the boy and ruffled his hair. Kendrick took note by the glare Bryant shot toward Dylan's back. He didn't appreciate the affection. "Where is your mother?"

"She said she needed to look for something, and that she would be right back. She headed upstairs."

Kendrick didn't hesitate, he took the stairs two at a time and knew she would be in Contrell's room. Sure enough, she sat on the edge of the bed with a note in her hands, tears running down her face. Kendrick no longer cared what happened to that selfish little imp, Amari, but Finna wouldn't cry as long as he drew breath. He sat down and wrapped her in his arms.

"We will fix this love; it will be well," he assured her.

She said nothing but turned into his shoulder and sobbed for a bit. After a moment, she cleared her throat and sat up.

"I did not mean for you to learn of Bryant in such a fashion. It was also not my intent to keep his existence from you, though few are aware I even have a son. It would not help him at school for his classmates to know who his mother is."

"I am not judging your decisions; they are yours to make —" he started.

"I saw your face when you were on the stairs. I hurt you by not saying anything."

"Finna, I have no right to expect anything of you. I am the last person you should trust with anything. What did the note say?" He decided changing the subject was best. This topic did not need to be hashed out now.

Looking down at the note, "She said she was going to show Michele her London. They have gone to the riverfront. There are many dens on that side, as you know, but I am certain I know which one they are at." She rose, looked at him, and gone was the fretful, vulnerable Finna. "We will finish our other discussion. I will not end things badly." And she quit the room, leaving Kendrick to wonder who was the vulnerable one now?

CHAPTER 14

*B*irch and Kendrick raced out of the townhouse to the address Finna provided. Silence descended. Lang and Reginald, although exhausted from their failed errand, sat silently in the parlor with drinks in hand.

Golding loomed at the front door where he would no doubt remain until everyone returned. Finna drank up the quiet, hoping to calm her nerves. Her small garden in the back of the townhouse was in full bloom, and if she propped open the window, the smell would set her nerves at ease, but they were battened down like a ship sailing into a storm. Twenty years of impulsive actions settled on her chest like rock. She had brought them all to this moment.

Turning from the view, she homed in on her son. He sat; legs sprawled out across the settee with a journal in hand. If she looked over his shoulder, she knew what he would be doing. His drawings were professional in quality. The one impulsive choice in her life she did not regret.

Finna made her way to the chair closest to Bryant and settled in. Sure enough, he created a scene with Lang and Reginald, capturing the essence of the current mood. He was almost an adult. Soon there would be no way to keep who she was from him, to shield him from the censure he would walk into. The fortune he would gain upon reaching his majority would go a long way in helping, though.

"Mother," he began, not looking up from his work. "Why is Mr. Birch and Lord Harwich here? And why is everyone so concerned about where Contrell is off to?"

Finna smiled a sad smile, because she had been expecting the questions to come. "Well, Contrell is off with a gentleman that both Mr. Birch and Harwich are hoping to protect."

"Is he bad?"

"No, in fact I think he quite likes Contrell, but he is very important to another country and it's fight for freedom."

Bryant looked up at that with a quizzical expression. "Master Fornier says that the average person does not want freedom from their rulers and that the king is there to protect them."

Finna clenched her jaw. She did not want a son who caused riots, but she wanted a man with his own mind, and didn't just spout rote philosophies. "And as an average person, what do you believe?"

He sat up then and looked at his mother with his head tipped like he had never considered that before. "I didn't know I could think another way. Master Fornier says—"

"Soon, my son, Master Fornier will be a memory and you will in the world making your way. Master Fornier has done an exceptional job at teaching you one way of looking at the world, but as America has shown us all, it certainly is not the only way to see it."

"I suppose you are correct. How would one go about learning other ways to look at the world?"

"Well, for one, doing as one's mother asks is a good start." He scoffed, but she persisted. "No, I am serious, Bryant. Have you never once considered why I may not want you in the city just now?"

"Well, ah no..." he admitted, knitting his brows together. "Probably because you are helping Mr. Birch and Lord Harwich and don't have the time to worry about me, or if I am in danger, but I can be of help. I am quite capable—"

"I know you are, and in a few years, I will no longer be allowed to dictate when you remain free of danger and trials, but for now, for just a smidge longer, I get the glorious burden of protecting you from all that the wider world can offer." She leaned in and cupped his soft, innocent cheek.

"I say," Reginald piped up, "do any of you smell smoke?"

Fear trickled down Finna's back. If they were being watched, it was obvious they were not being protected by the men that ran out together. But, if Contrell was as good at sneaking as Finna knew her to be, the watcher may not be aware that Amari was also vacant from the premises.

"I do, Golding, take Bryant across the street to the park."

The boy opened his mouth to argue but was stopped abruptly.

"Now!"

The stench of smoke was just the precursor to the plumb that billowed out of the smaller visitor parlor across the hall from the entry way. All three ran to the room, covering their mouths from the blackness. It was emanating from the back corner, by the window, which was pried open enough to throw a noxious soaked rag in on the edge of the drapes.

Without thought, Finna ran to the drapes, now threatening to become engulfed, and threw the window open wide, then grabbing at the top of the fabric just above where the flames licked and yanked with all her might. The rod and drapes came crashing over her, but by shear will she forced the smoldering bundle out into the garden, but they were not far enough from the house for her liking Before she could run past Lang to the back door, he grabbed her arm.

Reginald ran for the fire brigade. "They will be here."

"Lang, they won't be here in time." Finna wrenched her arm away as she lifted her skirts and flew to the back of the house.

She briefly thought she must look like a crazy woman flailing about screeching at the top of her lungs. Her ears whooshed, but in the distance, she recognized the deep clang of the fire brigade. She would not lose her home, she couldn't.

With no warning, powerful arms came around her and pulled her into a solid mass. Kendrick, the scent of his aftershave over the choking stink of charred drapes. She stilled, allowing him to rip the drapes, still smoking from her hands, and flung them to the middle of the garden.

"You're fine, it's fine," he cooed in her ear.

It was then she realized she was crying, ugly hiccup crying. "No, no, I will not lose my home." She pulled against him, unable to understand the threat was over.

He just held her and let her rail and scream and swear. All the while rubbing her arm with one hand, whispering assurances in her ear. It wasn't until three men dressed in grubby heavy coats and tall boots came around them with two buckets of water to dowse what was left of her French silk drapes now destroyed beyond repair. Watching the scene unfold while safe in Kendrick's embrace, she felt him rocking her as one does a crying baby. More men shouted from the open window where a slight charr or smoke stains encircled the window trim.

"Are you ready to go in?" he asked after some time.

"I think so, yes."

Kendrick stood and then took her hand and helped her up. Before they could make it into the house, one of the men from the fire brigade stopped them.

"You saved your house by throwing those drapes out the window. I would not think it the safest thing to do, but as my ma used to say, there is a fine line between bravery and stupidity. If you don't mind me saying so, ma'am, you may have crossed that very line today."

"Thank you. I am certain I did just that, but I could not lose my home."

The man bowed low and left to move the men out and back for their next fire. The two of them walked in silence through the house. The acrid perfume of burning oil and burnt fabric strengthened the further into the house they went. Birch greeted them at the stairs, but didn't say a word, just looked between her and Harwich.

They walked into the room that seemed like only moments ago was filling with smoke. Bryant took one look at his mother and flung himself across the room and into her arms. She felt Kendrick recede from them, but she didn't have the strength yet.

"You are a hero, mother," Bryant said with awe in his voice. "You saved us, and the house."

She looked into the eyes of her son that were now level with her own. She needed to see him as her grown son. "I did what I needed to, love. I will always do what I need to, to protect that which I love."

She assessed the room, still holding tight to Bryant. It wasn't as bad as she feared. The paper on the wall where the rags were flung had a dark scar of black soot and burned paper up to the ceiling and she noted the plaster where the rod had hung with large screws was crumbled with a gaping hole, and the beautiful floors were black, but it was not a loss. Nothing a few good workers and a sum of money could not repair.

It was then she remembered Contrell and Amari having gone missing. "Contrell? Did you—"

Birch put up a hand and then motioned for her to turn. Standing inside the doorway was a shaken Contrell with tears streaming down her face.

"Oh, thank God, you are safe," was the only thing Finna could think to say. This latest attempt had put much into perspective, and one of those things was her friend being safe.

"I am so sorry, my dear, I didn't think—"

Finna drew her up into a tight embrace. "It matters not. We are all safe and that is all I care about."

The housekeeper and several maids bustled in to begin the clean up, while all the men took to opening the windows.

"I have drinks poured in the other parlor if you would care to let the cleaning begin," Golding announced.

Once seated with a strong dram of whiskey, half drank,

she was more herself, she hoped. She noted Birch and Kendrick in the corner, talking in hushed tones. Amari sat like a scolded schoolboy on a chair just out of the circle of people. She did not care right this moment to attend him. He very well caused all of this to happen by his careless, selfish actions. Taking a deep breath, she turned away from looking at him.

"I need to leave," Birch announced, coming to center of the group. Kendrick, however, hung back. "I have extracted a promise from our friend that he will give you no more trouble."

Finna followed Birch's eyes to see Amari turning a bright red, but nodding, his double chin wobbling with the force.

"Thank you, but I couldn't help think when the two of you left in such a hurry today, it was obvious to anyone on the street that the house was not as protected as it might have been." This would be easier if not for Bryant sitting listening for any snippet of information.

Birch nodded. "We discussed that. From now on, we will leave from Contrell's hidden pathway, and I will have men stationed outside."

Finna's chest tightened, and she hauled in a breath to make her argument, but Birch raised a hand to stifle her.

"They will not enter the house unless there is apparent distress, and the neighbors will not know they are there. They would not be very good at their jobs if they did, now would they?"

"Fine," she acquiesced begrudgingly. It would be good to have an account of anyone coming or going when they were otherwise occupied.

"I will be back tomorrow with good news and a plan.

There are some leads to follow up on. I will be here well before the two of you leave for the Shelby's route."

"Thank you." And Finna meant it. It may well be his fault she had her current problems, but her choices had put her here, and Birch has done his best. They wished him a good night. Once he quit the room everyone else followed suit to lie down for an hour, since dinner had been pushed back two hours to air out the dining room. Even Bryant, who sat with his forehead knitted trying to piece together the story, said his farewells and left to find his room.

Before Kendrick could grab her attention, she rose. "Bryant, wait. I will walk with you. I wish to wash up and perhaps lay down to fight off a headache coming on."

Like an obedient son that he often was not, he waited in the doorway for his mother to loop arms with him, and she fled. It was pure cowardice, and she knew it. Not one to suffer headaches, even she was not above using every tool in her mother's arsenal that she witnessed as a young girl. Headaches were a favorite and one that father never argued with.

Once in her room, she locked the door just for safety's sake, and walked to the window. A fresh pitcher of warmed rose water already sat waiting with a clean piece of linen, but she ignored it. Peering out the window, the carnage that was her favorite drapes lay in a heap, waiting for someone to dispose of. Turning from the sad scene, her room also didn't seem like it should. It was silent and hollow. Not to mention empty. It was her sanctuary, but today it felt more like a prison, or even the den of a feral creature that shut everyone out. If she no longer could depend on this one place to be her bastion from the world, what was she to do?

CHAPTER 15

The clock on the mantle struck the hour. Kendrick had long since stopped counting what hour it was. It was well past the time he should be asleep, according to the moon peeking in his bedroom window. But when he closed his eyes he could get a whiff of the lingering burnt material and oil. Not to mention the look of Finna in her garden flailing the smoking drapes, long after she extinguished the blaze.

And, if he were able to set those two things aside, there was always the crippling replay of watching the fire brigade speed down her street and stop right outside her home. When that thought came, which it did in waves, his chest would tighten, and his gut would clench. Never, even when the doctor walked down from his wife's rooms and informed him she would not live the month. That had, to his guilt, been a relief. She had suffered, and wasted for so long, knowing she would soon be above her suffering was a comfort. Today, though, the thought of Finna not being in the world anymore made bile hot with anger and fear rise to his throat.

Kendrick threw the covers off for the hundredth time and padded to the window, past the dinner tray that lay forgotten and full. They decided after talking with all the adults it was best to let the dining room have as much time as possible to air out, so all took trays in their rooms. The night was as dark as a night in the city could get. He missed the country for that reason. Nighttime was just as it should be in the country; dark and quiet.

To his left, he noticed a glow from what must be Finna's room. He knew Bryant was not with her, because his room was on the other side of Kendrick's room to the right, and he heard the boy settle in and begin to snore at least three hours ago. He was not surprised she fought sleep. The trauma was severe enough for him, but Finna could be beyond traumatized. He doubted it, though. She was the strongest person he knew. Stronger than any man, even soldiers he had met over the years.

There was also the fact he was angry with her. When he wasn't dealing with the fear, he spent the rest of the time vacillating to red hot anger. She had no reason to not tell him about her son. In fact, he was also angry with the duke for failing to mention it. There was no way he didn't know about his grandson, bastard or no.

He never stopped thinking of Finna. Not one day of his life since he met her did he not have at least a fleeting thought. Not one. It was the one unspoken conflict in his marriage. Victoria understood, but he knew it hurt her that she was not the one in his heart.

Now here he was making a fool of himself, opening up, and considering his future in a way he never allowed himself to hope and it was all a farce. Lady Sarrafinna was above him, or marriage, or love, he wasn't certain anymore. Did she think he would be cruel to the boy? Judge him for the sins of his parents? She knew better. She of anyone in the Ton understood the whole of his story. Knew they disowned his mother for marrying for love, and that his grandfather never accepted him as anything but a bastard, though he wasn't. So much so he allowed the title to go into abeyance instead of allowing a street rat or the son of a street rat take his name.

He drove both hands through his hair, grabbing clumps to bring himself back to today. He was not a street rat; he was a Marquess. He had no intentions of ever treating young master Bryant as anything but the grandson of a duke, and if fate was not cruel, he was brought back to Finna to have the life they had taken from them, but he wouldn't move forward until Finna understood that.

Not bothering to put on a wrap or slippers, he walked to his door bare chested with only a pair of sleep pants covering him. At this late hour, or would it be early? No matter, no one would be shocked in the hallway.

Kendrick tapped on the door and waited. Footsteps, then silence and nothing, so he tapped again. The door lock clicked and Finna spied him by the candlelight washing around her, spilling into the hallway.

"Yes?" she asked, unsurprised.

"We need to talk. I do not care if it is in your room, in my room, or out here on the landing, but we will talk this hour." Brave words from a man who was betting his future on a woman who could shut the door in his face.

Instead of speaking, she swung the door wider and turned back into the room, allowing him to enter. He entered and shut the door, slipping the lock before he turned to face her.

She had cleaned and changed into a rather flouncy and demure night dress, but she looked comfortable. Her hair was down and shone in the candlelight. His hands itched to feel the silky strands in his hands again, remembered from the night before. Perhaps this was not the most stellar plan after all.

"Well, you said we needed to talk. What topic would you care to discuss?" she asked tartly. But he knew that was a sham.

"Us."

His honesty had the desired effect, because she stopped pacing the room and shot him a look that was a mix of desire and confusion. Now, that was something he understood.

"I have no idea what we—"

"For starters, I might enquire as to why you didn't bother to mention your son," he interjected. It was too late at night and there was too much at stake for gentleness.

She sighed and sat on the edge of her bed. "Because I was scared." She looked down at her hands, but he heard the self-hatred in her voice.

"Scared of what?"

She looked at him then, with a determined gaze and stubborn chin. "That you would judge me, or him, or I don't know. It makes no sense to me even."

"It seems everyone else knows the boy, but I am the one you keep it from?"

"Not everyone knows of his existence," she defended.

"All the people in this house are on a casual basis with him."

"All the people in this house are the only ones, save two others that know for certain."

"On that note, you and Birch?" He wasn't even sure how to word the question.

"Birch and I have run in similar circles for many years, and I have made connections for him in the past, and in return he has monitored my wellbeing. That is all. We were never lovers."

Kendrick hmphed, with nothing to say to that, but felt a great relief.

"I am not so foolish as to think Bryant will have his way paved with gold in this world. He is a bastard. Nothing will change the facts. His mother is one of the most well-known courtesans in all of England. I just wanted him to have a childhood without those worries."

"His father?"

She shook her head and looked away. "I was foolish—so foolish. Not to mention young. It seems like a lifetime ago. I had been working on creating a reputation as a woman who could move men in the direction they wanted to go in life. Contrell saw my worth and advised me it would keep me from the more unsavory experiences. There was a man who approached me with his aspirations, and I told him I could help him. We set a deal and so it began. At first it was like the other relationships, but the difference was we were familiar with each other before. I would not have considered him a friend, but an acquaintance. He was likeable and made me laugh."

He walked to the bed and sat next to her, to give her

support as she told him what he believed to be the first actual truth since they got reacquainted.

"It had been five years since you left. I had heard you and Victoria had a lovely daughter. You were moving on. I thought I was strong enough to let someone in. I convinced myself he had feelings for me beyond those of our agreement. By the time I was pregnant, I was so far lost in my own fantasy, I couldn't have found my way out. When I—"

Her voice caught, and Kendrick reached out, taking her hand in his. It was cold, and he rubbed it to get some warmth back in it.

"On the night I told him of his impending child, he had gotten some promising news about his career and came to share that news with me. In my mind, it was perfect timing. He was an up and coming, and now he would have a family and we would work together to make him successful. We could find a little set of apartments and be happy."

"He didn't see it that way?"

"No. After much yelling, and threats of forcing me to abort, he left, and refused to pay me for the last installment of our agreement, claiming I broke the contract and stole his seed from him. If not for Contrell, I would have been destitute in the months leading up to giving birth. That was when I began to care about my future, and I made a promise to myself that I would never need to depend on another person again. Until now, I have kept that promise."

"Depending on someone does not mean giving yourself over completely, you realize?" he asked. "I depend on several people all the time, but it doesn't make me weak."

She rose and walked across the room. The space she left turned as cold as her hand. He would not allow her to shut him out. Not this time, damn it. He didn't need her to depend on him, he needed her to love him. That realization almost knocked him off the bed. He walked to her and put his arms around her, pulling him to her. She didn't fight him, folding into the embrace.

"Today, when I saw my house burning, I realized I did such a good job never depending on anyone, I created a situation where they all depend on me. The weight of it was so great. Then you were there, taking it on. Holding me. It is too much. All too much." She stiffened in his arms. Comfort was not something she allowed herself to accept for too long.

He decided it would take a shock to her system for her to open up. She turned to look at him and he took his chance, crushing his mouth over hers and deepening the kiss until her body relaxed. Her relaxing was not enough for him, he needed to knock her senses so far off their axis it stripped her bare. He deepened the kiss, the flames of desire licking at him with relentless forcefulness.

Her hands landed on his bare chest, sending more desire spiraling. He needed to taste all of her and moved to her cheek and neck until he hit the little well at the base of her neck. It had the aroma of rose water, and he recognized the brininess of salty tears she had shed all afternoon. He knew when her mind was beyond building walls, when she laid her head back in his hand and opened to him.

She was the most beautiful woman he ever laid eyes on. Her long midnight locks tumbled from her head, cascading over her shoulders and around his arms. The column of her neck shone dark in the moonlight. He reveled at how her complexion always appeared sun-kissed, but that it was her Spanish grandmother's gift.

Not wanting her to gain back any sense of where they were or who she was with, he moved from her neck down until the layers of her night dress stopped him. He tried without success to slide it down more, but the sturdy fabric did not give.

Without warning, Finna pulled from his embrace. He froze and forgot to breathe, scared it would be a repeat of the night before. He couldn't withstand another night without giving into his desire for her. To his thrill, she silently undid two buttons at the top of the garment, and it slid down her body, forgotten on the floor. She stood as she had last night in his room, naked in the moonlight. The world slid under him and he thought he might fall off all together.

"Finna—" What did he say? The word love danced on his tongue, but he swallowed it quickly. One thing at a time. Tonight was not for that. Tonight was to show her the pleasure there was in his arms. "You are beyond compare." He chose instead. Certain any fool would see the same, he was sure it was a phrase that wouldn't make her uncomfortable.

He stepped into her space and placed a kiss on her forehead. "I want you, Finna, there is no surprise in that. I wanted you twenty years ago. Last night I let you leave. I will not force you, but I am only a man—"

Finna's expression softened. She reached up and put her hand on his cheek and he leaned into it. He expected her to say something, so when she slid her hand to the back of his neck and pulled him to her lips, no words were necessary. He savored the sampling of wine with a smokiness that was almost undetectable, but there still.

Her action broke the chains on the beast inside him. A

growl vibrated low in his throat and before he could pull back, he had swept her into his arms. His only focus was the bed. With the force of all his abilities, he eased her to the bed, but then stood back.

Between the moonlight and the spray of candlelight, her naked body was awash with a warm glow. To his relief she did not shy from his perusal, instead she opened to him and gave him a better view of all she was. There would be no shyness, and no shame in love making with Finna. No coaxing needed to help her open to pleasure. He could only concentrate on pleasure.

"You are overdressed, sir, I am at a disadvantage," she said, sliding her hand over her breast, languidly stroking her nipple to a rosy peak.

With no words because the beast in him was beyond the capacity of speech, he tugged with one hand and used his foot to pull off his thin pants. Left with her night rail, his erection making his desire obvious. She sat up and scooted to the edge of the bed, winding her hands up his body, around his hips and waist and then across his bare chest. The sensation transported him to a fantasy he lived nightly, but this was no fantasy, it was Finna.

He forced his head forward and watched her find her way to his penis. She took her time stroking it with a slow gentle touch, running her hand around his ballocks giving them a gentle squeeze which forced a moan from him. The smile she gave him might have a younger man nervous, but it sent a shot of electricity through his very soul.

Lowering her head, she took him full in her mouth and he was lost. His hands buried in her hair. He stroked her locks as his hands guided her movement, though there was no need. He feared the drapes would not be the only thing to be engulfed by an uncontrollable fire today.

"Finna," he managed, but the gravelly whisper was almost inaudible. "Finna, you need to stop love, please."

She pulled back and looked up with heavy-lidded eyes, filled with desire. There would never be another day as long as he lived that he would not allow her any damn thing she desired. He was forever hers.

It was time for Kendrick to show her what real pleasure could be. Taking her lips with his, he laid back, inching onto the bed and taking her with him as he went. Once again, with her spread out on the bed, but this time with him over her, he set to work. Finding the spot on her neck again, making her squirm a bit, then making his way to the destination blocked earlier by her offending night dress, which he decided was overrated and of no use to her from this point forward, he found a nipple.

The moan he wrested from her only added to the flames licking, demanding more of him. Her body was perfect in every way. It curved and plumped just as the female form should, giving him ample landscape to discover. Her breasts were larger than he suspected but filled his hand to perfection.

Her hips rounded and flared, giving away the fact she was a mature woman. He kissed his way down to her bellybutton where he dipped his tongue, eliciting a giggle and some squirming. Even her stomach, gently rounding as women's bodies did after having children and living life. It was soft and warm, and he thought the perfect place to rest his head after a long day. If he could end his day like that for the rest of his life, every bad day before would be worth it.

Below the rise in her stomach was his destination. Hair as dark and thick as he imagined her most private place beckoned him. But first he caught sight of her luscious brown thigh and couldn't help but nip at the flesh, pulling another giggle. He kissed to her knee, then moved to the other side and laid a trail of kisses back to the one place they both wanted him to be.

God, she was a perfect blend of all those things that made Finna the person she was—his. She arched her body and returned the favor of burying her hands in his hair and holding him to her.

"Oh. Oh, Kendrick—" she moaned.

His Christian name on her lips filled with passion urged him on. He lifted her buttocks for the best angle and continued his onslaught until he could barely keep hold of her. Breaking from his intimate kiss, he made his way up her body and stopped when his erection hovered at her entrance.

He doubted his ability to forgo but would force it if he thought her unsure. He checked her face for reassurance. Without a sound she wrapped her long legs around his hips and pulled him into her, in the same slow manner she had pleasured him. He was home. Nothing in his entire life had felt as right as this moment. So powerful was the sensation his arms shook, and he had to drop to his elbows to avoid crushing her under him.

"God, you are perfection, love," he whispered in her ear.

He kissed the side of her head, inhaling the bouquet of roses and the spiciness that would forever be his Finna. The slow tattoo of their rhythm only lasted a moment until it became apparent that this coupling would not be the slow onslaught into the hours of dawn he would like it to be. Just being with Finna made that impossible. It was twenty years of anticipation, after all.

"Oh God, Kendrick, yes," she whispered through clenched teeth, on the same brink as him.

Without so much as a second thought, he drove into her one last time and sent them both over the abyss. Once spent, he laid with his leg and arm still draped over her, not wanting to end the contact. They lay sweating and panting as the world settled back into focus.

After a time, he mustered the energy to draw the blankets over them. He settled into what he knew was the spot meant for him, with his arm tucked tight around her and his head nestled onto her belly. The constant of her breathing lulled him into what might be the best night of sleep he had ever had. Not for the sex, but for the fact he no longer had to depend on his dreams because she was next to him.

CHAPTER 16

*H*ow many nights could one chase the sunrise and survive? Finna thought perhaps two was her limit. The candles had long since burned themselves down and the moon no longer lighted the room, save for a small sliver across the floor highlighting the carnage of clothing left forgotten on the floor.

In all reality, her current situation should be pedestrian at this point in her life. She spent many a night wrapped in the arms of one man or another, but always knowing he would wake, sometimes an hour after love making, other times not until the sun was full in the sky, but always to leave and go back to his life and she hers. Once the initial shame of her reality wore off, she would sleep solidly those nights.

To her reasoning, if he were not with her, he would be with another. It was expected that a man take a mistress after all. They were offering each other a service. She got paid very well for her abilities in and out of the bedchamber, and much of the time they also did not disappoint her sexually. It was easy math. Good business.

Tonight was neither easy math nor good business. The last hour watching Kendrick Rutland, Marquess of Harwich sleeping, she wracked her mind trying to figure the exact moment she lost herself. So far gone she was, that she couldn't trace back to the point in time she let her guard slip and allowed her emotions to become engaged. Tears slid without notice down her face, as they had been doing since she first realized Kendrick was sound asleep with his head cradled on her stomach, holding her like he didn't dare let her go.

She observed like a voyeur as she twirled his dark, wavy, silky hair around her fingers. It felt so natural, like she had been doing it every night for her entire adult life. Would she have taken to doing this if they had married, she wondered?

There had only been a handful of times since she left her family that the urge to speak with her mother or sister pressed on her heart. This, ironically, was one of those times. She thought back to the first time she spied Kendrick at her father's dinner party for up-and-coming gentlemen. The two girls had giggled about this one curl that wouldn't seem to stay in place for him. He kept sweeping it back. His habit was endearing. Then, she and her sister spent the entire night talking about their scheme to get Finna to spend time with this new and interesting fellow. In truth, they giggled more than planned, but it was a memory she held dear to this day.

The last correspondence she had with Ginny was when Ginny asked her to not interact when she was attending her first Ton party as a married woman. Ginny had gotten word Finna would attend and didn't want it to be awkward. More tears fell on her pillow, but she didn't understand why. She had long ago come to terms with the decisions she made and the people it cut from her life. No, these tears were more for that young girl who wished she had someone to have tea with tomorrow and talk about her living the dream she had for the last twenty years.

She didn't even consider what her mother would say about them being lovers after so long. Would it redeem her in her mother's eyes? Would it redeem him? Her mother railed for days about irresponsible men and how men are so finicky with women. Finna, knowing her experience far outreached that of her mother, knew that men were not finicky. They, like women, were desperately searching for the one person who would make them whole. The secret though was that no one person could do that for you. If you were not the person you wanted to be, no one on this earth would make that happen for you.

Kendrick shifted in his sleep, but instead of pulling away he tugged her hip closer, pulling her more fully under his weight.

If he knew the truth, he would shun her. The real reason she was agreeing to be a safe house for a stranger she knew little of. It was all for her son. Bryant deserved so much more than the life offered him, and no matter how it made her look, she would make sure that his life would not be as unfortunate as her own.

Her biggest mistake though was to think she would remain unaffected by Kendrick. Four ways the fool, she thought. It was her arrogance that would be her demise every time. Always so certain she could turn every situation to her advantage or to control the outcome. Foolish girl, that's what she was. The fire proved just how out of control this entire thing was.

The fire was not even hinted at as part of a plan. She would never have agreed to put her house in jeopardy or her staff in danger. When next they met, she would call him out on that. Over the years of bedding men, one would think she would be more careful about bedding the devil, but clearly, she still had much to learn.

Bryant arriving also made things even more difficult. She had not spoken with him since they all retired to their rooms. Golding let her know earlier in the evening that he appeared tired from the excitement and that he would check on him from time to time. She assumed when she didn't hear again that he fell asleep. The sooner she got him out of the city, the better. After all, there was no point in her acting against her country to save her son, if he was too dead to appreciate her efforts.

Just as the moon faded and the first grainy stretches of sunbeams trickled into the room, Finna slid from her bed. She turned to see Kendrick snuggle in, but not wake. Her heart wept for what they could never have. Even if he forgave her for her past, her recent association would render her dead to him.

She would need to hurry to make her meeting time, so feeling sorry for herself needed to be abandoned. She tiptoed around the room, grabbed an easy walking dress she would not need help with and two ribbons to tie up her hair. She would sneak back in later to dress properly. Harwich was still slumbering. She could sneak into his room and dress there.

Throwing one last look at the sleeping man in her bed

and the urge to crawl back in bed and coax him awake burned so deep within her, but this path had been set into motion and could not be stopped as it always seemed to be in her life.

CHAPTER 17

Kendrick stretched and reached out to pull Finna close, but he was alone. Opening his eyes and then squinting to keep out the bright rays of the sun, he realized it was much later than he thought. As his eyes adjusted he saw the room was as empty as the bed. He noted a neat pile of clothes sitting on the foot of the bed. She must have made a trip to his room to make sure he didn't shock any of her maids.

He stretched and flung the covers away, stepping into the chilled room. Dressed, at least from the chest down, he made his way to his room and finished cleaning up and added a cravat with an easy knot. Fletcher would not approve, but Kendrick was in a hurry to see Finna. His Finna. Last night solidified in his mind that she was his future. Perhaps after his meetings today they would find time to discuss the prospects.

Downstairs, however, the breakfast room was empty save for master Bryant with a plate piled high with food. Kendrick had the impression it was not his first plate of the day.

"Lord Harwich, good morning." Bryant jumped up and bowed properly.

"Good morning, Bryant, I see the buffet is well stocked this morning."

"Well, cook knows what I like and tries to make it when I am visiting. I hope you don't mind."

"Not at all, in fact it looks as if you and I could eat happily together." Kendrick filled his plate with the hearty fare and sat waiting for the footman to bring his coffee. "Did you speak with your mother this morning?" Perhaps she was in the parlor and he simply hadn't seen her when he glanced in.

"No, I think Golding said she had stepped out. I am sure she will be here soon, because she is bent on me leaving and going back to the country today."

Bryant did not agree with her decisions but was too good a son to outright refuse.

"I could have a word with your mother if you like. I may be able to give her some assurances about your safety."

"You would do that for me? That would be deuced helpful."

"I am glad to do it, but I would not suggest you use colorful language such as that in her presence."

He blushed and smiled. "Suppose you have the right of that. She will never see me as a man grown."

"It has been my experience that when one tries to force the issue, that is when mothers pull back on the reins. If you just act as a grown young man, she will ease into the idea better."

"Perhaps so." He bit off a piece of toast with jam and seemed to think on the advice.

"So, ah, do you know when your mother will return?" What was it with Finna and all her meetings? Then an idea sat cold in his chest. What if she was meeting with a client and not telling him? He was an understanding man, more so than most, but the idea of Finna seeing men now that they had been together might see him hang at the gallows.

"Are you all right, Lord Harwich?" Bryant asked with concern on his face. "Did you eat a bad cherry? I hate overly tart ones myself."

"I'm fine, Bryant, thank you."

Just then Golding entered. "Ah, there you are, Lord Harwich. I have some correspondence for you. I left it on Lady Finna's writing desk, as I didn't want to wake you since you were sleeping in."

"Thank you, Golding. I will collect it as soon as I finish eating." Golding quit the room and Bryant seemed to be finished, but was lingering to not be rude. "Bryant, I came in late, please don't stay on my account."

"Thank you, my lord, but I was wondering if I might ask you a question concerning my mother?"

His morning meal was starting to not be as pleasant as he had hopes of it being as he dressed.

"Of course, what is it?"

"As I am getting older, before long I will on my own and mother will be alone." He paused, seeming to search for his words. Kendrick commended him for trying to act the adult but could tell it was new to him.

"Are you asking my what my intentions are with your mother?"

His expression cleared, and the relief was obvious. "Yes, I guess that is what I am asking. I would like to think my mother won't be alone when I am grown."

"I have only recently been reacquainted with your mother. We knew each other a long time ago, but she has done an excellent job at surrounding herself with people who care for her. I do not think your mother will ever be alone."

"I know that, and I appreciate all of those people who help to take care of her while I am in school, but she needs someone just for her."

This young man was more perceptive than Finna gave him credit and more grown than any of them realized. "I promise you if, in fact, I have any intentions with your mother I will come and discuss it with you beforehand."

"Thank you." He rose, satisfied with the outcome. "I will be scarce so you may have time to talk with her about letting me stay. If you need me, though, I'll be in the library."

"Very well."

Finishing his food, he went into the parlor to grab his letters and head back to his room. On the writing desk, the letters in question lay waiting, but an opened envelope caught his attention. Where had he seen the seal before? He knew it looked familiar, but in the breaking, the design was destroyed. The note also was missing. The scroll across the front held a familiar air as well, but he just couldn't place it. Giving up, he grabbed his letters and quit the room.

If he was lucky, he could get through his correspondence in time to talk with Finna before he had to leave to begin the process of setting her corrupt solicitor to rights. And he was also hoping Birch would have some answers for them about the fire. He tried to remind himself that he had no right to encroach on Finna's privacy. If she wanted to share something she would. He just needed patience. Because apparently twenty years was not enough.

CHAPTER 18

*I*n his room by the window, with a pleasant breeze to continue freshening a lingering scent of smoke, he grabbed the first letter. It was from Birch. He was no closer as yet to finding out anything about the fire. It seemed the traditional avenues of information in London had stalled, leading Kendrick to fear this went further up and closer to them both than they had first considered. Kendrick was learning Birch had a similar idea, but neither were ready to put voice to their claim. It would mean ruin for many if they were correct.

The next was a reply from the duke. Relief that Finna did not find these letters first flooded him. He would instruct Golding to give his missives to Fletcher.

The duke confirmed he was handing Reginald's name to several clients of Mr. Gilbert Knottingword. The man should be out of business within the week. Which meant Finna would need to give him an accounting of how much she should withdraw her funds before the man disappeared with her entire fortune.

The front door shut and Golding's voice welcoming Finna home echoed up the stairs. Satisfied with his communication he left the letters and went to greet her. He slowed his steps to a walk, not wanting to appear so happy to see her. He followed her voice into the parlor, giving Golding orders about bringing a tray for her to snack on.

"Good day, Lady Finna. I trust your meeting went well?" He entered and the look of surprise she shot him set him on edge. "I'm sorry, did I startle you?"

"No. Of course not," she rallied, but it was too late. "My meeting was fine. I was at the modiste talking with her about that dress I am commissioning for Contrell. She should come around later in the week to do measurements."

"With you out of the house so early, I feared I would have to sit in silence to break my fast."

"I am sorry," she said, as she unpinned her bonnet to show a simple low knot of hair, not her customary design. A woman of fashion did not meet with her modiste in such simple attire, of that he was sure. "I did not think to tell you. I am not accustomed to checking my appointments with anyone."

"Master Bryant was already at the table. He is quite a young man."

Her expression softened as any mother's would when talking about her children. "He is, isn't he? I am amazed just how mature he is getting."

"I know you are determined for him to be in the country."

"Yes, the country is the best place for him. I will go to him as soon as this is over."

"That is what I wanted to speak with you about. After yesterday, and the fire, we still do not know who did that, anyone could have seen Bryant standing across the way in the park. It would be an easy enough thing to follow any carriage leaving this residence. I think the lad would be safer here with us, than off in the country with staff who are not at all aware of the dangers we have put you and he in."

She blanched and sat down. He didn't want to frighten her, and though he was rooting for Bryant to stay so he could get to know him, he did believe that the town house was the safest place. He sat next to her and took her hand. Residual passion from the night before shot through his fingers and heated his body. By her intake of breath, he was not alone. The parlor was not the place, and he tamped it down.

"I hadn't thought of that. You may be right. If he is here, I can know that he is safe. No one would get access to him without my knowledge."

"Right, not to mention all the other eyes we would have helping."

She nodded and walked to the bell pull. Golding came in carrying the tray she had requested. "Perfect timing, mi lady, I was just grabbing up the tray."

"Oh, wonderful. Please Lord Harwich, help yourself. And Golding, please track down Bryant and ask him to come here."

"I believe he said he would be in the library, Golding," Kendrick added.

"Certainly, one moment."

She returned to the tray but didn't even look at it. He

assumed she ordered it for the young man in question who could eat his weight in food several times a day.

"While we wait for Bryant, I also wanted to invite you and he to my box in Vauxhall Gardens this evening. I know you have been preoccupied and had not chosen any more functions. I thought this would be a good time for us to see and be seen. We will be able to eschew most of the crowds."

She looked skeptical, like she was searching for an excuse. He leaned in to set her off guard as he was learning he had the knack for, and also the desire to do. "We could always just sup with the house and retire early."

Her face reddened, and he saw light goose flesh break out on her arms. Or they could just go to bed now.

She cleared her throat and slid her hand from his. "I do not think that a good idea either, so if I only have those choices—"

"You do not care to be with me again?" he asked, more affronted than he wanted to be, and his mind shot back to her appointment earlier.

"That is not the point. I do not believe it helpful if we ignore our reasons for all being together to romp."

"I will let the carriage know to pick us up by seven. That should give us time to arrive and get some food brought round as well."

"Mother, you are back, you wanted to see me. Lord Harwich, good to see you again." He bowed and entered the room. To his credit, he waited until she offered the food before he dove in.

An hour later, Kendrick was back in his room getting ready to go speak with Mr. Knottingword, to bring him the bad news. Finna had been happy to give him the amounts and her last letter from the late Mr. Henry as proof. He hoped to have good information for her when they met later.

Four hours later, Kendrick sat in the parlor with more questions than he got answers from Knottingword. But the short of it was that Knottingword was being paid a handsome profit to whittle down Finna's funds. He, like all the street rats thus far, could not give any solid information about who this person was, but he was understanding this person or people had a long reach and multiple purposes that perhaps was orchestrated to get them all in one place, which was disturbing.

"The carriage is here. Are you coming?" Finna stuck her head in as she fumbled with a pearl ear fob. She would never not take his breath away. He threw back his drink and rose to meet her.

"I would not miss allowing the world to see you on my arm whenever I get the chance."

Birch entered at that moment and settled in the chair he just left.

"You young ones have fun, and behave. Bryant is in charge, I already warned him to monitor you. He wanted me to tell you he was in the carriage."

They said their goodbyes and headed out to leave. Bryant was at a constant chatter for the entire ride, which was good, because Finna had been skittish since getting back from her appointment. Or perhaps after they had sex, he couldn't be sure. Why she would have nerves after having sex, he didn't know.

When they reached the entrance to the gardens the line was as usual long and at a standstill. So when the carriage veered and rambled down a side road, Finna looked skeptical.

"My man knows where the side entrance is, and it just so happens my box is close to that part of the park and I have an old acquaintance who works as a performer. I sent him a note asking for him to be close so that he could let us in. By the time when most enter, we will already be settled waiting for food."

"Brilliant!" Bryant complimented.

"I'm glad you approve," Kendrick responded with a chuckle. He realized the boy was happy to be getting to the meal sooner.

Finna had been silent on the ride. Kendrick didn't push her for conversation, instead he watched her from the corner of his eye and did not like what he witnessed. Something had her on edge. It could well be the current events in their lives, but he thought it more personal than that. Was she regretting their love making? She enjoyed herself, he knew. She had not rebuffed his advances or said they were through, but she may be pondering how to word it.

The carriage rolled to a stop and the side door opened. His friend ushered them in, and it took only moments to get settled. Kendrick had sent word in advance, so it was a matter of having the box attendant announce their arrival.

"This is a lovely box, Harwich." Finna expressed her approval while settling into one of the nicely appointed chairs. They watched as people began entering and milling about. Some noticed them already in their box with wine glasses in hand, and whispered to one another.

When the women would begin that, Finna would look away or study the nonexistent specks of lint on her skirt. If

Bryant were not sitting between them, he would have mentioned that it didn't bother him in the least. He spent his first go around in the Ton as the wastrel trying to infiltrate their ranks, when he only wanted to have his rightful place and reclaim the title for his mother's memory.

The meal was served, and they heard the first strings of music filtering through the chatting crowd. He ordered enough food to keep Bryant occupied and sure enough, he piled his plate high with the offerings and settled into the back of the box on the bench to give his concentration to the meal.

"Thank you, this was a lovely idea," Finna sparked up the conversation once they had a bit of privacy.

"I am glad it brings you joy. This is a way for us to be seen, but it gives us the buffer of a private box, so we don't have to engage if we so choose not to."

The servers extinguished the candles around the perimeter, letting the patrons know the show would begin soon. Kendrick motioned for the attendant to close the curtains to the sides. This would afford them even more privacy and allow them to keep a candle going to see their food.

As the play began and all attentions were turned to the stage, the warmth of Finna moving to the chair next to him pricked his awareness. Even more unsettling on the one hand, but promising on the other, was when she reached out and placed her delicate gloved hand on his.

To let her know he approved, he folded his hand around her and pulled it closer. Bryant was none the wiser as the table linen settled nicely around their laps hiding their actions.

As intermission came and the candles were lit once again.

Kendrick noticed Dameon two boxes over and wanted to touch base and set up a meeting. "I will be right back. I see Chesterfield in his cousin's box. I need to have a word. Can I have the attendant get you anything?"

"More wine would be lovely," Finna said as she turned to discuss the play with Bryant, an avid theater lover himself.

Kendrick left the box, gave his request to the attendant and wended his way through the crowd. Dameon had also emerged from his box, and Kendrick flagged him down. Stepping out of the flow of traffic, they greeted each other.

"I saw you with the beautiful Lady Finna. I need to reconsider giving you all the prime assignments. First Italy, now wining and dining London's most sought after Drury Lane Vestal. I often wondered if there was a term for the higher classed ones who frequent Vauxhall? Perhaps I could coin a new phrase."

The disdain in his voice sent hot anger through Kendrick. There was nothing about Finna that would ever make her a common doxy. Dameon knew this, however, and was goading him. Kendrick had too much life experience to play into his hands.

"I would like to come to the office in the next few days, but I don't have time to wait or be turned away. What day and time would be best?" he asked instead of acknowledging the comment.

Disappointment washed Dameon's face but was gone quickly. He wanted a row, but would not get satisfaction with Kendrick. "I don't believe I have anything on my schedule tomorrow first thing. Stop by around 9 o'clock. I will tell my clerk to expect you."

Kendrick nodded and opened his mouth to thank him,

but a commotion from the area of his box caught his attention. It was Bryant who, with no concern of propriety, was yelling and shoving at someone. Upon closer inspection the man in question had Finna by the upper arm in a manacle grip attempting to drag her from the box.

Dameon's expression was unexpected. Horror for the scene clear in his face. The man did not have the constitution for the work he forced others to do in the name of King and country. He would never play hero. He could only sit behind a desk and take credit for other people's actions. Kendrick ran toward the commotion, Dameon forgotten. Luckily, Bryant had made enough of a fuss that several gentlemen and a couple of the wandering performers had made a circle, not allowing the man to force Finna away.

Using the crowd and confusion to his advantage, he snaked his way around the group to get behind the man. He grabbed a large painted rock nestled in a flowerbed. He brought it down hard on the assailant's head. He motioned to his attendant, who stood in shock, to help drag the lump of a man into the box. Finna and Bryant followed, moving around the body to the front of the box, pulling the curtains shut to hide them from prying eyes.

"Thank you, please call the carriage around. We will wait until the intermission is over to move."

The young man nodded and slipped out of the box, shutting the door to the still assembled crowd. Bryant stood with fists at his sides. "I wasn't sure what to do, Harwich—" he said through heavy breaths.

"You did just as you should," Kendrick assured him. He looked beyond the boy to check on Finna. Though she was upset as anyone would be, anger seemed to prevail. He did not have to worry of her fainting on him.

"Will you be all right in the carriage with him?" he asked.

"Only if I can take that rock with me."

He couldn't help but smile. "I will get you as many as you like."

As soon as the lights dimmed and the crowd dispersed, they were in the carriage and back at the townhouse. Golding and Birch were summoned to help with the load.

In the house, the man roused. He was useless when it came to who hired him. Whoever this was, they were very versed at staying in the shadows. They found out that the intent was to capture Finna and offer her up as a switch for Amari. Which said to Kendrick that the person in charge understood Finna's importance to him.

The front bell rang, sending Golding to play his butler role and leave the bruiser role to the others. There were raised voices, then without being announced the duke and his wife swept into the room, bringing silence to all.

"Your Grace." Kendrick recovered first and bowed.

"Don't mind me, is this the brute who accosted Finna? If so, don't mind us."

Kendrick searched the room and found Finna standing in the back, more pale than when she was being kidnapped. Clearly, this was a first for their family.

"My dear, are you harmed?" The duchess walked past the bloodied man as if he was not there, only having eyes for her daughter. Kendrick decided the duchess's actions were lost on Finna, who turned from her mother and went to the window without answering.

Kendrick turned back to the duke. "I don't think we can

get any more out of him. As you can see, we have used significant power of suggestion to coax him."

"What did you find?" Rygate asked, towering over the man, making his presence and status known.

"He has no knowledge of who is behind this but gave us a why."

Birch added. "The information he could not give us, allows us some knowledge of the type of training the leader has though, so it was not for nothing. I have sent word, and there are men on their way to arrest him."

"Mother, I said, I am fine. I am, however, tired and would like to go to bed."

Finna's raised voice brought the gentlemen's conversation to an end.

"I will follow up in the morning with this braggart," the duke informed the group. "Come, dear. I think we have all had enough excitement. We can see Finna is being well cared for and she harbors no ill effects."

The duchess joined her husband and they let themselves out.

"I am going to bed. Thank you for all your help." Finna left without another word.

Within minutes Birch's men came to take the assailant and with the excitement over, everyone else found their beds as well.

Kendrick hoped Finna didn't think it was that easy to dismiss him. He would be in bed too, but not his own.

CHAPTER 19

"Well my dear, it is a wondrous shocking world is it not?" Contrell commented when Finna opened the note inviting her to visit her mother and have a private luncheon at the estate.

"I am certain it was the shock of seeing her daughter treated thusly and no unbidden desire to reconnect," Finna shot back.

"Now, I have never been one to comment on your family foils. Lord knows I am in no place to give familial advice, but if my memory is not waning as the years go by, it was not your mother who cut off contact. It seems over the years she just became tired of trying."

"It will not do for a duchess to be hobnobbing with a courtesan." She defended her choices. It was not good for anyone to have a connection to a woman like her. It was easier to bow out gracefully.

"Ah there you are, Mother," Bryant announced when he

entered. Kendrick also joined the small group, essentially changing the subject, which suited Finna fine. Contrell shot her a look that informed her it was not forgotten.

"Have you been looking for me long?" she asked her son, who smiled at the obvious jest. There were few places to hide in a city townhouse.

"No, this was the first place I looked."

"Not true, the first place you looked was the breakfast room," Kendrick said, chuckling. and tapping Bryant's shoulder as he walked past. "Lady Finna, I was hoping to have a word."

He gave her an unnerving look. They did not speak last night, at least not in audible terms, but once spent and drunk on the aftermath, he pulled her into his arms. There were no words needed.

A warmness swirled around her and shocked her from the want that built like a fire. There was no need to want something that was out of her reach. Once Kendrick left, Lang and Reginald would be there if ever Bryant needed a man.

"Bryant, can I speak with Lord Harwich, then find you?"

Bryant looked to Harwich, who nodded, and that was enough for Bryant, who said he would be in the library and left.

"What is it? Did Birch send word so early?"

"No." He sat in the chair across from her, but he was uneasy about something.

"What then?" She didn't like when people appeared uncomfortable to talk to her. It was never good news.

"Bryant searched me out this morning in my rooms.' He paused, she assumed waiting for her to respond.

"I am sorry, I will speak to him about bothering you."

"No, that's not a problem. I was happy he felt comfortable enough to seek me out. It is just that—"

"What?"

He glanced at Contrell who sat very interested in anything Harwich had to say. Contrell had formed quite a liking to him and was a constant bird in her ear singing his praises.

"Bryant overheard some talk last evening, when we were trying to get the scene under control."

"Oh, about what?" She had turned back to her mother's invitation. Perhaps Contrell was correct and she should accept the invitation.

"He overheard some women in the crowd calling you a common prostitute."

Contrell made a small strangled sound in her throat and turned to her task of writing with renewed vigor.

The invitation forgotten, Finna felt the room shift around her. Was this what fainting was like? The room spun, and she felt light, as if her weight no longer held her to the earth.

"Finna? Finna, don't faint on me, love." She heard Kendrick's voice very close. When she opened her eyes, he was a fraction from her face shaking her shoulder.

"No, no, I don't faint. I am fine." she said, brushing him off, trying to get her balance back, and not slide off the chair. "I knew it would happen. I had hoped to talk with him before, but I guess now is a good as—"

"I told him," Kendrick interrupted.

"You what?"

"If you all will excuse me. I would like to get this letter posted before luncheon." Contrell made the excuse, but didn't bother to wait scurrying out of the room. Finna would bet that the hall was as far as she got, and she was against the wall listening.

"I sat him down and discussed what he heard and probed him about it and what he understood of the situation."

"You had no right," she said flatly.

"I am right, but—"

"No, you had no right. You should have sent him to me. Do not claim to understand my mind or my reasoning for anything I have done in my life."

"Finna, calm down. I didn't and nor would I try to explain your decisions or your rationale for those decisions. What I think you needed to know, is that he was not coming to me because it was a surprise to him. He has known since he started school."

Finna lost the ability to speak, and perhaps to understand speech. It couldn't be that Kendrick just told her the one thing she hoped to protect her son from, was dashed upon his first entrance into school. It couldn't be. "But how?"

"I am formulating my own thoughts on that but will need more time. I wanted you to be aware of his knowledge. You aren't hiding anything from him. I also wanted to tell you just how mature your son is at ten and five. He came to me because he wanted to ask me how he might go about dealing with people in the future who may make rude and unchari-table comments. His words, not mine."

Her heart swelled and burst. A young man was thrown into the dirty underbelly of the world and reached out to figure out the most responsible way to handle the situation. How did she get so lucky to have a son such as him?

"I—" what did she say?

"I wanted you to know what I told him, so that you understand I will not lie to you when it is important."

She sat back and tried to calm her mind enough to hear him out.

"We talked a bit about how he found out and how bad it is at school for him."

"And?" she asked, fear gripping her. She would not send him back if his life was miserable.

Kendrick laughed, shaking his head. "He said one of the older boys took him aside and told him many of the boys at the school were bastards and if he was enrolled there, he either had a wealthy benefactor or he had a personal fortune that spoke louder than what his mother's profession was, so to not let it bother him. He summarized that since he was one of the better polo players on the team, the older boys wanted to keep him happy."

The air whooshed from her, spinning her head again. He was not wounded. Her choices had not destroyed him. The joy from knowing that made her almost drunk on relief.

"We then discussed his thoughts on the subject of courtesans, and I talked a bit about why men chose to spend time with you."

She shot him an uneasy glance, which he waved off.

"We discussed nothing above the fact that you are politically savvy and have many connections to help men get ahead in their endeavors."

"He is unaware he is from 'that' Lennox family, or at least I don't think he knows." She admitted. She knew nothing that she thought she knew about her son anymore.

"No, I don't think he realizes his mother is the daughter

of a duke. I didn't tell him that as he got older that was also a connection that would shield him a bit."

"Thank you. I am glad he came to you and not Lang or Reginald. I doubt they could easily assist him in handling things with aplomb. Reginald, not being of the Ton, does not have that protection, and since he grew up on the streets, he has seen his share of poor treatment for his life choices, and he sees anger before understanding in most cases, and Lang has been lucky enough that his family connections have shielded him, that and being a third son. No one has found the need to judge his choice of companion, so he would not have relevant advice."

"Well, I am certain he wants to talk with you about all he has learned. I didn't want you to go into it not knowing."

"I appreciate that," she said.

"And I wanted the room to be empty so I would be at my leisure to do this."

He took one step from the chair and leaned in with a kiss. A kiss filled with promises and memories. A kiss as it should be, she thought, leaning in, allowing her body to react. After so many years of only allowing kisses on the cheek, her lips buzzed with the novel sensation.

A noise from the stairs had them scrambling like young people being caught alone. But, if Lang noticed, he didn't say.

"I just spoke with Reginald and you will not believe it. He has had no less than three of the oldest families in London reach out to him. They want to move their accounts to him. Can you imagine?"

"That's wonderful!" Finna was thrilled the business Lang set up for Reginald was taking off.

"Well, I think Harwich deserves most of the credit. It

seems they are all unhappy with their current solicitor, because there are rumors he is playing it fast and loose with some accounts. The man is Knottingword."

Kendrick didn't argue against it.

"You are turning people from Knottingword? For me?"

"Well, I needed to show you that people with wealth change who they allow to handle it all the time, and that you can too."

"Perhaps I should move my funds as well with Reginald?"

"I was hoping you would say so. If you give me leave and the amounts you feel you should have in the accounts, I will go there today and get things completed. I don't want to wait too long, because he is a slippery sort and could vanish with what money he has available."

"Of course, I'll get those numbers for you now."

Finna jumped up to get her ledger and have a moment to herself. Working so hard to keep every aspect of her life in a certain nice neat box and not melding had worked until now. She had cut off contact with her family to not force them to make the hard decisions to defend her in public and risk their own reputations. Now her mother wanted her for luncheon. Her perfect, never did anything to raise an eyebrow mother. Not to mention learning her son knew the one thing she sought to keep hidden from him until she could not anymore, and now she was giving her financial information to the man who propelled into her choice of life to fight a battle for her. If a dog wearing a waistcoat and watch fob were to walk around the corner by her study, she would not think twice about it right now.

On her desk, settled on top of her blotter, lay a note with her name scrawled across the front. She looked around and noted one window was ajar, letting the warm breeze flutter the drapes.

Her first instinct was to alert Kendrick, but then she thought better of it. The note only had a time and place. She knew the handwriting and decided it was best to wait on calling the alarm. It was just a messenger this time.

Grabbing the ledger, she was happier now that Kendrick would leave to handle her accounts, because she could make her meeting without fear of being followed by the one person she needed to stay unaware. How did life ever get so complicated?

CHAPTER 20

$\mathcal{H}$e just made it to Dameon's office by 9 o'clock. After the excitement of the almost kidnapping, the appointment slipped his mind until Bryant mentioned it last night, jogging his memory. This would be a meeting to update him and figure out next moves and an attempt at perhaps moving Amari to a more secure and less Finna filled location?

"I thought you would stand me up," Dameon drawled once Kendrick was escorted into his office.

"To be honest, once the attempted abduction of Lady Finna distracted me, I had forgotten until this morning, but I am here now."

"Yes, indeed, you are. Horrible turn of events for Finna, but it was only a matter of time before her low connections caught up with her."

"Excuse me? I was not aware you didn't hold her at a

higher esteem. I have heard nothing untoward about her connections."

"Have you not met Mr. Cedric Langley and his," he cleared his throat, "companion, Mr. Chesterfield?"

"Yes, in fact I have been introduced. They have been deuced helpful with this mess," Kendrick pointed out.

"Yes, I am sure. They are a helpful sort."

Kendrick knew what Dylan was implying, but he would not be goaded. It has been well known that Dameon Chamberlain was an ineffective clerk who saw his worth well above his station. Such rude behavior with no warrant to whom he was speaking made it obvious.

"Listen, Dameon, I am not here to argue the merits of either Lady Sarrafinna or her choice of friends. I think we need to consider moving Amari to a place that is more secure and with fewer opportunities for manipulation. The braggart from last night clarified that he was to take Finna as a bargaining chip to trade for Amari. This cannot continue."

Dameon heard that and perked up. "Really? Interesting, did you get any more information from him?"

"No, just like all the others, he had no way of giving any names or descriptions. Whoever this is, they are good."

Dameon sat back in his chair and steepled his hands, considering. "I am inclined to disagree with you about moving Amari. I think any attempt would raise eyebrows. Instead, I suggest the opposite. Have Lady Finna host a dinner—"

"Are you daft? Did you not understand—"

"Hear me out before you send me to Bedlam," he said with a calm that irked Kendrick. "If in fact there are men trying to gain access to a house that is locked away from everyone, then if they manage to infiltrate it, there are fewer there to be protective. If, however, Lady Finna holds a dinner party, it doesn't have to be huge, but enough so we can position some of our men, then there are more eyes. Also, they would be more of a help to secure the house at the end of the night."

Kendrick still didn't like it. It was inviting someone to come in and harm anyone in the house. He liked having more eyes but wasn't sure just inviting the ton into her home would solve their problem. It would also help Amari's wanderlust, that threatened to be their undoing when he acted on a whim.

"See, you are seeing the brilliance in my plan," Dameon said after watching Kendrick consider.

"No, I hate your plan, but having more men in the house to help make it secure would be helpful. But what about all the nights after the party? We are back to having just a handful?"

"Yes, that is a bugger." Chamberlain pondered this. "I know, what if it were to be a series of dinners? Perhaps leading up to Parliament starting. We all know how much Lady Finna loves to get her fingers in that pie, by parading her recent acquaintance around as if she found the next prime minister. I think if you played it on her vanity of you being her next success, she would be happy."

Dameon's attitude toward Finna raked against his need to protect her, but what Dameon Chamberlain thought about a duke's daughter was not something he had to worry about. On the social ladder, Dameon would be several steps below her.

"I will bring it up with Birch and see what he suggests."

"Yes, speaking of Birch, seems he went underground.

There is no news from his front. Do you know anything about this?"

Kendrick trusted Birch more than he would ever trust Dameon. "No. He checks in from time to time. I know he was struggling to find passage out, but that is the last update I received."

Chamberlain nodded and rose. Kendrick allowed him the act of power. It meant little to him. He noted that perhaps he would look further into Dameon once he was a member of Parliament. It was time for a change of guard, in Kendrick's opinion.

Once on the street, his carriage rolled up and he jumped in, heading to Bond street and his next stop of the day. He hoped this one would be more productive.

London bustled along as it did yesterday and the day before that, oblivious to what the Dameon Chamberlains of the world did to good honest people. Had he been oblivious? No, wrapped up in his own drama perhaps, but he above anyone saw the mistreatment firsthand. His mother died not knowing there was redemption and retribution in this world. He had lived it, and therefore would make certain he passed that on to others.

Bryant's bright face danced in his mind. That was a boy who was unaware how lucky he was. Kendrick assumed that, though his grandfather shouldn't know about him or anything about his life, he was involved. Rygate was no doubt the driving force that helped to pave the boy's way at school. Kendrick knew how cruel boys of an age could be and how relentless. Forces greater than Bryant or his polo prowess were at play. Kendrick admired Rygate more in that moment than he already did. It took a powerful man to embrace a bastard grandson, especially a duke, where lineage was more important than anything.

The carriage rolled to a stop, and the driver jumped down to let him out. "I plan on being at least two hours, but do not go far in case I am mistaken."

"Of course, mi lord. I'll drive around and park just up there. There is a pasties cart. I'll get me some meat pasties and a drink."

"Good plan. I haven't had a meat pasty is a very long time," Kendrick admitted.

The bell on the door rang as he entered. The outer room was empty. Not even a secretary to herald new clients.

"We are closed! Go away!" Knottingword yelled from the back. Kendrick let himself in and continued through to the office.

"I am afraid that is not an option, Mr. Knottingword. You see, we have business to attend to."

"Augh, tis you. You've done enough."

"Whatever do you mean?" Kendrick asked, playing along for a moment.

"You, it had to be you. Now they are all leaving. Moving their funds. And why? Because I mistreated a loyal client, just because she was defenseless. That is what they are all sayin'."

Kendrick noted his refined speech no longer held true. "It is unfortunate for you, that you did not do more research on your uncle's clients before you chose which ones to mark as your private funds."

"I did. She is nothing but an expensive doxy. I was assured her status as a duke's daughter was not relevant, since they disowned her."

"I am afraid someone misinformed your informant. Lady Finna has never once been disowned by her family."

"Now, speaking of Lady Finna, she, as you were witness to just the other day, has given me permission to speak on her behalf."

"Ye want to collect her accounts and move them."

Kendrick nodded, but there was no need.

"They are gone."

"No, they are not."

"Yes, they are. I may be a bad solicitor, but I am not a poor thief. Whatever your ledger under your arm says, I have plenty of others that say different." He was a smug one.

Kendrick stepped closer, until he was toe to toe with the man. "I hope then you are as good a shot with a pistol." Even he was impressed by the deadly tone to his voice.

"Now, see here. I am a young man, you are not. I wouldn't suggest you go around making threats—"

Kendrick took another step toward the man, proving at least that he towered over the whelp. "You are correct, I am not a young buck anymore. I have had many, many years of practice with a pistol, and I lived a good life. I am right with my king and with my God. Can you admit to either of those?"

"I, ah, I—you are not seriously calling me out over a common whore?" he spat, trying to find anything that would make Kendrick see reason.

"I am calling you out, unless you find your seat and find the funds you misappropriated over the last several months and return them to Lady Sarrafinna's accounts. I would also like to point out that I appraised the Duke of Rygate of the situation and even if you were a lucky shot, I do not think

His Grace would stand on such formalities as meeting you on a dueling field."

The duke was a fair man, but it was widely known he rarely took no for an answer and suffered fools even less of the time. And being a close cousin to the king, he had Prinny's ear from time to time.

Mr. Knottingword's mouth worked, but no words materialized. After but a few moments he grabbed two ledgers and sat to figure. As he worked, Kendrick made no move to walk away or give him a moment to formulate a plan. The ledger he worked in had only initials, and Kendrick thought several of the columns' initials were interesting. He made a mental note to look into those more.

After working, and drafting a letter, he turned to Kendrick. "Here, this will sort it out at the bank. If you have any trouble, let me know and I will be glad to—"

"You will join me at the bank. Once her accounts are put back to rights, I will have no more need of you. I would suggest, however, that if those initials belong to the men I think they do, a long trip on the continent might be a safer bet for you."

Knottingword swallowed. "My passage is already paid for."

An hour later, after dismissing Mr. Knottingword from the banker's office once they finished his part, Kendrick left with papers for Finna and new accounts with Reginald's firm. Her accounts were now as healthy as they should have been all along, and her blasted notion that she needed the money from this job to protect Amari was no longer stopping her from being safe.

"Here you go, mi lord," the driver said, presenting Kendrick with two still steaming meat pasties.

"You didn't need to buy me any food, I am—"

"I didn't, when I told the woman about my employer the Marquess saying he missed them and hadn't had them, she gave me two to give you."

"Well thank you." He got into the carriage. He would send Fletcher back tomorrow with a payment, certain she would be in the same place, as his mother always sold her wares in the same place to get return customers.

With the smell of cooked meat, bread, and cinnamon, sage, and other familiar scents filling the carriage, he sat back and enjoyed the flavor of his childhood. He was not one to prognosticate, but he took his wins today as a sign his destiny was upon him and it included one headstrong courtesan.

CHAPTER 21

Finna's carriage sat with a hidden view of rotten row. Few people knew she kept two carriages. One that was her flagship to the Ton, announcing her in all her glory, then the carriage she used when she wanted to go about the land unnoticed. It was not safe for a woman to hire a hack, so this was the next best thing. She didn't want to not be home when Kendrick arrived back. That would just cause issues, so he better hurry. She gave him only five more minutes.

Three minutes later the door to the carriage opened and Dameon Chamberlain entered. The curtains were drawn so no one could see, and the driver had parked the rig so that one side faced the foliage hiding the door.

"I almost left, you are late," she pointed out.

"It is fortuitous that you didn't. It wouldn't play well for you."

"What do you want, Dameon? I am assuming you were the one who paid some street rat to kidnap me?"

He smiled at that. "You know you would come to no harm, but you have not done your part, so I had to act."

"You also tried to burn my home down," she said, her voice raising with anger, but she caught herself and dropped her tone.

"Again, if you had done what I paid you to do, we would not be meeting."

"You realize you hired two of the most reliable and effective men in all of London? You might lower the bar a bit. It would help your cause."

"I do not need strategy lessons from a woman and a whore."

The last bit stung, it always did, but she was used to it, and almost considered it a term of endearment from him. How had she ever compared Dameon Chamberlain to Kendrick? That right there showed the dregs of which she had succumbed to.

"We need to use more caution now than ever. Bryant has arrived and is staying in the house."

"And why does that need to be any of my concern? He is your son."

"He is also your son," she said the words, but knew they were hollow. Dameon did not acknowledge Bryant, even though the resemblance was uncanny.

"We have been down this road. There is no more proof that bastard of a son of yours is mine. Now, if he came with an ear to the duke then perhaps, but as he stands, he is no more important than the street rat you have living with you."

"You mean Marquess Harwich?" She smiled when the

note of his title, being leaps and bounds above where Dameon would ever be, made him crawl.

He ignored the barb and moved forward. "I am certain both Birch and Harwich are suspicious. Birch has gone to ground, I can't get a wind of him anywhere or what he is planning, so you need to finish this and soon. Harwich will return and suggest a series of dinner parties at your townhouse to be more in the public eye. I have convinced him it will give you more protection. You will agree then I will send word when you are to make certain Amari is available.

"What if I tell you I have straightened out my accounts and am no longer in need of the funds? I think it best if you move Amari and I go back to my life as I am used to it."

The expression on Dameon's face told her it was a surprise that she no longer had money issues, which proved his involvement there as well. The scowl he formed told her she was not getting out that easily.

"Let me make this clear. You are not being let out of your obligation to me. You cost me enough already. If you so much as attempt to thwart my plan, you will find yourself alone, burying all those who you love. Foremost that bastard son that you keeping saying is mine, and second, possibly with the same bullet so I don't waste my own fortune, will be that upstart who for no other reason than he had a lucky streak will follow."

Finna went cold, perhaps it was fate telling how her death would feel, because if she lost either of them or anyone she cared for, because she fancied herself in love years ago, then behaved recklessly when he turned away from her, she could not live in this world.

"Very well, then you and I will be finished. Do not expect

COURTESAN'S WICKED DESIRE

to come to me again, Dameon. I will get a pistol and shoot you myself."

The look she shot him was that of a future duchess, as she was trained. Her mother did not give her many skills to use as a courtesan, but the withering I will kill you and eat your young while you watch expression was all her mother.

Without a word, a much paler Dameon Chamberlain chose retreat and left the carriage. Once the door shut, the vehicle lurched forward. She knew the driver heard more than he should, but she also was certain that Dameon's foot had not yet left the step before he let the horses loose. She smiled bitterly. The carriage rumbled around the park. She could have walked back to her townhouse quicker. Finally, it stopped and deposited her down the street. Since this was her secret carriage, she preferred no one see her near her home.

Once back at the town house, she expected Kendrick to be waiting, sullen faced, in the parlor to reprimand her for leaving again. To her relief, he had not returned. She hoped that didn't mean he had more trouble than he expected with the solicitor. Her one fear was that the wastrel would steal all her money outright and disappear. If Kendrick could orchestrate moving her funds to Reginald's firm, she would not worry in the least.

It was less than an hour when Kendrick walked in. "Oh good. I don't have to search you out. Did all go well for you and Bryant?"

Her heart warmed that he even remembered her concern and thought to ask before all else. When he left, it might well break her once and for all.

"Yes, quite well. He is old enough that he understood and did not need to ask many questions. Not that he would."

"He is a bright young man, and very inquisitive, so I would think questions he might have had, he searched out people to give him satisfactory answers," Kendrick assured her.

"How did it go with Mr. Knottingword?"

His grimace was not reassuring. "That man deserves the gallows for his behavior. However, your money has been re-located and transferred to Reginald's firm. I have informed the bank that Mr. Knottingword need not worry himself with your accounts from here on out. We went to the bank to make sure it properly handled the transaction. I believe that Mr. Knottingword is about to embark on a grand tour of the continent."

That surprised her. "why, I cannot imagine he is threat-ened by retribution by a mere courtesan?"

"No, you are correct, you do not set fear through him, which is the first indication there is something amiss, but the threat of His Grace, myself, and also of the man who paid him to ruin you were all great motivators."

It made her angry that it took three powerful men to make him scared enough to act, because a woman in her world held no power in his eyes. Finna well knew the power women held over men, but it was not power that paraded in a drawing room.

"There is no place in this world for men like that. You said he told you someone paid him to drain my funds?" That was more upsetting.

Kendrick sighed and shook his head. "Yes, and like our

current luck, he did not have a name. He had a description, though, so I am working to see who fits it."

"Well, if they were targeting me, perhaps if you share the description, I can help."

"I had hoped I wouldn't have to make you consider it, but I am afraid I still sit in the wings of most Ton affairs since my return. He was tall and on the thin side, with straight blond hair and bright blue eyes."

"Yes, well, that just described half the gentlemen in London," she pointed out. She could come up with a list, and she also knew who would be at the top. If she couldn't confide in Kendrick about her other dealings, this was off the table as well.

"Could you think on it?"

"Yes, I will see about getting you a list. How did your other appointment go?"

"Much shorter, but no less frustrating. I tried to convince Chamberlain to move Amari to a more secure location for everyone's safety. His answer however was in fact the opposite."

She waited, knowing what his suggestion was about to be. She decided on shock as her reaction, because the man made no sense, so agreeing would set off alarm bells in Kendrick's mind.

"He suggested we, well you, host a series of dinner parties with Ton guests. He said that way it would be easier to bring in people to watch the goings on without having an increase in numbers at the house seem odd."

"I do not see—" she started, then pivoted toward defensive. "I told you I didn't want a bunch of strange men overtaking my house. And I do not appreciate being told I have to entertain society. It has served me well to not attempt to be a socialite. They do not think I am reaching." The last was true, so it bolstered the rest, she thought.

"I know. The only part I agree with is getting more eyes on Amari. Nothing about that could be bad. He is worse than an errant child at times. I wouldn't ask if it wasn't the only choice. Hopefully, Birch will come through and he will be out of your hair before you have to entertain more than once."

Kendrick leaned in and with those pleading dark pools of brown almost the color of a cinnamon stick once it has soaked in brandy, she could not refuse him anything.

"All right, but if I am to hold a dinner, it will be black tie only. I will expect a small quartet as well, they can set up here in the parlor. It is not large enough for dancing, but if we move the furniture out, there will be room for mingling. How many should I invite?"

"I'm not sure. Victoria always handled those details, and Zoe after Victoria took ill. I just dressed and appeared as I was told. I would think we will want at least a need for five more footmen to mill around."

"Very well, are there any men you are interested in speaking with before the opening of Parliament, or should I just choose those I feel are the most important?"

"I will defer all to you. Whatever you need me to do, I will be at your service. I would think we need to do it as soon as possible."

"Yes, I agree." The sooner she did this, the sooner she would be free. Free to live with the guilt of lying to Kendrick and possibly getting her friend's love interest killed. "I will have Contrell assist me with invitations and send them out immediately. There is a musicale tonight, and three days from now, Lady Jersey is holding her annual ball. I think two days from now will be optimal, as most people do not attend gatherings the day before Lady Jersey's ball."

Kendrick nodded, uninterested in the details. "I will have the invitations posted later this afternoon, so that by the musicale tonight there should be some buzz. Will Dameon have time to arrange enough men who can handle a serving tray?"

"I will pen a note right now, so he has time to. I will leave you to your work then."

"Thank you, please ask Golding to fetch Contrell when you pass him in the hall, and be ready by 7 o'clock. The Smythe musicale is always a crush, and they do not keep well stocked of champagne. If we do not arrive early, we will be left with tepid lemonade."

With that, Kendrick left. Finna blew out the breath she had been holding. Every bone in her body screamed for her to trust Kendrick and tell him everything. She knew, though, how deadly serious Dameon was. He would follow through with his threat if given the chance. And now with her knowledge that it was no doubt him trying to destroy her financially, she had even more at stake.

CHAPTER 22

Finna could read people. It was what made her good at what she did, and it would have made her an exceptional duchess. She enjoyed reading people until she didn't and tonight when Kendrick escorted her to the musicale, she knew he was aware.

Perhaps he didn't, but he suspected. What he suspected was unknown, however, she could not allow him prying. Like any man, he would not understand it was as much for his wellbeing as it was for her and Bryant. Dameon made it clear he would include Kendrick in his edict if given an excuse to do so. Never would she be able to fathom what Dameon held against any of them. She understood Bryant, which made her ashamed, but to a man Bryant would be a reminder of his transgression.

"The talent this evening was much improved from the last musicale," Kendrick chatted.

"Yes, on the surface a musicale is very appealing. An evening of music and singing, while young ladies show their talents. If only the young ladies who were foisted in front of a crowd had any talent to begin with."

"I remember several musicales when you were a deb. If I recall, you had both an exceptional voice, and you were quite skilled on the pinafore."

"Well, I would call none of my skill exceptional. Let's just agree I would have had less luck joining a theater or musical troupe when I went rogue."

They both laughed, then she looked up and Kendrick's eyes pierced to her soul. "Why?"

Neither of them needed any more of a question. She had considered it over the years, but never pinned down the exact moment.

"To be honest, I am not sure at what moment I thought becoming a courtesan was a smashing idea," she answered honestly. If he was grappling with their past, he wasn't trying to ferret out their present.

"I thought perhaps when Victoria told me that you were taken advantage of—" He cut off his words. His emotion so close to the surface she read it in his face.

"No. Nothing so dramatic. Mother sent me to Bath while she handled the scandal. She did it because she didn't want to see my pain. Her idea was to join me after a few weeks, but when I arrived it was such a social whirl that I was taken up in all the parties and salons. An acquaintance pointed out to me the women who seemed to be all the rage with gentlemen."

The carriage rocked and jostled, sending her forward.

Kendrick's strong arms steadied her, then guided her the rest of the way to his lap. His arms holding her. If only for the moment Finna would take the comfort they offered.

"I was reeling from losing you and my emotions were raw. Those women appeared to be enjoying themselves, not the least worried about trying to impress or behave a certain way. I was at a crossroads. If I went home, I would have the scandal to contend with. No matter what my mother did, I knew the looks I would get. I would also be bound to what my parents thought best; buck up and find another suitable husband."

She turned and looked into his liquid eyes, like pools of warmed brandy. If things were different, if their present was different, she would be happy with her choice, because it would free her to be with Kendrick. The sadness filled the cracks of that story, because after her years of loose behavior and her current active lie, she took her chance to be with him away.

"I met Contrell, and though she was older and more experienced, she didn't dissuade me when I expressed an interest. In fact, she thought it a marvelous ploy to attract clients. The daughter of a duke. She took me under her wing, and before my mother considered coming to get me, I had written her a letter and left Bath for Bristol."

They sat in silence, each in their own thoughts about what seemed a lifetime ago. As the carriage made the last turn onto the thoroughfare, Kendrick pulled her down for a kiss. This kiss was gentle, probing, questioning. This was not a kiss that led to anything, but one that made promises; promises of long languid mornings spent making love, promises of quiet evenings spent with wine by a fire, promises of all those things never allowed to a courtesan.

As the carriage came to a halt, Kendrick set her on her side and just like that they were the epitome of the uninterested couple. The separation made her heart ache for what she knew was to come. Inside, Contrell and Amari were still up and wanted an account of the musicale. It interested Contrell to hear anyone who accepted their invitations. Quite a few had expressed their excitement of being invited and assured her friend they would get responses first thing in the morning.

Amari had left their side and instead sat with the gentlemen. Birch and Kendrick were in deep conversation about whatever was the most important item to date. Finna didn't care anymore. Soon, this business would be done, and everyone would go to the winds. The next move on this chess board was obvious. She had no desire to stay and listen to their plans.

"I am exhausted, and with the planning that needs to happen tomorrow rest is needed. I will bid you all a good night."

"Good night, my dear, I will endeavor to be about early to assist where needed," Contrell declared. Finna appreciated the declaration, but in all her years Contrell had not been out of her rooms before 10 o'clock in the morning.

Birch, Amari, and Kendrick rose and bid her good night. Her gaze lingered on the marquess with a silent invitation she was certain he understood.

An hour later, Finna lay naked in her bed, staring up at the canopy. Years ago, determined to make a private life for herself, she had painted a lovely warm summer scene on the ceiling of the canopy. She had long since covered it with silks, annoyed with the whimsical young girl who thought she could create a haven that would protect her from the cruelties of the outside world.

She almost missed the click in the silence had it not been for the shaft of candlelight from the hallway. "Finna?" Kendrick whispered, not moving more into the room.

"In the bed. We are alone."

Once he shut the door, she couldn't see him but heard shuffling and the sounds of clothing hitting the floor. Before she expected it, he was slipping under the covers to join her.

Not that it mattered, but she had to ask. "Did anyone see you?"

He kissed her forehead. "No, sweeting. This is your home, and therefore your decision when to announce our relationship."

Relationship. Only once on her journey had she dared to call her connection with a gentleman a relationship. The bitterness stung her tongue. Now, that same man threatened to kill their son and the one man who never treated her as anything other than a lady.

He lay so he was above her, searching her eyes, looking for a truth, a clue to what she was hiding. Kendrick was an intelligent man, but she was exceedingly good at what she did too. Wrapping her hand around his neck, she pulled him down for a kiss. Unlike his kiss in the carriage, hers offered no promises of long romantic nights. Instead it was greedy and hungry, demanding then demanding more. As her tongue licked and stoked the flames, her hands spread over his tight hard body adding fuel.

Finna had been with an array of men. She would never consider herself indiscriminate with her lovers, but she never had to spend a night alone if she so chose. Men, like women, she supposed were different. Some, like Kendrick, were all hard plains and angled edges like a marble sculpture. Kendrick was a perfect specimen of the male form, soft and smooth skin covering tight muscles not hindered by extra layers.

She ran both hands down his body until she reached the small ridge that sat on either side below his bellybutton. From there she ran a gentle finger along each rigid raised line until her fingers met in the middle just above his manhood.

Sucking in a breath. "Finna, you slay me," he whispered in her ear, nipping it and working his way down her neck. She leaned to give him better access but continued her own perusal of his body.

Without pausing, she continued moving her hands to her destination, spreading her fingers through the patch of hair and to the prize beyond. Holding his balls with one hand, she began at the base of his penis and stroked with a firm grip.

"Oh god." He stopped, throwing his head back to enjoy.

She let go and raised up to whisper in his ear. "Roll over, love."

He took her proximity to steal a kiss but did as she instructed. She slid, so it splayed him out in the middle of the bed, filling the large mattress. He was glorious. Over the years most men softened, but not Kendrick. If the women of the Ton knew what lay under his suit, he would not have a moment's peace.

A rush of power flowed through her, as it always did

when she sat hovering over a man in bed. This was the one place she was in charge. Her partner would never admit that, and Kendrick was no different, but she knew the power she wielded. Tonight, it was the power to muddle his brain so much with desire that he left behind whatever notions he had.

Leaning forward, she slid her mouth around the tip of his erection and took her time covering the length. The moment he gave into her she took mercy and sped up her ministrations.

"You will kill me love," he moaned after a while and took her by the shoulders, dragging her up his naked body and splaying her on top of his chest. He put his arms around her and held her. "Mm, I could wake like this every morning for the rest of my life and it wouldn't be enough. I love you. I never stopped. I don't care if you are not ready to hear it, I won't lie to you any longer."

Finna had to bury her head in his chest to stop the tears from spilling over. Her lips burned with the words to return, but she swallowed hard. Soon enough he would hate her with just as much passion. She would allow the words to wash over her now and cushion the pain that was to come. Instead, she took one of the smooth nipples and suckled it to draw a moan from him. She would give anything to have the world he envisioned. But life had proven once again destiny would not allow her to have a love for herself or happiness beyond contentment with what she had. These last few days would be all she would take with her.

Determined to have a piece of him on the dark days to come, she threw away all reserve, and decorum which she had lived by as a courtesan. She would drink him in and take in the greediest of ways everything she could steal before that happened. Dameon be damned. He would never take their love for each other. Her thoughts and memories were things he could not destroy or steal from her.

"I need to taste you now," Kendrick announced as he turned them in one fluid motion, making her heady with the sensation of him all around her at once.

Throwing back her head, allowing him to return the favor, she let the emotion take her. Silent tears trailed and disappeared in the waves of hair surrounding her. Never had she allowed herself to just feel. Always, she was calculating and gauging how to make the experience good for her partner. That was after all the fundamental task a man paid his courtesan for, was it not?

When she could hold back her orgasm no longer, she tugged at his arm and he knew, rising over her and with a thundering moan buried himself inside her. His rhythm was perfect with her own as if they were meant to, if not be soul mates, at least revolve around each other for eternity.

When they were both spent and laying, staring up at her painting panting, she knew if the world stopped tomorrow her last memory would be the first time, she made love and was made love to. Instead of steeling her reserve she turned, wrapping her naked body around his and wept from the joy of having someone love her, the anguish of knowing it wasn't meant to be, and the righteous anger of the unfairness of it all. Tomorrow, he would try to save everyone, including Amari, and she would be back to sacrificing her own soul and Amari's life to save the two men she loved the most. Tonight, though, she could lock that out.

"Make love to me again," she said as she stroked her leg up and down his thigh.

"Always," was his response and so they spent the night in each other's arms.

CHAPTER 23

*M*orning broke and exposed their hidden world to the reality they both wanted to ignore. He lay on his back with Finna's head on his chest. Her hair spread out like a blanket, he marveled at how the sunbeam danced along the strands making the black locks appear almost blue in some places. Sometime around 3 o'clock. She was asleep. Her breathing slowed and her body relaxed.

Thinking back to their night, it was the closest either of them had ever had an honest sexual interlude. While he spent his marriage trying like Hercules to enjoy his wife, in return showing her how to enjoy him, she clearly did not. Finna had spent all of her sexual experience guarding her emotions to not feel anything.

Two fools they turned out to be. More buoyed than ever that a life together would work. But Finna held back still. She had not returned the 'I love you', and though he was certain she enjoyed their activities, and that it affected her beyond the physical, she refused to trust him.

This time he was the one awake first, and he slid out from under her, almost falling clear off the bed in his attempt. Age had not made him a more agile lover; of that he was certain. Gathering his clothes, he snuck through the hall to his own room to dress. Though not sure why he bothered anymore, Contrell had them pegged, he was certain.

Whatever was holding her back was tied up in the mess with Amari. She was hiding something. Both he and Birch were aware. She was a masterful courtesan, but she was not adept at hiding things from an old spy and the man who loved her. The question was, what? He had the suspicion all their hard work was being sabotaged. He trusted Finna. Her loyalty was to those she loved and was not the kind to harm another. So, if she was the one causing issues, it was under duress.

Fletcher came when beckoned and dressed him in his most marquess outfit. Never adhering to the foppish styles, which included a waistcoat of mahogany velvet with embossed ivy leaves covering. He tugged on a dusty grey over jacket with threading and buttons to match the waist-coat. His breeches matched the jacket and the pin holding the too complicated knot in place, a large ruby encased in diamonds. It was time that he embraced the power that was his title.

Birch was meeting him at White's to break their fast and discuss what to do about Finna. If he was going to White's, he would need to look the part of being a parliament member. In all of this, he had not forgotten that goal. If she agreed to marry him and she asked him to not take his seat, there would be no question which he would choose, but with no declarations he was not ready to become a country gentleman just yet.

He had a stop to make along the way, because it was paramount that Finna stay so busy with these foolish dinners and the planning that she not see the counter measures Birch and he were formulating. It might be underhanded to use her mother's invitation against her, but she used their love making last night to control the narrative and put him off course.

The house remained quiet as he made his way downstairs and into the back dining room where Golding often hid to read the morning news sheet. He wondered if Finna was aware Golding read it before he placed it in the dining room each morning. Not striking him as the sort to know how to read, it impressed Kendrick.

"Golding, I have to step out this morning, and Birch will not be coming. Are you set to man the house in my absence? Fletcher is also available if needed."

"Awk, aye, mi lord, not much happens here in the morning anyway, unless you count master Bryant doing a sizable amount of damage to the breakfast buffet."

"Very true. Regardless, I will not use the front door or call my carriage. I wouldn't want to give the assumption the house was not being guarded."

"Very well, mi lord. What should I tell Lady Finna, if she asks?"

"Tell her I had a meeting with my solicitor that skipped my mind with all that has been happening. Tell her I will be back when I am finished, but I wasn't sure when that would be."

Golding nodded.

"Golding, do you mind if I ask you a question?"

"No, mi lord."

"Where did you learn to read? I don't mean any disrespect, but I had the impression you were not raised in the upper classes."

"Awk, nay, you have the right of that. Lady Finna taught me. She said if I was to be her butler instead of a common pick pocket I'd have to learn to read, write, and do my numbers. I hated every minute of it, I did, but now I can read the news sheet and see what is going on for myself."

"Very good, then. I am glad you see the worth."

Kendrick said goodbye and continued to the back of the house and the garden door. He would sneak out the back and walk the back street until he came out on St. James. He missed walking. In Rome he often walked wherever he needed to be. On St. James he flagged down a hack and made a stop at his first destination. Once satisfied with that, he then headed to White's.

Birch was already at a table with a full plate and a hot pot of coffee sitting next to him. Kendrick sat and ordered from the extensive menu. Birch poured coffee into his cup, and the waiter soon brought a fresh pot to replace that one.

"So, did you learn anything to confirm your suspicions from our talk last night?" Birch asked, not wasting time. This was coming to a head, and they needed a plan.

"Nothing that will help us know what she is planning," he admitted.

"But you learned something?" Birch asked.

"Yes, I learned that when persuaded Finna can put an

awful lot of energy into distracting a man from his real purpose."

Kendrick had not admitted to Birch they were lovers, but Birch was perceptive, and privy to their background. Chuckling, he said, "She was the bell of the Ton's underbelly for a reason, you are aware?"

Kendrick just grunted, knowing her profession was forever a part of who she was, but would rather not be reminded.

"Well, since we both are certain Finna is working for Dameon, or they are both working for someone else, it stands to reason these dinners will be a smoke screen. I hope that I am close to having a plan to move Michele. I have gotten confirmation from my contact in Belgium that they are ready when he arrives."

"I do not believe Finna is a willing participant in all of this," Kendrick said pointedly. If she would not defend herself, he would.

"I never thought she would," Birch assured him.

"You two have become close over the years."

Birch looked up from his plate to study Kendrick. He did not need to know if they were lovers, in fact he quite liked Birch and would not want to put his assurances he has given Finna into practice just yet, in case it did not go well.

"We were never lovers, so put your hackles down," he said with a chuckle, shaking his head. "If you react to every man who either has been with her, or even those who claim to have bedded her, because there is a large contingent in that corner as well you will either be a top marksman from all the dueling or you will be dead and no longer able to enjoy the lovely Finna for yourself."

Kendrick winced. "I will not lie and say it is not a work in progress but thank you for understanding."

Kendrick's food arrived and Birch caught him up on all the times they bumped into each other over the years.

"At first it was deuced awkward, because we were acquainted, she knew my family. I got the impression it was no different for her. It is so much easier to act out of character when no one knows what your character is. Over time, she stepped in when I was close to giving up my cover. I wasn't always such a spy extraordinaire."

"I would never have thought it," Kendrick chuckled. He was glad to have this time away from the house and all the chaos. Although, if Finna stayed with him, his life would never be ordered again.

When they parted, they agreed Birch would bring men in to handle the perimeter and at all entrances. They would also need to put men upstairs. Birch would be there under the guise of being Amari's personal assistant while he visited, that way he could remain at his side. They could not trust the men Dameon would send. Kendrick hoped he was wrong. Dameon Chamberlain was not a good man, but it was sad to think he would have fallen this far.

Once back at the house, Finna was not home, having been summoned to her family home for luncheon with her mother and sister. The tone Contrell used was clear. "I find it curious that Finna has not tried to be in her family's sphere until you return."

"I take it you do not approve?" Kendrick said, not wanting to make an enemy out of the woman closest to Finna, but Finna needed the love of her family.

"On the contrary, I have attempted over the years to push

her to reconnect. She would hear none of it. So much so, she believed the stories she told herself about them not wanting her. I have kept her mother up to date over the years."

Kendrick raised an eyebrow on that. "Finna would have seen that as a lapse in trust."

"Yes, she would have, that is why she never knew." She shot him a look that said she wanted to call him a dolt but left it off.

"I did not reach out to her mother. The issue at Vauxhall Gardens promoted her mother to act. But I am not above helping things move along."

"I knew you would come up to scratch eventually. It took you years, and not months as I had thought back then, but here nonetheless."

Contrell filled him in on the progress with the dinner. As expected not one invitation went unanswered. Finna's first non private gathering of her life would be a crush, it appeared.

Now, if Kendrick could keep them all alive and save Finna from herself, it might be a success.

CHAPTER 24

"Golding, I do not want to follow you around this evening." Finna heard Contrell scolding Golding about his penchant for relieving people of their unneeded valuables.

"Golding has come a long way, haven't you?" Finna interrupted, joining them in the dining room. The last layer of plaster was added yesterday and would be ready to paint before luncheon, and dry by the time the guests arrive.

"I 'ave, Lady Finna. I promise to make you proud tonight. Fletcher has been helping me with all the rules. A lot more than just a dinner of friends, I might add."

"Yes, there are, and I am sorry I was so distracted that I didn't think to advise you. I will thank Fletcher personally. This isn't even his household after all."

"That one is a good bloke. Stiff, but after a fashion he loosens up."

"Very well, now Finna we need to discuss your greeting

line. I suggest you set yourself by the stairs. It will allow for many people to be in the house and not cooling their heels on the street."

"I agree, thank you."

Contrell locked arms with her and headed her toward the parlor and a tea service. Finna spent much of the afternoon in her room when she returned from her mother's, to avoid discussing something she had yet to process. Contrell would want a recounting.

"Now love, how did it go yesterday? So much has change right now, I don't know if we are coming or going half the time."

Finna looked around the parlor and the hairs on the back of her neck rose. "Contrell, where is Mr. Amari?"

"Lord Harwich took him to buy a new hat and also to get his good suit taken in. It seems he has eaten little since being in England."

Her heart stopped hammering in her chest, but only just. "Thank goodness. I did not want to have him go missing. Poor Lord Harwich would not take that well." She sipped her tea, knowing she had bought all the time she was going to.

"So?"

"It was as I remembered, warm and welcoming. Father was not home, but I saw some staff that were happy to see me."

"Your mother? Your sister?" she prodded.

"It was nice. Awkward at first, but mother was the perfect hostess. We talked about the current season, and Ginny's two children. They are now nine and ten. I couldn't imagine. Time goes so quickly."

"Does time also heal as they claim?" Contrell asked, chewing on a soft cake.

"I suppose it does. Mother has reached out over the years, but I never wanted to make it difficult for them, especially Ginny. She was so shy as a child; it would put her in a hard place. It wasn't fair."

"I told you, didn't I tell you?"

"I know you have been in approval of it for many years," Finna admitted.

Before Contrell could probe more, the gentlemen entered. Amari with a garment bag over his shoulder, and Birch the same. "I suggested Birch be here to get ready, to help go over things without worrying about not being ready, and Amari will not look like someone's grumpy bachelor uncle."

Amari laughed and excused himself.

"Fletcher offered to give him a long-needed grooming, you will not see him until the dinner."

"Well, I think then it is time for us to retire to prepare. All is in order down here," Contrell assured everyone. "I will let cook know that you are ready for your bath."

Finna didn't argue. She had no desire to spend the day with Dylan and Kendrick. A coward of the worst sort, but there was nothing to do for it. Her time away would be spent to rest and gather her thoughts.

The group met in the parlor for drinks before the appointed time. The modiste managed to get the dress for Contrell finished in time. She looked stunning. Mr. Amari no doubt agreed. He had not taken his eyes off her since the women entered the room.

"I spoke with all the men sent by the foreign office, they

know what they are doing well enough," Birch said while he sipped from his brandy.

"Ready?" Kendrick walked up to Finn and rested his hand on the small of her back, sending a fissure of awareness through her, chased by a stab of guilt.

"Yes, I think so."

"You look beautiful," he added.

"Doesn't she?" Contrell jumped at his comment. "I insisted she wear the red. It is her home, after all. Everyone should see her. Kendrick smiled and nodded his agreement.

As the group faded out to their perspective spots Kendrick guided her toward the window overlooking the garden, "Are you sure you are ready? This is the first large gathering you hosted?"

She tried not to give him an annoyed glare, but knew she failed. "The reason I never entertained in my own home was not for lack of ability. I am and have always been capable of being a hostess."

He smiled. "I never thought otherwise, love," he assured her.

"Hmm," she sniffed. "Honestly, I didn't entertain because I never wanted to be censured under my own roof. It is painful enough to let hurtful comments pass. I wanted a place where I had no hurtful memories to contend with."

"That makes perfect sense."

"It does?" She knew it sounded like a firm argument in her head but was happy he agreed.

"We all want a place where no one judges us. Most of us are not self-aware enough to be protective of that place, however. I commend you." He pulled her hand to his mouth and placed a kiss in the palm. Even through her glove, she could feel the heat and promise.

The doorbell sounded, and that was the end of her calm. Before she could rise and greet her guests in her chosen location in bustled her father, mother, sister, and brother-in-law.

Her mother walked over and kissed her on the cheek. "No need to get up. We came early, thought it would be a sound showing of solidarity."

Had she invited them? Had Contrell? They were not on the guest list she created. Her sister wrapped her in a warm hug, while her father and brother-in-law greeted Kendrick. Golding took hats and shawls, and it was done. Relief flooded over her, followed by pointed fear. It was good of her family to rally around her first attempt to enter back into the Ton, other than as a tolerated outsider. However, if things went bad with Amari, her mother and sister would witness it. She would have to stay aware and keep them safe.

"If you will excuse me, I forgot something in my rooms, I will be back," Kendrick said and left.

Finna made sure everyone had drinks and were settled, and she made introductions. Father started up a discussion with Amari about his politics and where he saw relations with England in the various possibilities. Birch stayed close to his target, but chatted with her brother-in-law, David, Lord Temple. They seemed to at least be acquaintances.

When Finna turned back to the ladies, Contrell sat next to her mother, the duchess, and they chatted like they have been debutantes in the same season. Her heart constricted. Did her mother harbor any resentment to the woman who took her place? She knew Contrell pushed over the years for

Finna to reach out, but she also knew Contrell was jealous of the relationship between a mother and daughter. Kendrick walked back in the room, but within moments the bell rang, and the dinner party had begun.

The first half hour past like a whirl, with guests coming in a constant stream, and champagne flowing. She had made a list based on men who would pave the way for Kendrick. In doing so, she also had a group of people who were more progressive in their ideas. There were a few women she would need to steer clear of, but that was easily done.

She found Kendrick and linked arms with him, moving around the clusters of guests injecting just the right questions to give Kendrick the floor.

The strange footmen in her livery, representing her, were unsettling. Birch had vetted them, but she knew Dameon had put them in her home for one reason and one reason only. Many gave her unfriendly glances when they passed her. Bryant had promised to not attend this evening and was holed up in his rooms. He surprised her by agreeing without argument, but a large group of adults only wanting to talk about politics would not be a draw to a boy only ten and five.

"This is smashing, sister. Well done. It was several botched attempts before I managed a reasonable success." Ginny came up next to her when Kendrick had left to check in with Birch.

"Thank you. I have held many smaller gatherings, but none this large or this public." The women then stood in awkward silence. Perhaps her sister wasn't as much a champion for her but being forced by her parents. Oh well, that was not anything Finna could control.

"Dinner is ready, my lady," Golding came and announced to her in a very formal manner. She smiled at his good job.

"Thank you, Golding. Everyone, dinner is being served in the back parlor, shall we?"

Kendrick arrived at her elbow from out of nowhere to escort her.

All was going well, but the panic she could not leave off from not knowing when they would act was working on her. The entire party ate, drank, and laughed throughout the meal. When all were finished Finna directed them back to the front of the house where the quartet was playing the first strains of a melody. Kendrick again went to check on things, and it left Finna to wander through the guests.

She noticed her sister standing with another young woman she knew was married to one of the younger lords, but she was not well acquainted yet. Deciding this was a good time to get an introduction, but as she approached, she overheard the discussion.

"I understand she is your sister, and as long as your father refuses to disown her, there is no choice but to accept her. All I am saying is that it is such a shame to have an important family stained by such a pariah."

"Well I—" Ginny started, but the young woman just talked through her.

"I mean the shame you must carry into decent upstanding social gatherings knowing your sister is nothing but a common doxy. My Thurston would never be so crass as to pander a mistress in the same circles. I mean, that is why those dens exist to keep them away from decent people. We should never allow them to mingle in good company."

"Well I—" Ginny tried again.

"You are a dear to hide the shame so well, but I cannot imagine how you will handle the impact it has on your children."

"My children, what have my children to do with this?" Ginny bristled. Apparently, for Ginny to gather her muster, someone had to bring her children into an argument. Finna had been about to step in, but she held back to see if she could find out her sister's true feelings.

"Well, you can't think they will find successful matches with such a lineage. The competition for marriageable titles is fierce as it is. I am certain they will find some nice country gentlemen who may even own land, but—"

Ginny rounded on the woman. "I'll have you know my daughters already have interested mothers looking to connect their titled sons to good lineage. And the problem you had finding a husband had more to do with your sour expression and uncharitable behavior toward anyone who may challenge you or make you look less than you think you are." She stepped toward the woman, sending her stepping back into a potted palm. "As for my sister, we, as a family have made the choice to support her. She has made her own way in a world that would eat most women alive, without the added difficulties of her vocation. She is more of an example of a strong titled woman than you will ever be. If I hear that you ever have said anything disparaging about my sister or anyone in my family, or for that matter in my circle of friends, I will make sure Lord Temple is informed."

The woman paled at the threat. Finna's brother-in-law might well make prime minister and even if he didn't, he had the ear of some of the most powerful men in all of England.

Apparently, her meek little sister was coming out of her shell and opening up an arsenal.

Finna watched to make sure the woman was apologetic and left her alone. While she was proud of the strength her sister showed, Finna could see the toll it took on her. If it wasn't for who she was Ginny wouldn't have had to be so out of character.

It was time Finna admitted the pain she always caused to those she loved. If she stayed, her family would forever defend her to the world. If she stayed, Bryant would have to contend with a limitless amount of hardship because of the circumstances of his birth and who his mother was. Then there was Kendrick. He loved her. The knowledge of that made her chest ache. She had done everything in her power to be undeserving of all these people and yet they stood true. If she could get out of this with no loss of life, she was leaving. She could take her fortune. Now that Kendrick reconciled her accounts and adding this payout plus selling the town house, she could keep the country home. Bryant would have land in his home country that way, but they would be very well off in Spain. It had taken some time and many arguments with herself about how she could make it work if she stayed. This was the deciding factor. Never again would her poor sister have to come to her defense.

The weight of it almost sent her to her knees.

"Whoa, there, are you not well?" Kendrick took her arm and held her steady. Where had he come from? He had a troublesome habit of being there when she most needed him.

"I think it is the heat in here," she covered. It was then she noted some guests heading in her direction and just like that they were filing out, thanking her for a splendid time and hoping she would host again, and many promising to send invitations for their next gatherings.

Her family had been the last to leave and her sister did not appear to have any ill effects of her altercation, but it solidified things for Finna. How she loved her family for their show of support, and it would make her missing them hurt more once her and Bryant left the country.

Contrell fell to the sofa with a melodramatic air. "Lord, am I exhausted. These hob nob types are tiring indeed." Everyone laughed, except Birch, who entered just as her family exited.

"Well done, Mr. Birch," Mr. Amari offered to his protector. "You got me through the night without a knife in my side or bullet in my head."

"Don't thank me just yet," he said angrily. "Harwich, you personally locked every door and window yourself?"

"Yes," he said, unaware of where Dylan was going with this.

"Someone unlocked the back door by the kitchens. No one exited, and no one has yet to enter from there. The man I have outside that door heard the latch click and has not left it since."

"So, someone is planning on coming back?" Finna said, trying to seem surprised.

Birch shook his head grimly. "No, Golding and Fletcher counted the extra hands we were assigned and one was missing when they all filed out."

"Are you sure?" Finna was certain Dameon told her someone would come in, but if he thought she would change her mind...

"Yes, I am sure. Fletcher was asked to watch the main

entrance to the kitchens from here and he said no one passed."

"So, how could the door have been unlatched then?" Contrell asked.

"The priest holes. Only members of the household knew where those were and how to maneuver around the house with them."

Kendrick sat next to Finna and rested his arm on hers between them.

"Are you saying someone living here made it possible for an assailant to enter?" Contrell said with shock.

"Well, we do not believe it to be Michele, unless he has a desire to die before he gets to Belgium but, other than him, it is all possible."

"Who do you think would do such a thing?" Contrell argued.

"That is what we will figure out right now. First, I will rule out everyone here and then I will move to the servants."

"Oh, this is ridiculous," Finna piped up. She refused to have her staff treated like common criminals, many of them came to her because of their circumstances. "Next thing you will drag Bryant down here and accuse him."

"I hadn't thought, but you are correct, I will send someone to—"

"Stop," she said, pulling her hand from Kendrick's safe embrace and putting it with her other hand in her lap, clasping them. The gesture had always given her quiet strength when she needed it. "It was me. It has been me the entire time."

CHAPTER 25

*I*f Kendrick could acquire one supernatural power, it would be to take another's pain. When his mother wept, hungry and cold in their cramped room in Cheapside because she missed her family after his father died, Kendrick prayed every night to let him take her pain. When his wife lay wasting with no end in sight; he would sit by her bed and wish her pain to travel from her hand into his. Now was another one of those times.

Finna sat next to him with her shoulders back and her chin out, ready for censure. The room fell quiet, but no one appeared outraged. They just waited. After a moment she collected her thoughts and began.

"I want you to know, Mr. Amari. When I agreed to take you in and help protect you, I was fully invested in that endeavor. I never intended to put you in danger."

"Well, thank you, my dear," he said in a strangled voice.

Looking at her clasped hands she continued. "It started

with a note here and there about leaving a window open or being out of the house. But once the fire happened—" She looked up at the ceiling.

Kendrick saw the tears sparkling in her eyes and wanted nothing more than to pull her into a safe embrace.

She pulled her head back and faced the group with a defiance that was pure Finna. "What I did was inexcusable, but I was given an untenable choice. I do not expect any of you to trust me now, I need you all to understand if I felt I had another choice I would not have gone along with it. Now that I am caught and it is out of my hands I will deal with the consequences."

Contrell was the first to act. She rose and walked to Finna, sitting down next to her. Without a word, she wrapped her arms around her and just held her. After a moment she spoke with heavy emotion.

"My dear girl. None of us think you acted purely for your own gain. Whoever the bastard is that put you in such a situation should be drawn and quartered. But might I ask how many years does one need to be acquainted with people in this room before we are trusted? The world was not made for a person to survive it alone. You must know that by now."

The tears flowed freely then, rolling silently down her face.

Birch moved the conversation forward. "I have a plan finally. I could not find anyone to take you from ports close to London. There are forces much stronger than us pulling strings there. I will need to find a hack that I can procure—"

"I own one," Finna interjected in a meek voice.

"You? You own a hackney?" Birch asked in surprise. "Why wasn't I aware?"

"I own a hackney so I might cross town or travel without being noticed," she pointed out. "It is unmarked and very well sprung, if you need it please make use of it."

"Thank you, I will. It will make things go more smoothly if we don't have to depend on outsiders."

"Mother? Mother? Are you unharmed?" Bryant came bounding down the stairs with Golding fast on his tail.

"I tried, mi lady, to keep him in his room, but after a while he just wore me down," Golding admitted.

"It is fine, Golding, thank you," Birch dismissed him.

Bryant sat hugging his mother, noticing the tears. "What did they do to you? What did you do to her?" he yelled, staring at Kendrick.

"You should not be down here. There is still danger in the house, and they did nothing but support me. I have done some things and put many people in danger because of my need to be independent. To protect you..."

Kendrick couldn't help get the impression there was more to that statement, but this wasn't the time.

"We found the wastrel, my lord." Fletcher came hurrying in triumphant in their quest. "He was hiding in the small alcove cubby. Have to give him credit for getting himself into that small space."

In the hallway stood two of Finna's footmen, and between them was none other than one of the men put in the house by Dameon. Kendrick's temper flared anew. That man needed to pay for his years of apparent abuse of his position, and his lack of regard for the safety of women and children.

"Thank you, Fletcher, well done. I think it best if I take our newest prisoner and question him off the premises. Thank you all for helping."

Birch chose not to go into any detail with Finna present. That way she would not be culpable to anything if pressed. It mattered little; Kendrick knew that plan. The only question left was if Amari would need him to join in. Not running off to Scotland was his choice, but he would see this to the end.

"I will leave you all to your rest," Birch said, rising and glancing at Kendrick, which he acknowledged with a slight nod. They would meet in the morning to deal with the outstanding issue that was Dameon, but not tonight. He took his captive in hand and made his way out to his carriage.

Finna rose first and walked with her arm around her son up the stairs, not saying a word.

As Reginald and Lang made their way out of the room, Lang slowed. "Thank you."

"You are most welcome, but for what?" Kendrick had a hard time understanding his gratefulness, because since Kendrick had resurfaced in Finna's life only trouble followed.

"For being there for her. For not judging us. For taking great lengths to keep everyone alive. She pushes so hard against you because she loves you deeply. In case you wondered."

Reginald smiled a tired smile and guided Lang out of the room.

Amari and Contrell were next, not bothering anymore to hide their amorous intent. Michele stopped in front of Kendrick and waited with an uncomfortable expression.

"Do not worry, Michele, Mr. Birch has things well in hand."

"I am hoping you will travel with us, my friend. Mr. Birch can be sullen and not overly conversational."

Kendrick smiled at the assessment of his friend, but inwardly sighed at the direct request. "I am uncertain if there will be room for me to join you," he hedged.

"I know it is too much to ask, I am sorry."

"No, no, it is not too much. I have taken on seeing you safe to your destination. I will talk with Dylan in the morning and we will get it sorted. Have no worries."

In his own room, Kendrick collapsed in a chair, throwing his head back. Now what? He doubted, once out of her house, that Finna would even accept his suit. Not to mention his unease about her resignation of the entire situation niggled at his brain.

He got up to stoke the fire and noticed the glint of ribbon on the floor in front of his door. A note. He had heard no one walk by. Finna's elegant script sprawled across the page. It was an invitation.

Bryant was a persistent young man, like his mother. There would be no confiding in him about her plan, though. He never could keep a secret.

The realization of it all hit Finna in the parlor when Birch said he now had a plan for extracting Mr. Amari. It was almost over. For them, at any rate, not her. She would be the target of Dameon's wrath when he lost. And there would be retribution. She would need to leave using Amari's escape to shield her own, both from Dameon and Kendrick.

If Kendrick found out her plan, he would not let her leave. He harbored some insane notion that fate had brought them back to each other. Ever the romantic, she was glad life allowed him the hope he still had. She was not so lucky. Finna saw the world as it was, with all the tarnished bits and broken pieces, their once budding love story among the remnants. It was easy to allow herself to be pulled into his lovely fantasy for a moment, though. Now she understood if she wanted any remaining memories, she would have to steal them.

It was uncertain when Birch would whisk away with Amari. He would not trust her with that information any longer. And she was uncertain if Kendrick would travel at least part of the way to see him safely away from Dameon. She hoped he would. It would make her departure so much easier without Kendrick's watchful eye on her. Tonight, however, it was like they were suspended in time. All that was to come, not yet known, and all that had transpired dealt with. If there was a time for her to let her guard down and experience all that love has to offer, it was tonight. If she could let all her walls fall, she would have the memories. It was all she could hope for. Tomorrow would be about planning for them all, tonight could be only about them.

The knock sounded, jumping her from her reverie. "Come in."

"I didn't expect to be summoned," Kendrick said once in the room. "Considering how tonight drained you."

"Honesty is the most tiring of the virtues, but having the weight lifted no longer taxing my countenance is a relief. I wanted to say sorry for all the smoke and mirrors. You didn't deserve it."

"You were protecting Bryant. I could never fault a mother's love, and I have been out of your life for a long time. You were uncertain if you could trust me."

She walked to him, done with words, or at least so many. "Make love to me Kendrick." She stood on her tip toes and took his mouth with hers. No guards, no barriers. With that kiss she told him tonight they would strip bare, exposing all the pain, frustration, and passion they never knew with each other.

The passion blurred the room and their surroundings, enveloping them in a blanket of desire. Not able to restrain her need, Finna ripped at Kendrick's robe, then her own dressing gown to have nothing between them.

Kendrick's passion soared with her own, and he backed her against the closest wall and dined on her naked body. Finna fought herself to hold back, to not feel. She had worked so hard at it, now she feared she could break. Kendrick bent, taking one of her nipples in his mouth and sucking hard, while trailing his other hand to her center and inserting two fingers. The world shifted and all her reserve shattered like a pane of glass. His body read her need and greed and matched it.

Feeling both his hands now on her bottom, she wrapped her legs around his hips without hesitation. In one move he was inside her, leaning her into the wall he moved like a man possessed and she his protege. The spiraling heat made her dizzy with his every thrust.

"God, Finna, you drive me to distraction. I may die from desire here in your arms." One arm bracing them against the wall, the other held her weight from under her.

With every motion, kiss, and lave of his tongue, she spiraled higher. Never, in all her years had she allowed herself to be taken on the wave of desire to the point of no return.

"Kendrick, I can't, you need—" Her words jumbled in her mind, replaced with flames licking at her resolve.

"I know, love, let it go. I've got you," he whispered in her ear, then threw his head back and gave into it himself until she exploded into a million pieces and his mouth crushed down, swallowing her cries of pleasure.

Both panting and sweaty, he stood with her in his arms, her back against the wall for several minutes, until he turned and walked them to the bed, never putting her down. Once on the bed, he continued his onslaught until she rose to the pinnacle of ecstasy again and split into a million pieces. He had taken what was left of her soul. The small piece she kept for herself hidden deep within. He pried it out and took it like a thief in the night. Never would she experience this again, because she would never again be with him.

All of her rash decisions over the years came crashing down on her. Every night filled with loneliness, every time she had to see the hurt in her family's eyes at a social event. Every instance where she envied her friend to the point of hating for circumstances out of her control. This man, this moment boiled down her entire life to now.

Laying in the safety of his arms after, both spent from all the raw emotion torn from them, she had no more to hide. They were both raw.

"Do you ever wonder what we would have been like as a couple?" she asked, making swirls on his chest with the springy hair.

"I would dream about it night after night. You were beautiful, heavy with child, of that there is no question. And you would have been the task master while I would have helped the children plan pranks on their nanny."

She swatted him. "You would not. You clearly spent your life following the rules, while I skirted them at every turn."

"Did you ever wonder what would have happened if we had runaway together?" he asked out of the blue. He never offered that as an option at the time.

"I would have run in a minute," she answered without hesitation, a smile warming her lips.

"I know. That is why I never suggested it. You were safer here, even at arm's length from your family, than you would have been trying to live in a hovel away from your family."

"You can't be certain of that," she pointed out.

"I am, I watched my mother suffer for that very reason. I hated doing what I did, but in my young mind it was the only option." He rolled up on his side and looked down at her then, love clear in his eyes.

Her first reflex was to look away and ignore it. Love had no place between them... Tomorrow, love had no place between them tomorrow. Tonight, it was about it all, love included.

She reached up and cupped his cheek, letting her own love for him show in her eyes. She did not let the irony of it all escape her. Last time he left just when their love began, and now as their love bloomed from all the years of harboring it in secret, she would leave him. She would hurt him, she knew, but he had his daughter and soon a grand-child to dote over. He was still a striking man, who wore his virility on his sleeve. No doubt women of the Ton would slip their addresses in his pockets at every event he attended. He would survive.

She would find a quiet corner of Seville or Barcelona and absorb the calmness, watching her son become the man she knew he would. It was not a poor end to a courtesan. Perhaps not a fairy tale ending, it could make a good tragedy in Shakespeare, or a gothic novel with the sad end for the main characters. The first strings of morning played in the garden.

"Make love to me as the sun comes up?" she asked.

He searched her face for an answer to a question he couldn't voice, but knew her well enough to understand, he kissed her on the tip of her nose.

"There is nothing I could refuse you, love."

In the still darkness of the bedroom, she accepted his love, draining herself dry of emotion and greedily taking all he offered.

CHAPTER 26

hree days later the town house was still a flurry of activity. Finna canceled their plans for any additional events and ignored the summons from Dameon on two occasions, sending back an excuse each time. Kendrick stood in the garden with Birch weighing their options, because now they had two objectives. Escort Michele safely to Belgium and make sure they left Finna unexposed to whatever retribution Dameon may be planning.

"If it were a day's trip with no stops, I would not see the need, but even changing horses throughout it will take well on four days."

"Just so, and Finna cannot be left unguarded for eight days or more," Kendrick pointed out, pacing. "You know she will refuse anyone else."

Dylan nodded. "What then?"

"You won't be fond of my assessment," Kendrick warned.

"I haven't been fond of any of our options. Might as well add yours to our list."

"What if, instead of racing to get Michele out of England, we deal with the threat here on our own grounds?"

"You mean use the object of our protection as bait to protect the woman you love?"

Kendrick jerked around to see that no one was listening, then back at Dylan with a scowl. "You were the one who recruited Finna for this erstwhile assignment. I am trying to save everyone involved."

"Fair enough," Dylan chuckled.

"What are you finding humor in?"

"You," he said, slapping him on the back. "You are so in love you stink from it, but I guess that is what twenty years of pining does to a man."

Kendrick only grunted in reply. It would improve his mood if the object of his love at least hinted at her plans. As it stood, their night of passion after her dinner party was the last they shared. It was not clear what she was planning, but he understood in his bones that he wouldn't like it.

"If we did what you are suggesting we would need to appraise every one of their plans. I will not put someone in danger without them understanding."

Kendrick glared at Birch. "Now see here, I spoke to Finna that there could be attempts on his life. She withheld the fact that Dameon had her by rights."

"Fair enough," Kendrick conceded. "A situation must be set up that there be no time for Dameon to send some of his henchmen, not that they have been successful. I would have left them off days ago, but he is not one to get his hands dirty."

"I agree. If we don't make a situation such that Dameon thinks he may lose we will never catch him."

"I promised Bryant I would work with him on his shooting today, so once we have this set, I must attend to him," Kendrick said once they seemed to have a viable plan.

"He's a good enough lad," Dylan commented.

"He is a very good sort. I quite like spending time with him."

"Imagine, you having a son at your age. Bouncing your grandchild on your knee and teaching politics to Bryant."

The two men made their way back to the house. Kendrick had to admit the image Dylan explained was one he hoped for, but that would be up to Finna.

The topic of their discussion emerged from the kitchen door. "There you are," Bryant waved. "Mr. Birch, how are you today? Any updates?"

"I think we have the workings of a plan, but we will need to talk to your mother first," Dylan explained.

"Good luck. She has been too busy for anything in the last few days, and when I get a moment with her, she is a bear."

Dylan laughed and ruffled Bryant's hair. "Thank you for the warning, I will enter with caution."

They said goodbye to Dylan, and he left them in the garden. "I asked a footman to bring the target and the pistols out. I hope that was not presumptuous," Bryant said with enthusiasm.

"Not at all, it will save time doing it now," Kendrick assured him. Within a minute a footman arrived with the pistols. While they waited for the target to be set in the back of the garden, Kendrick fished a bit.

"Do you know what is upsetting your mother so? I have noticed she is off."

"Haven't the foggiest. She never tells me anything. To her I will forever be a boy of five in leading strings." The frustration was evident in the poor boy.

"It is difficult for a mother to see her child grow up. She cannot protect you once you are left to make your own decisions. And all her fears that she herself didn't make the right choices in the raising will show up then. Just be aware that whatever your mother does, she does with love."

Bryant nodded at that. The target ready, Kendrick handed him a pistol, and they took turns taking aim and firing for a bit. When it was a moment of quiet while they reloaded Bryant jumped in. "Lord Harwich."

"Please, call me Kendrick, at least when we are in private."

"Kendrick," he corrected, "do you think once you leave, I could continue correspondence with you? You seem to know my mother well enough to understand things others might not."

The question warmed his heart. "I would like that very much. Thank you for thinking of me."

"I love Mother, but at an age there are things that she just doesn't understand."

Kendrick was sure that Bryant's mother understood many things about the male sex that other mothers did not, but he didn't point that out.

"I was impressed by the way you instructed me to handle any rude remarks against her. I feel that a man needs someone like you to have an ear."

Kendrick laughed at the wisdom spouting from such a young man. They continued shooting for another hour until

Kendrick was certain Bryant could handle a pistol in an emergency. He would not tell either the boy or Finna that was his plan, but it worked.

Once back in the parlor, Kendrick made sure Bryant saw where in the parlor he tucked the pistols, and also taught him how to load and ready a pistol for firing, so they were both charged. Now, here's hoping Bryant would be as quick thinking on his feet as he portrayed.

After dinner the entire family unit settled in the parlor waiting to hear what Birch and Kendrick had come up with.

"You mean to make us all bait in your little fox hunt?"

Kendrick didn't argue with Finna's estimation.

"If by bait, you mean we are making you part of our plan to see Dameon taken care of once and for all, then yes," Birch answered with as much disdain as he was handed.

"Listen, we," Kendrick motioned to both him and Birch, "understand that it puts the very people we are attempting to protect in the direct line of fire, but it will allow us to control the parameters and not be divided in our endeavor, which would happen if we left with Michele right now."

Finna glared openly, while Amari sat in quiet contemplation. He was no stranger to these situations, as they had smuggled him out of Italy and then smuggled to their care. Finna, on the other hand, was not used to anyone dictating any part of her life.

"May I speak?" Bryant asked in a quiet voice.

"No," Finna answered.

"Yes," Kendrick said at the same time. Glaring more at him, she nodded to Bryant to go ahead.

"Well, I think it makes more sense to lure the braggart here. We all are familiar with the house and its hidey holes, we know where things are, and there will be all of us instead of mother and me, and then Michele and Mr. Birch and Kendrick."

Finna sucked in a breath to call him on his use of Kendrick's Christian name, but Kendrick caught her eye and shook his head.

"Thank you, Bryant, but I would feel better not putting any of us in danger," Finna pointed out.

"I am sure we all feel that way, but it doesn't look like that is going to be an option. Sometimes in school when dealing with a difficult set of figures it is more prudent to just handle it head on than attempt to get around the calculation," he answered his mother.

Kendrick noted the weary smile on Finna's face as she gave into her son's clear logic. "You are correct, of course, my dear."

"Then it is decided?" Dylan asked, looking around the room. But everyone knew the only one needed to agree was Finna.

"If possible, I would prefer Lang and Reginald take Bryant out of harm's way—"

"Mother, no!" he shouted. Kendrick should side with Finna to help his cause, but this was not his discussion to have an opinion on.

"Bryant, I can't have you—"

"No, I refuse. You must see me as the man I am becoming. Soon enough I will have my majority and be out in the world. You cannot continue to protect me from every slight or danger. You may banish me, but I will run from Lang and come back. Wouldn't it be better if you knew where I was instead of worrying where I might be?"

Kendrick and Dylan shared an appreciative glance. There were few men in power in all of England who would so easily go toe to toe with Lady Sarrafinna as Bryant was doing now. He would do well in the world indeed.

"I swear I did not spank you enough as a boy," she complained. "Very well. Anyone who wishes to remain may, but if this is not something you relish, please do not feel compelled to remain. Both Mr. Amari and I were familiar with the dangers when we took on our roles the rest of you are not beholden to us."

Kendrick nodded in agreement. "Finna is correct. If you wish to leave, we ask that you do it tomorrow because after we put our story out, we cannot promise when the strike will happen."

They decided that Lang and Reginald would leave to make it appear as if the house party was breaking up. Reginald suggested that, but Kendrick was aware Reginald worked hard to protect Lang from the cruelties of the world as he would like to protect Finna. To his frustration, Lang was more willing to lean on his partner than Finna.

Birch and he stayed late in the parlor to set the rules for the game now that they knew the players. By the time Birch left, the candles were burning themselves out. The hallway upstairs was dark, but without seeing where he was, his feet slowed at Finna's door. He wanted nothing more than to sleep one more night with her safe in his arms, but he would not be welcome.

Once this situation was out of the way, her stubborn self be dammed, he was making her his. To the world, she had been his for twenty years already.

CHAPTER 27

"Golding, catch this please and hand it to Reginald to go in the carriage with us," Lang called down from the top landing as he let fly a pillow he liked to use on the bumpier roads.

"Of course, mi lord, shall I just huck it at him, or would you rather I walk it out?" Golding asked in a cheeky tone.

Finna hated seeing her friends leaving, but again, none of them realized it would be their last farewell. She sat at her writing desk trying to find the words to explain to her family why, after reuniting with them, she would leave the country. After which she would need to pen a letter even more difficult.

Kendrick left before dawn, and Birch was off as well. She would only admit it to herself, but she felt safer when Kendrick was nearby. That realization last night in her room alone was enough to make her rise and begin making a pile of clothes for packing. Loving him she had dealt with long ago and to this point buried it deep, but needing him was another thing all together. If she allowed herself to need him, she would never survive. The funny thing about a broken heart, when it healed the scars were hard and stiff and difficult to break again in the same place. But, when you allowed someone to make you need them, that is when it could do more damage.

"And we are off, my dear," Lang said as he strolled into the room, a big smile on his face.

"I do always hate it when the two of you leave. You take a piece of my heart every time," she said, rising to engulf him in a hug.

"Well, I do wish we could stay and watch the excitement, but this will be an indication that you are vulnerable, then that brute of a man of yours can come in and save you all."

"Brute of a man?"

"Yes, my dear Lord Harwich, I do like watching him save the day. Do not let him get out of your web. Keep him around this time." He hugged her again and didn't give her time to argue.

Finna walked to the front step to wave them off. The couple had been her rock through many years. Without her parents' love to witness daily, she may have forgotten that love that strong still existed, but they reminded her. No matter how difficult or dangerous it could be, they showed her that a love that strong was possible. Not for her, but for others. She hoped that Bryant would find a love that strong with someone. She had to believe it possible.

"Finna? Finna, where are—oh, there you are," Contrell called as she wandered in and out of the parlor.

"I was just waving off Regi and Lang. It will be quiet in

here with them gone." She walked back into the parlor and took up her pen again. "What was it you wanted?"

"Well," she started, then stopped and walked to the parlor door and shut it. Privacy was never something Contrell worried about in anything.

"What is it, Contrell?" Finna asked, worry spiraling up her spine.

Contrell perched on the edge of the settee and Finna joined her, taking her hand to reassure her. "What have I missed?" Finna asked. "I am so sorry if I missed something, I am so caught up in my own troubles—"

"No, no dear, this is nothing like that, and you are never too caught up in your own troubles to forget those you love. I, I need to tell you something and I am uncertain how to do it."

"Well, just tell me. Even if it is bad news, I would rather know."

"It is not bad," Contrell assured her. The older woman's cheeks blazed red, which was not a good look for a red head, even if it was more grey than red these days. "Michele has asked me to accompany him to Belgium."

Finna blinked, then blinked some more, trying to find words. "Contrell, that is wonderful—wait, he isn't trying to make you his—"

"Wife, he asked me to marry him once we get settled, and he feels it is safe." Finna's dearest friend said the words with sparkling tears of happiness in her eyes.

She pulled Contrell into a tight hug and held her. Of all the people who deserved a happy ending, it was Contrell. And Finna had an idea Michele would treat her like a queen for the rest of her days.

"After all this time you were holding out for an Italian," Finna joked with her.

"Well, I do prefer his accent to the French," she reasoned. "Now, what about you? I am not leaving until I know things with you and Lord Harwich are solidified."

"Really Contrell, that is not an avenue I can allow myself down. We enjoyed each other these past weeks, but it cannot go further."

"Why not?"

Finna shot her friend an exasperated look, which was returned by a perturbed one. "It is not destined as you all seem to think. He has aspirations that I will impede."

"Pish posh, that is an excuse only you believe. After all, it is because of you half the men in power are where they are."

"Yes, but you know as well as I men have short memories when it comes to their success and they would just as easily use my past against Kendrick as for him."

Contrell shook her head. "You are a foolish girl who will end up alone if you are not careful."

That comment hit a bit too close to Finna's own thoughts and fears. Without better judgement she countered. "It will not matter in a day's time, because Bryant and I will be on a boat headed to Spain." Contrell gasped, bringing Finna to the realization of what she had just done. "And do not say a word to Kendrick. Not a word, not an utterance. Do you understand me?"

"No, I never understood you. I never understood why you have so much yet spit in the face of it. The only person who will make you miserable is yourself. All of this will be over soon and there is no reason you can't be happy for once."

Before Finna could come to her own defense, Contrell

stood and marched out of the parlor. It was not lost on Finna that Contrell made no agreement to keep what she knew to herself. It mattered not, the passage was paid for and the arrangements were set.

The letter to her family sat waiting for the last few lines, so she went back to it. The last lines were the hardest. There would be some very difficult last moments in the next few days, so she would need to get a thicker spine than this.

"Mother," Bryant greeted her as he strolled in. The house had grown quiet and his voice in the void jumped her.

"Oh, Bryant, you startled me. How are you today?"

"I am fine, I was going to take the pistols in the garden and practice if that is all right."

"I would rather you wait until Kendrick or Birch are here to assist you," she said in as pleading a voice as she could.

"I am deuced bored, Mother. I—"

"Lady Sarrafinna, I hope I am not interrupting."

From behind Bryant a cold deep voice washed over her, leaving a panic in its wake that was acid on her tongue. Dameon. Where was Golding when she needed him to appear?

"Mr. Chamberlain, what a surprise." She rose to greet him and put herself in front of Bryant. Just having them both in the same room made her skin prickle with fear.

"And you must be Master Bryant." He ignored Finna and reached around her to shake her son's hand.

"I am, I am sorry, but I do not know you, Mr. Chamberlain. My mother keeps me locked away in the country or at school as much as she can, I am afraid."

"It is because she loves you, my boy. She knows what a

cruel world it can be. I am certain your mother is the best of the best."

"What is it I can do for you, Mr. Chamberlain?' She asked, diverting his attention back to her. She glanced at Bryant and knew he saw the resemblance. With them in the same room, it was hard to miss how much the son looked like the father.

"Well," he said, moving back to the parlor door and shutting it with a deafening click of the latch. That door had been closed a total of two times since she owned the house. The thought flitted through her mind for no reason. "I am afraid I have learned you have been keeping secrets from me."

From where it came, she didn't know, but suddenly Dameon stood in her parlor holding a gun on them. If there was ever a time to faint it was not now, but Lord, she wished she could close her eyes and have this go away. However, if there was one thing, she needed to make sure she protected Bryant from it was the evil that was his father. She could not fail this one. Again, she stepped in front of Bryant, this time making sure if the gun fired it would have to go clear through her to get to him.

"Dameon, is that really necessary? You and I have always been able to speak cordially."

"We have, but of late I am getting the impression that your choice of house guest has filled your head with ideas a woman like you should not have."

"I say that smacks very close to an insult. You will not insult my mother. Gun or no." Bryant came around her and stood his full height, which proved in a few more years he would tower over Dameon, as it was, they were equal in size.

"Bryant, no, it is fine—"

"No, Mother, it is not. I have a feeling this man would treat any woman badly, but you have thought you had little recourse to fight back and I will not allow it in my presence."

"Bryant, for the love of everything for once in your life just listen," she snapped, done with all outspoken troublesome men. They could all go to the devil.

Both men stopped staring off and instead looked at her with matching expressions of utter surprise. It was just enough time for Finna to once again step in front of Bryant and put herself in harm's way.

"The boy has nerve. He'll need it to get by in a world where his mother is a whore, and he is a by-blow ignored and reviled by all."

Grabbing Bryant's forearm, she forcibly held him back. "What do you want, Dameon? I know it is not that you had precious time in your day to come have a tender family reunion. Get on with it."

"No, in fact I tried my damnedest to remain as far from this mess as I could, but your heathen group of rejects would not be towed. The plan was to ruin both Harwich and Birch, and when Birch thought to bring you into the mix, well if you died by a stray bullet who would care. Nice and tidy. Then, when I heard your bastard was in town, the moment crystalized. If I could arrange for him to die as well, I would no longer have my seed running around in a useless vessel any longer."

"Finna? I'm sorry to interrupt but—"

CHAPTER 28

ear gripped Kendrick when he walked through the door. Finna stood, as one would expect, between Bryant and Dameon with his gun. Reinforcements would arrive, but not soon enough.

"Ah, Harwich, nice of you to join us."

"Just leave Kendrick, leave now," Finna shouted, before Dameon turned and glared at her.

"Harwich will not leave you. He loves you, and probably your bastard as well. He has an overexaggerated sense of loyalty and responsibility. Precisely why he has been so easy to lead over the years. Come, come join us." Dameon smiled, which looked more like a grimace.

Kendrick put his hands out to his side and walked around the settee and table arrangement.

"Are you harmed?" he asked Finna, making eye contact with her. The wild fear he saw in her eyes punctuated the severity of their predicament.

"No, I am not."

"And you?" he asked Bryant.

"He is hearty as well, Harwich, stop talking," Dameon interrupted.

Kendrick came around and stood next to Finna, shielding Bryant. It only took one look with the two of them in the room to make the connection. Dameon was the man Finna thought she loved. He was Bryant's father. All the pieces clicked into place.

"What do you want?" Kendrick asked, hoping to keep him talking and not considering murder.

"The world," Dameon said, waving the gun with a flourish, "but I will settle for an elevated post in the government to start with."

"This is about you getting a promotion?" Anger flared, tamping down the fear for the moment. All the people he hurt or put in danger over a better job?

"Well, that and ruining you, of course. That has been my long-held goal."

"Why?" Kendrick didn't understand why someone would spend their life trying to bring him harm. He was no one.

"Ha, you do not understand, I am sure. You were protected by the ugliness of life, by those who loved you."

The only person who protected him was his mother, and she did not do a bang-up job of it, for her efforts. "What in bloody hell are you talking about? I was raised a street urchin at best, and a dock rat on bad days. I am certain the world's ugliness did not escape me."

"No, brother, you are wrong." Dameon said the words and let them hang in the air. In the silence, the chill that caught

Kendrick earlier returned. "That's right, you and I had the same sire. I was all of four when he left my mother to marry a debutante he fell in love with. One day he was there, then the next we never saw him again."

Just as Kendrick opened his mouth to reply, two gun shots rang through the house rattling the windows. Finna gasped and stiffened next to him.

"What in hell—" Kendrick looked around.

"Finally, it is done!" Dameon shouted with a look of triumph on his face. "Oh, you didn't think I came here alone?" He looked at Finna. "I was a distraction, a decoy for the real danger. Now that Amari has been dispatched, those who do not approve of a unified Italy will pay me handsomely, and I will no longer be left to rot in the damned foreign office."

Finna put her hand over her mouth, tears spilling now unabandoned. "Contrell. Contrell was with him. Oh God, Kendrick, they killed them both."

Dameon laughed out loud at Finna's pain. Never had Kendrick wanted to cause another person's death more than he wanted to rip Dameon limb from limb, but to win the day he must keep his calm.

"All will be well, Finna, just hold on."

She nodded through her tears and drew in a staying breath.

Kendrick kept pushing Dameon for information to keep him talking. "I was not aware that I had any siblings. It would have brought great comfort to us both to have someone to lean on, but I assure you when our father died, we were not in any better shape than you and your mother."

"I am aware. You see, my mother held a hatred for our father and your mother until the day she died. We often found ourselves near your mother's pasties cart. On several occasions, she even gave us free food. My mother would not have denied me a full belly, but the pride it required her to swallow that putrid food affected her."

"How, then, did you get to school? I was not even afforded such a luxury until I found a benefactor?" Kendrick asked, interested in the journey that makes someone come so far in their lives only to fall into madness as Dameon obviously had.

"The only saving grace for me was the fact that when my father left, he left all his belongings, and the deed to property, however small, on the edge of a small farm outside of town. My mother couldn't read, so didn't understand what it was. I, however, spent three years being taught to read by a woman who saw it as her duty to come into the dregs and educate the poor." The last Dameon said through gritted, gnarled teeth. Even such a kindness he saw as something dirty. "I knew enough to understand I could gain funds. However, I was about to be evicted from my mother's home. So, I went to the closest landowner and offered to sell. Then I found a small solicitor's office and begged for a position to learn and a place to live. They gave me a room in the building's attic, and I worked to learn anything I could after paying them all my money from the sale of the land. From there my employer knew someone in the government looking for a secretary, and from there you know the rest."

"Amazing," was all Kendrick could say. It amazed him how a man with so many paths afforded to him would wish it all away just to get revenge on an innocent soul.

"Remarkable actually, that both of us began as we did and now stand here in the parlor of a duke's daughter, though a whore, but the breeding is there nonetheless. Pity she was already tarnished when I found her, or I might have married into my life's dream. You made her so vulnerable I easily came in with a kind word here, reassurance there, but soon realized her reputation could only harm my aspirations. It was quite the coup, though, don't you think? I not only was able to become your superior and dictate your actions and decisions, but I also could have had the life you so desperately wanted."

Next to him, Finna sucked in a shaking breath, trying as she might to not break down. Kendrick on the other hand needed to move this forward. Dameon may have been smart enough to put himself in a position to play him like an instrument, but now Kendrick and he were on the same page, and Kendrick had something Dameon had lost knowledge of a long time ago, the love of a family.

"Well, then. You have what you came for. Amari has been killed, you will get paid, there is no reason for us all to remain here. I admit defeat, brother. You were the smarter and more cunning of the two of us. Well played."

Dameon raised the gun more fully at them. "I am afraid this does not end well for you. I mean, I would be a fool to let you all live. By killing you now, it will get swept up in the Amari business and I will be the one who finds the tragic scene. I will say that I stopped over to check how things were going and found you all dead."

Finna reached her hand over and took his own, squeezing it. He squeezed back, trying to decide if it made more sense to dive for Dameon or to step in front of Finna to take the bullet for her. He was well out of options.

Just then, two loud cracks rang out and smoke filled the room. In that second Kendrick thought his life was over. His life with Finna never meant to be.

CHAPTER 29

*T*he smoke burned Finna's throat while bile acrid and bitter rose to meet it. Her loud cry rang her ears, but she was removed from the scene as every regret she held spilled out. In the end, she failed them. In a second, with two bullets, her world was over.

"Finna? Finna talk to me love, are you hit?" She heard Kendrick's voice, strong and forceful. She blinked the tears from her vision to focus on his face, his beautiful, handsome, weathered face. He wasn't dead, but—

"Yes, but what happened?" As the room cleared, she saw Dameon laying out in her parlor, a red stain spreading across his cream-colored waistcoat in two places. Kendrick and Finna turned and standing behind them was Bryant and behind him to his left stood Contrell in a dressing robe. Both holding pistols. Both white faced and in shock.

"Contrell, you aren't dead," Finna cried, but strode straight to Bryant standing, still holding the pistol at the ready. Kendrick took the gun from his hands and it was only then that her son looked into her eyes and wrapped himself around her.

"It is done, sweeting. You saved us all. You brave man," she assured him. He hugged her tighter.

Kendrick took the other gun from Contrell and led her to a chair where she collapsed still staring at Dameon's body and the blood now oozing on to the floor.

"Contrell, is Amari hurt?" he asked her.

It took her a full thirty clicks of the mantel clock before she looked away from the body and up at Kendrick. "Michele is fine. He is in the priest hole, waiting. A, a man burst into his room, we were caught off guard. He had a gun—" she was rambling, but Finna didn't want to stop her for fear she would not be able to finish.

Kendrick prodded her a bit. "We heard the shots and thought the worst, but we could not come to your aid."

"Yes, we assumed as much," she acknowledged. "I have always carried a revolver in my reticule for protection. Today, though, was the first time I used it. My bag was on the night table and I grabbed it and shot. He shot as well, but mine hit him and threw off his aim." She turned and looked at Finna. "I am sorry, love, but you will need to have the plaster repaired in that room."

A laugh escaped Finna. It came out more as a strangled mix of a cry and a laugh, but it was a relief. Bryant pulled away from her and went to Kendrick who pulled him into a fierce embrace, then Bryant moved to hug Contrell. From the priest hole hidden in the wall next to her writing desk, Amari emerged wide eyed.

"Is everyone safe?" he asked.

A resounding crash came from somewhere deep in the house, sending renewed panic through Finna and everyone else.

"Go," Kendrick pointed for the priest hole. "All of you. Do not come out unless I tell you."

Finna took Contrell's arm, as the woman was not steady on her feet still and the four of them shuffled into the hiding place. Before Finna pulled the door shut.

"I love you," she said to Kendrick. She could not take one more moment away from her chance. "I need you to know, whatever happens from this point forward, I have always loved you."

He kissed the side of her head, and she felt him breathe in her scent. "I know. And we will have plenty of time to discuss it later. I love you too." And the door shut, leaving them in inky darkness.

The silence made the waiting worse, as no noise from outside their place in the wall came through, until a few minutes later and many voices filled the outer parlor, all talking at once. Then the door opened, and light flooded the space. Finna's eyes ached from the sudden brightness and she blinked, trying to see. Kendrick stood, holding the door, and the other voices were those of her staff.

"That braggart locked us away in the food cellar and slid the massive dish hutch in front. We were awhile before we could topple it," Golding explained.

"I am just glad you are unharmed," Finna said, feeling grateful it was over.

"What in bloody hell?" They all turned to see Birch and the Duke of Rygate standing in the doorway to the parlor, looking at the now very dead Dameon.

"It is over," Finna declared, feeling the weight of it all lifting.

"Finna, my dear, are you harmed?" her father asked, walking past the body and through the throng of servants, taking her into an embrace. Not since she was a young woman of eighteen had she smelled the mix that was her father. Expensive shave cream that her mother still imported from Spain, along with his cologne and sweet cherry root cigarillos. She was a young girl of five again, with some type of calamity that only a father's hug could cure. The tears rose again, but this time happy ones.

"We are all unharmed, Father. Today only those who deserved to be harmed were." He kissed the top of her head but didn't let go.

"Well, Harwich, what happened?" he asked.

"Bryant and Ms. Contrell saved the day. Bryant saw where I had stored the dueling pistols we had been practicing with and at some point got one of them, and Contrell snuck down through the priest hole and took up the other. When well enough distracted they both shot, and it was done."

Rygate stepped from Finna and walked over to Bryant. "Thank you, my boy, for saving my most beloved daughter. I believe it is well pastime we were introduced. I am your grandfather, the Duke of Rygate."

Bryant stood silent, looking from Finna to his grandfather to Kendrick, who nodded and smiled. Bryant bowed low to his grace and then grabbed him into a heavy embrace which made everyone laugh, including the duke. But it wasn't to last, as Dylan cleared his throat.

"I know we all would like to think this business done, but

we are still a day away from getting Amari out safely, and those who hired Dameon will still try to get the job done."

"You are correct," Kendrick agreed. "What now?"

"Simple, you will all come to Rygate castle with me." The duke spoke up, silencing the group. "It makes the most sense. We have a full staff, so put with your staff," he motioned to Finna's servants, "there would be added protection. It is also out of the city and closer to your destination. It is decided. I will go back to our townhouse and get the carriages moving and inform your mother, you and your—" he faltered a bit, but rallied. "Your family will join us. You can pack quick enough for a few days, I trust?"

"Yes, thank you," Finna said, in awe of how easy it was for her father to step back in as a protector, but she was learning, as a parent, one never left that role.

With all decided, the duke left to arrange things on his end while Birch and Kendrick devised how to keep the death of a foreign secretary as quiet as possible, at least for now.

Since Finna and Bryant were already packed for her escape to Spain, she had nothing to do but assist her friend. In Contrell's rooms, it seemed a world away from the chaos they just witnessed.

"I am going with him, you know?" Contrell said.

"I know. I knew you were before this, but the way he looks at you, with such love. You would be a fool not to," Finna assured her friend.

"You don't need me anymore, dear," she said, sitting next to her on the bed. "You have your family back, Bryant, and not to mention that man who looks at you with just as much ardent love as Amari does me."

Contrell was correct, Finna's life had shifted in just the

last few hours. Her head spun from it. But was it really all that different? The Ton would not forget what she was. Bryant was still a bastard, and now a bastard son who killed his father, with a whore as a mother. Could a fortune and a connection to a duke really cancel that all out for him? Then there was Kendrick. Could she dare taking the chance to let their love grow as it may? Did she even deserve a chance to love him again? Her sins were great. Could their love be greater?

CHAPTER 30

he great hall in Rygate castle hummed with the guests who ascended on it in short order. Before Finna knew what happened, Kendrick had called for his carriage, her carriage, and her hack to be brought round, but then there were several other hacks lining the street for her staff as well and then they were off.

Finna and Bryant led the way with their servants following behind, while from behind the townhouse, Contrell, Amari, and Dylan snuck away in the hack all to descend hours later in the country. She looked at the mess of carriages with bags and trunks littering the courtyard but didn't find Kendrick. He wasn't in the hall either. He had not said he wasn't coming, but then he no longer had to protect her or Michele. His job was done.

"He will be here. He had to sort things out with his household and pack," Dylan said as he came up beside her.

"What? Who?" she replied, trying to sound oblivious.

"Right," was all he said and walked away.

The duchess entered like a storm of will and metered out orders and room assignments, sending the once unorganized group into a frenzy of dedicated tasks. Finna smiled at it all. She and her mother always had their differences in how they wanted the world to view them, but her mother was a rock. Meek and quiet until the situation called for her not to be.

"And you need a hot bath and a nap, my dear. Same for you, I am afraid." Her mother came up to her with Bryant not far behind. Finna smiled and warmed at the thought of a hot scented bath, but Bryant recoiled at his grandmother's idea, which she had already expected with her comment. "I ordered the water to be started ahead of us leaving, as some of our servants traveled ahead to start preparing. They just informed me your bath is ready in your room, all it needs is to be filled and one has been set up in the room next to yours for your son." She looked at Bryant with tears in her eyes. Another mark against Finna for keeping her child from his family. A family that would clearly not care one whit about the circumstances of his birth.

"Thank you, Mother. I would love a bath. I am tired."

The duchess pulled her into an embrace that said far more than words and went to order the bath to be filled. In thirty minutes time, Finna relaxed in the steaming water scented with lavender and rose water and a mind whirring with the decisions she needed to make.

"Would you care for help?" Kendrick's deep voice filled the void that was her childhood room.

She turned to see him, still in his riding clothes, dirty from the road. "I wasn't sure you would come," she said with a smile so wide it pulled on her cheeks.

He walked in and shed clothes as he went. First his hat, then his greatcoat, then outer coat and waistcoat, until he knelt by the tub shirtless, with just his breeches and boots. "Where would you think I would be?"

She shrugged, allowing him to take the sponge from her hands and begin washing her body. "I thought perhaps Dylan told you he needed your assistance."

"I am not one to not see a project through to its completion. And he still needs me to help him get Amari safely to Scotland and on that ship."

It wasn't a declaration of undying love, but it was Kendrick. She would take his company any way she was able.

He didn't say another word, but took his bathing service seriously, not leaving an inch of skin unattended. Then he moved behind her with the soap and dripped water over her head, washing her hair. Had she not wanted to catalog every moment to her memory, she easily could have fallen asleep under his hands.

"How are you holding up?" he asked in a gentle voice that washed over her nerves.

"Better than I was. The bath helped," she answered with her eyes closed. Her head lolled at the bend in the tub, her hair heavy hanging over dripping into a basin, so she was not ready for the sloshing of the water, when Kendrick, naked, stepped in and slid down around her legs.

"You looked so relaxed, I thought it a waste to leave this half of the tub unused. Do you mind?" he asked, a devilish crooked smile. One she would never forget. It brought her back to his face, so much younger with fewer lines and wrinkles, but still his eyes held the sparkle of youth.

"Well, it stands to reason, so the servants' work wasn't for not. It is perfectly reasonable."

They spent the better part of an hour, turning the servants knocks away twice in that time, enjoying each other in the bath. As they lay in the now cooled water, her reclined back against his chest, with his knees on either side of her poking out, she had the distinct feeling of being where she belonged. The unsettling feeling made her itch to move and gain her footing, but the languid circles he made with his finger on the top of her breast were enough to hold her down.

"You and I must make some decisions," he said out of the blue. He was not wrong, but the cocoon they created in the bath was not where she wanted to ruin their peace.

"I know of no decisions I have yet to make."

He ran his hand under the breast he had been toying with and took it in his hand. "You, my lady, have avoided this for far too long." He bent and kissed the side of her neck.

Before she could stop them, the words tumbled from her mouth. "I am leaving for Spain in two days."

However, it was drowned out by him saying. "I love you, Finna. Marry me."

Silence fell in the room. Finna could feel him behind her, every muscle reacting, but still he said nothing.

"I have to leave. It is the only way," she tried to explain.

He met her explanation with a bitter laugh. "I will follow you." He said the words as a declaration of intent.

She turned then, sloshing cold water up the sides of the tub. "You cannot. You have your career, your daughter and soon to be grandchild. It makes no sense for you to leave."

"It does if you will not be here to share it with," was his simple answer.

She looked into his eyes. If she wanted to find a speck of doubt, she wouldn't see it there. She turned back around, settling into his embrace to fortify her argument, but doubt seeped in like the chill from the water. Did they have the right to even expect a chance at love? Could she be welcomed back into her family and their lives without repercussions? And what about Bryant?

"Bryant can't stay here, there are too many blocks to his success—"

"Bryant is a smart, capable, and proving today to be a brave young man, with a personal fortune almost as large as his grandfather's. He will make his way in this world just fine regardless of where he is, but here—here he has a family that loves him." He ran both his hands up and down her arms, making it difficult for her to keep her train of thought. "If there is one lesson I am taking away from all of this, is that life would be easier for us all if only we had strong families to cushion the hard blows of life."

"But your career. If I stayed and you married me, I fear it would hold you back from your aspirations." She tried once more to reason.

"My aspirations were to gain back my family's title and sit in parliament as the marquess. I have met all of my aspirations. Nothing you could do now or in your past will take those from me."

She sighed. He would thwart her every reason she knew, so the one argument she had left would have to open his eyes.

"Kendrick. The choices I have made in life have hurt all

that I care about. For that reason alone, I do not deserve to be happy, not to mention all the sins in and around those decisions. I am the last woman in England that should have a happy ending."

He took her shoulders and guided her around to look at him. His eyes were deadly serious, and his frown showed his annoyance. "You listen to me. Sarrafinna Lennox, every person no matter their sin deserves redemption. I don't give one whit about your sins of the past. Your choices made this," he waved a hand, "possible, when I finally chose to do what my heart has desired for years. I don't believe your sins are any greater than my own; trying to make a marriage work with another while I refused to give up on my love for you. We may both be damned to hell, but we can be together and try to make amends to those we love, or we can go to the winds and die without even trying. Marry me, Sarrafinna Lennox, I have already gotten permission from your father and your son."

For the hundredth time in a day the tears fell unbidden down her cheeks. "What did they say?"

"You father said I could not back out this time, or he would meet me on the dueling field. And Bryant said it was time that his mother had someone to make her tough decisions with her and not be alone."

"Well then, I guess it is already decided."

The next hour was a blur of kisses and wet limbs, but when they finally emerged from the freezing tub, Finna was no longer a fallen woman.

As they dried, she began to plan. "I guess I will talk to mother about getting the banns read."

"Yes, well about that," he interrupted.

"About what?"

"Well, one reason I was a few hours behind was that I needed to make a detour to acquire a special license. Also, while we have been up here, your father left to find an officiant. If you will still have me, I would rather not wait one more minute. Neither of us is growing any younger. If there is one bit of wisdom, I plan to hand down, it is that every minute you are allowed with your loved ones needs to be counted and cherished." He walked up and pulled her to him, kissing her nose.

Would there ever be a time she could say no to him? "Well then, Lord Harwich, what are we waiting for? We have a marriage to start."

EPILOGUE

The next morning Kendrick woke to a bustling castle. He woke alone in the bed he and Finna shared the night before on their wedding night. Well, they slept little, but what transpired was a washing away of their collective pasts and christening of their future together.

"Good morning." Bryant beamed with a plate filled precariously high, threatening to topple sausages across the table if not handled correctly.

"Good morning, Bryant, I see you are replenishing your stores."

"Yes sir," he said, unsure. They had yet to discuss what he should call his new father.

Kendrick loaded his plate and joined his stepson. "Bryant, you may call me whatever you choose. I want you to be comfortable."

"Is it wrong that I am uncertain?" the boy asked, with soulful eyes.

"Of course not. You have been thrown into much lately. Until you decide I do not foresee a situation where you would need to call me anything in particular."

"Thank you."

"Have you seen your mother this morning?"

"She was helping Contrell get the last of her things loaded on the hack," he said around a mouthful of egg.

That's right, Finna had told him last night that Contrell would go with Amari. She would miss her friend terribly. Then the thought of four of them fitting into that small vehicle for the long ride to Scotland made him groan. He wanted nothing more than to find a quiet corner of the vast castle and lock Finna away for a month with no interruptions, but duty called, then they could find a place to hide and just be together.

After eating, he took a fresh cup of coffee with him to the courtyard. What he saw when he got there was not the hack, but the duke's finest carriage with six horses attached that would make any horseman in England drool with excitement.

"Oh, there you are," Finna greeted when she looked up and spied him on the steps. "I'm glad you didn't miss them."

"Miss them?" He thought they were waiting for him.

The Duke of Rygate came to stand next to him. "Son-in-law, good morning."

"Your Grace," Kendrick greeted.

"I do not think it appropriate for my daughter to wed, then be abandoned the next day all in the name of duty. Your services are no longer needed," the duke declared. "I spoke with Dylan last night and by using my most regal carriage and adding several of my most proficient men, they will be well protected in name and sheer force of manpower. And six horses of excellent stock will also move them along better than one of questionable lineage."

Kendrick chuckled at how easily his grace slipped into the role of father, protector, and got things done.

Kendrick walked down the steps and to the group milling about.

"I will ship those other dresses to you," Finna was saying as the two women hugged. "And I will send a footman to personally deliver your note to your sister."

"Thank you, my dear. I am so happy to be leaving you in such a state. You deserve every happiness you are offered from here out. Do not forget that, love."

Finna stepped back, eyes glistening with unshed tears for a woman whose protection saved her many times over, Kendrick could only imagine. Then, without warning, Contrell grabbed him, pulling him into a fierce hug, almost spilling his coffee.

"I knew you would be back; I knew it. You love her like every day is your last day. She deserves at least that," she whispered in his ear.

"Never worry of that, Contrell," he assured her.

Dylan came around and the two men shook hands. He wished Dylan the best, but secretly hoped the man would find another vocation. He was to the point he deserved a quiet life in the country with the only untoward thing to deal with would be a fox stealing the eggs in the hen house.

Finna stood tucked into Kendrick's side as they waved their friends a farewell watching the carriage majestically disappear from view.

"You know, with Contrell leaving, it seems like that entire

part of my life has been wiped away. It is an odd feeling," Finna admitted.

Kendrick kissed the top of her head and turned her into a full embrace, looking down at the woman's face he envisioned in his mind every day for the last twenty years. He understood exactly what she meant. They had a new beginning. Nothing mattered but what life offered them going forward. It had taken twenty years, but now that he considered it, the next twenty years would be even more sweet, as they knew what a gift their love was.

"I think, wife, that you should give me a complete tour of Rygate castle. I would be interested to see what the tower rooms look like in the morning light."

"Mm, I bet you would, husband. You are aware a virtuous wife would tire of a man so amorous." She rose on her tiptoes and kissed him.

"Well, tis a good thing I have never had a need for a virtuous wife then. Shall we go find what other excitement you can bring into my life? I am certain there is something. Even courtesans must have a wicked desire or two."

ABOUT CLAIR

Author of 7 Historical romances, including the Improper Wives for Proper Lords series, Clair Brett lives in NH with her ever emptying nest which includes her children when they visit, two cats, one willful dog boxer/beagle, and a mean Pitbull mix, that will lick you to death and run into her kennel when you speak loudly, and one grand dog who one day just moved in. And one ever harassed husband who takes it all in stride. A lover of all things Regency, Clair, was hooked when she first read Jane Austen. She is a firm believer that a reader finds a piece of who they are or learns something about the world with every book they read. She wants her readers to be empowered and to have a refreshed belief in the goodness of people and the power of love after reading her work

CONTACT CLAIR

Website: www.clairbrett.com
Facebook: http://facebook.com/@AuthorClairBrett
Twitter: http://twitter.com/@clairbrett
Goodreads: https://www.goodreads.com/clairbrett
Pinterest: www.pinterest.com/clairbrett

Join Clair's Newsletter
https://www.clairbrett.com/newsletter-sign-up

ALSO AVAILABLE BY CLAIR BRETT

Winn's Fall– Stand alone novel— Common Elements Book

Ruination of a Rogue—Haute Ton Readers Society—Anthology:
Once upon A Twelfth Night

Visions of Pleasure— Stand alone novel - Enduring Legacy Series

Improper Wives for Proper Lords Series

Dealing with the Viscount

An Heiress by Midnight

Marked for Love